# AGE OF GODS

*Descendants of the Fall Book III*

## AARON HODGES

Edited by Genevieve Lerner
Proofread by Sara Houston
Illustration by Eva Urbanikova
Map by Michael Hodges

# ABOUT THE AUTHOR

 Aaron Hodges was born in 1989 in the small town of Whakatane, New Zealand. He studied for five years at the University of Auckland, completing a Bachelors of Science in Biology and Geography, and a Masters of Environmental Engineering. After working as an environmental consultant for two years, he grew tired of office work and decided to quit his job in 2014 and see the world. One year later, he published his first novel - Stormwielder.

## FOLLOW AARON HODGES...
And receive TWO FREE novels and a short story!
www.aaronhodges.co.nz/newsletter-signup/

# THE KINGDOMS OF HUMANITY

# PROLOGUE

Nicolas screamed as an explosion shook the world, hurling him to the ground. Flames rushed overhead, scorching, violent. They vanished as quickly as they had appeared, leaving only the stench of smoke burning in his nostrils, choking his lungs. Gasping, he forced himself back to his feet.

Screams came from around him as fellow soldiers fled in every direction, all semblance of order lost in the face of an unstoppable enemy. The battlements of Fort Illmoor loomed above, its great blocks of stone torn apart, leaving a hole the width of several houses. Soldiers dressed in red poured through the breach, swords held high as they fell upon Nicolas's comrades.

Another explosion rocked the fortress, though now it came from farther off, as the enemy catapults turned their terrible weapons on a new section of wall. Gasping, Nicolas stumbled in the opposite direction from the soldiers. Black smoke obscured his vision and he struggled to distinguish friend from foe, to find a path to safety. Somewhere above, a horn sounded the retreat, though few defenders were still standing their ground against the terror of the enemy.

Even as he fled, Nicolas struggled to understand how this could have happened. The Gemaho had thought themselves secure behind their giant walls. The Illmoor Fortress had never fallen. Against man and Tangata both, it had stood strong through the centuries. Not even the Flumeeren queen could defy its might.

How wrong they'd been.

Forcing his way through the press of men, Nicolas cursed his king for a fool. Nguyen should have given up the false Goddess, should have surrendered the Calafe princess —whatever it took to appease the mad queen.

Instead, the Gemaho king had goaded Queen Amina, rebuffing her demands.

Now the full strength of Flumeer came against his kingdom.

And Gemaho would fall.

The screams of the dying chased after Nicolas as he picked his way through the rubble. What new power the Flumeerens had discovered, he could not begin to comprehend—only that it was terrible, destructive, unstoppable. The first explosion had blown blocks of granite the size of horses a dozen yards across the inner grounds of the fortress. Nicolas shuddered to think what had become of the soldiers manning those ramparts.

A roar came from nearby and he swung around as a group of soldiers emerged from the smoke. Red and yellow battled furiously as the melee converged on Nicolas. Cursing, he dragged his sword from its scabbard and leapt at the nearest of the red-garbed soldiers, desperate to cut a path to safety.

The blow connected, slicing through the enemy's unprotected forearm and lodging in bone. As the man screamed,

Nicolas tore his weapon free, then stabbed the soldier through the chest. He fell, but another was already stepping forward to take his place.

Nicolas grunted as the enemy's sword slipped beneath his guard and struck him in the chest. The chainmail vest he wore *crunched* with the impact, absorbing most of the blow, though the air was still driven from his lungs. He staggered, struggling to breathe, and swung his blade in a clumsy arc to fend off a second attack.

The enemy soldier parried the attack with a contemptuous swipe of his sword, then stepped in close, blade aimed for Nicolas's throat. Before the blow could fall, a woman in yellow appeared alongside him. Her short sword leapt to meet the enemy's, and steel rang on steel as the weapons clashed. Carried forward by his own momentum, the enemy staggered, and the woman's blade buried itself in his throat.

Blood gushed from the wound as the woman freed her blade, allowing the enemy to crumple. The Gemaho woman flicked a glance at Nicolas as he straightened. Silently he nodded his thanks. She vanished back into the melee before a word could pass between them.

Finding himself at the edge of the chaos, Nicolas took a moment to take stock. An opening between the blocks of granite beckoned, leading away towards the docks. If a resistance could be mounted, he would find it there. He staggered between the chunks of stone—

*Boom.*

A terrible force struck Nicolas in the back and flung him from his feet. The bricked ground rushed up to meet him and this time Nicolas felt something go *crack* beneath his chainmail. Pain sliced his chest, even as the air turned to fire, his inhaled breath burning, searing...

...the flames vanished, leaving again the cloying smoke, the scorched stone, the moans of the dying. Ears ringing,

Nicolas forced himself to move. To stay still was to die. His vision spun as he regained his feet, but even as stars danced across his eyes, he found himself looking upon a sight of horror.

One of the enemy's explosive projectiles had landed a dozen yards behind, where his fellow soldiers had still been battling with the enemy. The explosion had torn through friend and foe alike, leaving them scattered in pieces across the bricked yard. Some still moved, clawing at the ground, their screams just now becoming audible over the ringing in his ears. The woman that had saved him was dead. Only the great blocks of granite had protected Nicolas from the same fate.

Stifling a moan at his own pain, Nicolas stumbled on. A part of him yearned to turn and make a final stand, to die facing the enemy with courage. Yet his duty was clear, even now that the trumpets had fallen silent. If Gemaho was to survive, some needed to escape, to regroup, to warn the cities. The fortress was lost—there was nothing he could do to change that. But he could still serve his nation.

A staircase beckoned, leading down from the plateau upon which the walls had been built. Relieved, Nicolas started down, his body aching, chainmail torn and twisted by the blows that had struck him. Blood was trickling down his side, though he could not feel the wound. Perhaps he was already dead, his body yet to realise it. He'd heard tales of soldiers that fought on with mortal wounds, driven by adrenaline, until they finally dropped dead.

Nicolas thrust the thought aside as the staircase twisted, the port coming into view below. Sails rose from the murky waters of the river and he glimpsed dozens of his comrades already gathered on the pier—those who had escaped ahead of him. They were struggling to board the galleys docked in the river, their only chance for escape.

There was surprisingly little panic, and Nicolas continued down the stone stairs, trying to estimate the numbers below. Between those still on the pier and the others already aboard, there had to be at least a thousand. More than he'd dared hope, after the disaster above. Perhaps there might yet be a chance for resistance.

He forced his weary body on.

Then his eyes alighted on the flag flown high atop the largest ship. He paused in his stumbling, grasping desperately at the stone railing, straining to see, to know whether it was true...

*Yes!*

Despite his earlier reservations, Nicolas's heart soared at the sight of his king standing on the gunwales of the warship. Whatever Nguyen's failures, he was the only one who could unite Gemaho against the invaders. Perhaps they might yet repel the mad queen's invasion.

Filled with renewed hope, Nicolas resumed his descent, desperate to reach the safety of his comrades. Normally the pier could have been reached in minutes, but slowed by his injuries, he struggled on, time racing by with each pained step. He could feel his injury now, a dull ache radiating from his ribs, draining the strength from his limbs.

Finally, he reached the stone docks that led along the shore of the Illmoor. A dozen piers already stood empty, but near the end a group of soldiers still waited to board the last of the galleys.

Blood pounded in Nicolas's skull as he struggled towards them, forcing himself to pick up the pace. The pain grew and he clutched at his side, feeling the hot blood soaking his tunic. Dark spots danced across his eyes, but he forced his vision to focus on the king's flag, still flying high above, the last hope of his broken nation.

He was halfway along the pier when a sharp pain tore

through his calf. His legs collapsed and he cried out, crashing to the stone. Sprawled on the dock, Nicolas's gaze was drawn to his injured leg, where an arrow now protruded from his flesh. His head swam at the sight, not quite able to believe what he was seeing.

A scream tore from his lips as an agony like red-hot fire swept through his leg. The sound rang from the walls of the fortress, drawing the eyes of his companions on the nearby ships. Shock showed in their faces, before gazes shifted, turning to the stairwell he had just descended.

Nicolas twisted to follow their gaze and glimpsed movement on the stairs. Cries carried from above as a dozen archers appeared. One was already stringing another arrow to his bow, while others raced past him, bounding down the stone steps, eager to place themselves in range of the ships on the river. The rattle of shields being raised came from out on the waters, even as the first arrows flashed towards the king's fleet.

Clenching his jaw against the pain, Nicolas forced himself to hands and knees, then reached down to grasp the wooden shaft piercing his leg. With a sudden wrench, he ripped it free. Despite his best efforts, another scream tore from his throat. Thankfully there were no barbs in the arrowhead, and it came out cleanly. Even so, blood coursed from the wound as he dropped the shaft to the stones.

Nicolas gritted his teeth and began to crawl towards the nearest ship. Dark spots floated across his vision as he watched the last soldiers on the pier fending off arrows from above. Nicolas knew he could not reach them in time. The archers were too close, the Gemaho cause too desperate to delay for one man.

Yet he kept on, eyes on that distant flag, on the soaring eagle on a yellowed background. Nguyen was an honourable man, often seen walking the ramparts of the fortress, joking with the men, enjoying their company. He would not leave a soldier behind.

And so Nicolas crawled on, the darkness growing, vision narrowing until all he could see was the single figure standing atop the gunwale of the king's ship. Hand clutched to a rope for balance, it seemed to Nicolas that the king was watching him, that there was recognition in those green eyes. No, Nguyen would not leave. He was a hero to the people, was going to save them all from the mad queen, from the Tangata...

Nguyen turned away, dropping to the deck of the ship.

Above the soft ringing in his ears, even above the roaring of enemy voices, Nicolas heard the order given:

*Set sail!*

He crawled on.

In the distance, the last of the ships drifted away from the pier to join the rest of the fleet. Wind filled the great sails of the Gemaho ships and the cries of the sailors carried across the racing waters.

Nicolas continued.

On the waters of the Illmoor, the ships turned slowly, the king out of sight now, though his flagship led the way. Sails cracked as they caught the wind, and shouts came from Nicolas's comrades as they taunted the enemy trapped upon the shores.

Then they began to race away, heading...downstream.

Even through the haze of agony, Nicolas frowned, lifting his head a notch. Gemaho was upriver—downriver was only Flumeer, only the enemy. What was Nguyen thinking?

But already the fleet was nearing the river gates of the fortress, which swung open on their approach. Dark figures swarmed away from the control tower and hurled themselves into the waters, only to catch ropes thrown to them from the galleys. Too late, the Flumeerens realised the

Gemaho were escaping. Shouts chased after the departing fleet, but Nguyen was already away, fleeing west.

Abandoning his kingdom to the mad queen.

Despair touched Nicolas then, and he slumped to the stone dock, the last of his will fading. His king had betrayed him—had betrayed them all. The other kingdoms had long accused Nguyen of cowardice, that he had abandoned their alliance in the time of their greatest need. But the people of Gemaho had never believed those claims.

Now the truth lay uncovered for all the world to see.

The patter of approaching boots came from behind. Nicolas didn't lift his head. His death would come by the hands of the Flumeeren archers, but he no longer cared. Instead, he turned his eyes to the mountains above. The snow-capped peaks made even the great walls of the broken fortress seem tiny by comparison. The other kingdoms called them the Mountains of the Gods, and perhaps there was some divine beauty in them. A fitting sight, for a dying man.

The footsteps fell silent, as though a dozen men had suddenly frozen in place. A single pair continued, their tread falling softly on stone, the odd rattle of metal betraying the bearer's armour. Despite himself, Nicolas looked around for a glimpse of his killer.

And found himself looking upon the face of a woman. A strange sight, given that the Flumeerens did not permit women in their armies, but as he looked closer, Nicolas saw the helm the woman carried beneath her arm, the golden wire bound into the steel, forming the impression of a crown. His eyes were drawn to her face, taking in the emerald eyes, the brunette hair woven tight against her scalp, the narrow cheeks and arrogant smile.

Amina, the Queen of Flumeer, stood before him.

"Where has your king gone, soldier?" she asked,

crouching beside Nicolas. "Tell me, and I will make your passing quick."

Even through his pain, Nicolas reached for his sword. The queen kicked it away before his hand could close around its hilt. Her steel boot fell upon his wrist.

"I will give you one last chance, soldier," she admonished.

"I would rather burn in your so-called hell than help you," Nicolas spat back.

Amina sighed. "I feared as much."

Nicolas flinched as she raised a fist, but to his surprise, she held no weapon. Instead, a gauntlet covered her hand, its metal threads woven so finely they almost seemed to merge with her flesh. In the full light of day, it shone a soft red...though the light did not seem to be a reflection of the sun.

"Sadly, your resistance matters not. You will tell me everything, by the end."

Baring his teeth, Nicolas made to spit some fresh insult at the woman. Before he could form the words, though, she opened her fist. Light flashed—and then a terrible shriek filled his ears, shearing through the roar of the distant battle, through the distant explosions, until all he could hear was the screeching. It drilled through his eardrums, seemed to slice into his skull itself, to ignite a furnace in his mind.

A scream tore from Nicolas's throat as he clapped his hands to his ears. It made no difference. The flames spread, burning, tearing at his consciousness, until he arced against the stones, until his whole body was aflame, until blood filled his mouth and he could no longer even scream.

Standing over him, the queen leaned closer. He heard her whisper through the briefest lull in the shrieking.

"Tell me, soldier, what is Nguyen planning?"

# I

## THE HERO

C rouched in the shadows of a pine tree, Lukys looked across the gravel beach to where a row of fishing ships lay stranded on the shore. They could not have been touched by human hands in the year since the kingdom of Calafe had been abandoned, and not for the first time, Lukys wondered whether he had chosen the right course for his companions. Most of the ships looked worse for wear, their sails hanging in tatters from broken rigging, boards of hulls broken by passing storms.

Had he led his friends to disaster? Those ships were their only hope of escaping this land, of evading the Tangatan hunters that might even now be closing in on them. He was surprised they'd made it this far. No human could outrun the Tangata in the wilderness, not with their unnatural endurance, their heightened senses.

A shiver spread down Lukys's spine as he glanced side-long at the figure crouched alongside him. Sophia. With her curly brown hair and softly tanned skin, she might have been mistaken for human—if not for the entirely grey eyes.

Like all members of her species, they were the only distinguishing feature that marked her as different, as Tangata.

But the differences ran far deeper than mere appearances, deeper even than Lukys had realised before their escape. Confronted by the Tangata Adonis, he had felt the full force of the creature's power, its whispers in his mind, the pressure on his emotions, filling him with sheer terror, sending him to his knees.

That was the true power of the Tangata. Beyond their inhuman strength and agility, their supernatural senses, behind the grey eyes, they possessed mental abilities unheard of amongst humanity.

*I don't see any guards,* Sophia whispered into his mind.

Lukys had long since grown accustomed to her touch on his consciousness—an ability that he alone of his human comrades apparently shared with the Tangata. Only recently had he begun to understand what that truly meant. For it was not just words that Sophia and her brethren could press upon his mind.

They could also touch emotions, manipulate how another Tangata or human felt.

And in doing so, control them.

Lukys's gaze was drawn to his fellow Perfugians, hidden behind him in the undergrowth lining the shore. Dale and Travis crouched on his other side, their Tangatan partners close by. He had rarely seen the partners separated since they'd fled New Nihelm. The terror of the escape, of their battle to survive, seemed to have only strengthened their bond.

Or had the Tangata been influencing them again, pressing on the emotions of his friends?

Anger touched Lukys as he recalled the long days he'd spent in the cells beneath New Nihelm, Sophia his only visitor. He had come to trust her in that time, to believe the Tangata were not the monsters he'd thought them to be.

And all the while her brethren had been manipulating his companions.

With his newfound ability, Lukys alone had been immune—or so Sophia claimed. There was still so much he did not understand, it was difficult to pick the truth from the lies.

For the moment, though, he must focus on the task at hand. Sophia and the others might have manipulated them, but those they'd left behind in New Nihelm were far worse. A new power had taken control of the Tangatan city, an ancient creature from the time before the Fall, when the Gods had cast humanity down for its sins. That Old One had no desire for peace, no wish for union between human and Tangata.

It wanted only death.

Lukys and his comrades had barely escaped with their lives. The other humans in the city, those who had found peace amongst the Tangata, would not have been so lucky.

*Where are your people?* Lukys directed the thought at Sophia. It was a strange sensation, reaching out with his mind to touch another, but over the last few weeks it had become almost as natural to him as speaking out loud.

A dozen huts of wood and thatch stood amongst the trees across the beach from where they crouched. There was no sign of movement, but Sophia had been sure this village was occupied by Tangata.

*They...won't be far,* Sophia's response came after a moment's pause.

Lukys's jaw tightened and he struggled to ignore the flutter in his stomach caused by the touch of her voice.

*We'll have to move quickly then,* he replied, tightening his grip on the spear he carried. The spear Sophia had given him...

He pushed the thought aside and focused his attention on the village. For the most part, the Calafe had been a nomadic people, before the Tangata had forced them from these lands. But for the capital of New Nihelm, their villages tended to be simple constructs, built from local materials. Now the Tangata had taken up residence in these abandoned villages, though fortunately they had not yet filled all of them. The Perfugian recruits had managed to salvage some supplies in another farther upriver: thick furs to protect them from the last of winter's chill, even some tools and knives they could make use of.

They needed only one thing from this place.

A ship.

Lukys gaze was drawn past the rocky shore to where great dunes of sand rose in the distance. They loomed over the river like small mountains, concealing the ocean beyond. Those endless waters offered safety, freedom—but without a ship, they may as well have been beyond the Mountains of the Gods.

Drawing a breath, Lukys tensed and was about to launch himself toward the line of ships when a hand caught him by the shoulder. He flinched away from Sophia's touch, muffling a cry, and glimpsed a flicker of pain in the Tangata's eyes. Guilt touched him, but he crushed it with an iron hand.

*What?* he growled, glaring at her.

Sophia said nothing, only nodded to the shore. Teeth clenched, Lukys followed her gaze. Movement flickered amongst the huts and he quickly waved the others down. The dense undergrowth of the forest would shield them from view, but one could never be too careful when it came to the Tangata. Fortunately, the breeze was blowing from the dunes, putting them downwind. Even a whiff of human scent would bring the creatures down upon their hiding place.

As Lukys watched, two figures emerged from the huts. They held no tools or weapons, and their clothes were of the same rough-spun cotton that Sophia and the other Tangata wore. They didn't appear alert to the Perfugians' presence, but Lukys held his breath all the same, grip tight around the haft of his spear. These creatures were strong enough to tear him in two, should they wish. The weapon was his only advantage—the Tangata fought with their hands.

The pair wandered down to the shore. The Shelman River was sluggish here, pressed up against the dunes, its currents sapped by the broad plains of Calafe. An estuary had formed in the shelter of the coast, running a mile behind the sand dunes before finally spilling into the ocean.

Lukys watched as the pair crouched in the shallows— one female, the other male. Warrior pairs, humanity had come to call them on the frontlines, though they had not understood their true significance. Lukys knew. It was the great secret of Sophia's, one they had kept from humanity for generations.

The Tangata were almost impotent, rarely able to breed amongst themselves. Their Matriarch had tried to preserve them by partnering youths as they marched to war, in the hope some would produce children. But all too often the efforts had proven futile. That had been the case for Sophia and the others who joined them now. That was why they'd come to be partnered with the Perfugians.

To create the next generation of Tangata.

A splash drew Lukys's attention back to the Tangatan

pair. His eyebrows lifted in surprise as he saw that the male now held a shimmering fish above his head. A second later, the female dived, her hand darting out to break the water and clutch at something beneath the surface. Then she too was lifting a fish high.

The two exchanged smiles. From their hiding place, Lukys couldn't sense the thoughts that passed between them.

*Gatherers,* Sophia's words came to him. *Those who refuse to fight may still partner, but they will not be assigned with a human. If they fail to produce a child together, their lines will come to an end.*

Lukys flicked her a glance, but did not respond to that silent look in her eyes, that longing.

Below, the two left the water and started up the shore with catch in hand. No children appeared from the village as they disappeared into the buildings, and Lukys wondered if that meant their partnership had been unsuccessful.

Shaking off the thought, he turned to Travis. The recruit's usually tidy blonde hair was matted with three days' worth of twigs and dirt streaked his face. His eyes were fixed on the ships below. Travis claimed he knew how to sail, but...

"Are you sure you can sail one of those things?" Lukys asked softly.

"He'd better," Dale muttered from Travis's other side. "Given we're all dead if he can't." At six feet, the man was taller by a good three inches than either of them. His bulk looked awkward crouched amongst the shrubbery, but Lukys had come to rely on the recruits strength these last months.

"You know, I'm starting to see why you lot were sent away," Travis said, his eyes dancing. "We *all* had to learn the basics of sailing, you know."

"You do realise they sent you to the frontlines with us, right?" Dale growled.

Travis waved a hand. "Clearly a mistake was made." He rose to his feet, eyes on the distant ships. "But yes, I think I'll manage." He hesitated, his eyes lowering a fraction, and for the first time Lukys thought he sensed doubt in his friend. "With a bit of help from the others, of course," Travis added at last.

Lukys eyed his friend, wondering just how far the man was over his head. But it was too late for second thoughts now. For better or worse, their path was set. He clapped Travis on the shoulder, then gestured the other Perfugians forward. There were fifteen left, their Tangatan partners making them a party of thirty. Rejects all. Lukys couldn't help but wonder how their people would receive them. What would their Sovereigns think about the reappearance of recruits they'd thought long dead?

Not to mention the Tangata who accompanied them.

No, he couldn't think about that, not yet. First they needed to escape the lands of Calafe. Shaking his head to dislodge the distant worries, Lukys gestured to the line of ships.

"Which one?"

Pursing his lips, Travis studied the gravel shore, though from a hundred yards out Lukys wondered how much his friend could truly tell about their condition. He said nothing though—Travis would only make some joke about having the razor-sharp vision of a Tangata. There was no point questioning him in front of the others.

"The one on the end," Travis said finally as his partner, Isabella, came alongside him. Absently, he placed an arm around her waist as she drew close. "The sail looks to be intact, and I can see some oars on the decks. We'll need them to navigate the estuary."

Lukys nodded, but before he could address the others, Isabella caught his eyes. Her words whispered into his mind:

*He is worried,* she said softly. *He is not…certain he can do what you are asking.*

Her words gave Lukys pause, though they echoed his own earlier thoughts. He watched her, wondering if she was reading Travis's mind. Sophia had assured him that was impossible, that not even the Old Ones possessed such an ability, but…Sophia had lied to him before. Glancing at Travis, he took in the tightness of his friend's jaw, the way his eyes did not waver from the distant ships. Finally Lukys let out a sigh and returned to Isabella.

*Welcome to the human condition,* he said softly. *You're right, he doesn't know. We might very well fail to even get the boat off the gravel. But…we'll try it anyway.*

A flicker passed across Isabella's face and when she spoke again, Lukys sensed her fear.

*How do you stand it?*

*Stand what?* Lukys asked.

*The uncertainty,* Isabella's reply came as a whisper, even as she turned from him, her grip tightening around Travis's arm. *The not knowing.*

Lukys frowned. *If no one ever did things they weren't sure would succeed, we'd never do anything new.*

Isabella's eyes widened a fraction and Lukys found himself smiling. This was a side of the Tangata he hadn't seen before. Sophia and the others were always so confident, so self-assured. Even the way they moved—like fluid grace, always in balance—bespoke their confidence. These were creatures capable of running for days, of swimming across the wildest of rivers. At times it seemed there was nothing they *couldn't* do.

He supposed it made sense then, that they would find the prospect of failure disconcerting.

*There are others in that village,* Sophia interrupted. *Perhaps…*
*they might wish to join us, when they learn what has become of New*
*Nihelm.*

*No,* Lukys replied sharply, with more force than he'd
intended. Sophia flinched, and he drew a breath before
continuing. *We can't trust them.*

*Can't trust them?* Sophia snapped. *Or can't trust me?*

Before he could reply, she spun and slipped away
through the others. Lukys cursed silently to himself as he
watched her join Dale and his partner, Keria. But Sophia's
anger would have to wait. Travis still stood tense beside him,
and the other Perfugians were beginning to shift nervously
on their feet, awaiting his command. How they'd come to
look to him, Lukys could not understand, but he would not
let them down now.

"Travis, you and your crew will board the ship and
make ready to sail. The rest will work together to push it
from the sand. Dale, you're with me." He hesitated, eyeing
the others. "Kloe and Warren, you too," he finished,
naming two of his best fighters.

Lukys waited for the three to join him before turning
back to Travis.

"We'll stand guard, in case those Tangata realise what
we're doing."

Silence answered his words, and looking over the group,
Lukys could see the fear, the trepidation in their faces. In
that moment, he wished he were one of the generals from
the history books at the academy, able to give his followers
courage with an inspiring speech, to lift their spirits, quell
their fears. Instead, all they had was him.

"I know the last few days have been hard," he said softly,
"but we're almost there. Just one more push, soldiers."

He met Travis's eyes and the man nodded. The heads of
the others seemed to lift a fraction. Jaws clenched and grips

tightened on pillaged weapons. Nodding his satisfaction, Lukys raised his own spear and pointed it at the distant ships.

"Let's go find ourselves a ship."

## ❧ 2 ❧

## THE EMISSARY

W ind tugged at Erika's hair as she soared upwards. Wings beat down as she left the Mountains of the Gods far below. From so high above, the largest of boulders became no more than pebbles, the raging mountain rivers seemingly reduced to a trickle, the sheer slopes no more than rolling hills. Not even the glacial peaks seemed to tower so high, though they surrounded her still, their chill piercing, even through her thick mountain clothing.

Watching the ground passing below, she allowed herself to embrace the glory of flight, if only for a moment. Blood pounded in her ears and she wondered at the marvels of the earth, the seemingly endless mountains. Soaring so high, the troubles of her world seemed to recede into the silence, leaving only the fluttering of wings, only the cracking of feathers striking the air, the sharp intake of breath.

If only the wings belonged to her.

Her shoulders were already aching where the strong hands held her beneath her arms. The view was worth the pain though, and it was with sadness that she realised they were beginning to descend, as the God holding her aloft angled for the basin below. The racing of her heart slowed as the valley floor approached, the glory of flight fading as her worries returned.

Erika had trespassed on forbidden land, had journeyed farther into the Mountains of the Gods than any human living. She had searched all her life for proof that the Gods still lived, that they might come to the aid of humanity, might save them from destruction at the hands of the Tangata.

Now she had finally found them.

Any other time in her life, she would have been enthralled by the creature that held her. But everything had changed these last few days.

Wind tugged at Erika's blonde hair as her gaze was drawn to where another of the Gods flew. Cara's auburn wings stretched wide as they caught the air, her amber eyes fixed on the ground. Erika had come to know the Goddess well these last few weeks, but she could not read the expression in her friend's eyes now.

It was Cara's appearance that had drawn Erika to this place, all those weeks ago on the River Illmoor, when the Goddess had first revealed herself. Erika had still been an Archivist then, servant to the Queen of Flumeer, a fledgling noble, with fame and fortune written in her future. But that had been before these past few weeks, before she'd failed, before she'd turned her back on the queen.

Before she'd betrayed Cara.

A tremor shook her at the memory of her own treachery, a shame she felt deep in her stomach. How desperate she had been, how contemptible. To avoid retribution for her failures, Erika had attacked the Goddess, taking her prisoner and fleeing for the lands of the Gemaho.

Only nothing had gone as planned. It hadn't taken long for Queen Amina to follow, launching an attack against the very kingdom in which Erika had sought sanctuary. Seeking an ally against his new enemy, the King of Gemaho had sent them into these cold, unforgiving mountains, to the lands of the Anahera, of the Gods. He hoped to earn their friendship by returning Cara to her people.

But even in the Mountains of the Gods, there was no escaping the reach of the Flumeeren Queen. Her assassins had followed them here, setting an ambush that had slain their escort, had almost slain Erika herself. Poisoned by a traitor in their midst, even Cara had been laid low by the queen's assassins.

If not for poor, brave Romaine, they would have all been killed. The last warrior of the Calafe, of her own people, he had been the best of them. He hadn't run away like Erika, hadn't abandoned his kingdom to the Tangata. He had stood to the last against the darkness.

Now because of her he was dead, buried in a shallow grave, left behind in the mountains. Alone.

Erika would never forget his sacrifice, his bravery. No more would she flee her responsibilities, her heritage. When she finally left these mountains, she would seek out her people, the refugees of Calafe, and take up her father's crown. She would lead them back to the light.

She felt a pang in her heart at the thought of her father. His death had come more than a decade ago, and for all that time she had thought it the Tangata who had slain him. Now she knew the truth: the King of the Calafe had fallen to treachery, stabbed in the back by the queen's agents as he led a charge against the Tangata. The Calafe army had been broken that day, the human alliance fractured, weakened. All so Queen Amina could gain ascendancy.

A shudder ran down her spine at the thought. For the better part of a decade, Erika had served her father's killer. The man that had delivered the blow was dead now, struck down by Cara in her rage, but it was Amina who was responsible. She had already succeeded in seeing Calafe destroyed. Now she threatened the lands of the Gemaho. The woman needed to be stopped before all the land fell beneath her heartless rule. There was only one force, one power left who might yet oppose her.

Erika let out a breath as her feet touched down. Released by the God, she sagged to the ground, taking a moment to recover her balance. The Anahera that had carried her said nothing, only strode past to where the City of the Gods waited.

Although now that she had seen it herself, it hardly deserved the title of 'city'. Instead, she found herself standing before an enormous building that dominated the floor of the valley in which they had landed. Smooth walls of the strange grey stone she had come to identify as the material of the Gods stretched some thirty feet above them. There were no windows or embellishing features she could see, though the harsh mountain elements had left their impression, wind and ice opening cracks in the stone.

The erosion came as a surprise to Erika. She had spent her life exploring the ruins left behind from before the Fall, chambers carved beneath the earth by the Gods when they had once lived side by side with humanity. In those places, this same stone had stood untouched by the passage of time.

It was in those chambers that she had first discovered the magic of the Gods. Even as Erika looked upon the city, her thoughts were drawn to the knapsack she carried at her side. Covered in dust and blood, it held the gauntlet she had wielded until today, the secret artefact that had been forgotten to the ages. Only by its power had Erika survived the past months. She had removed it under duress by the queen's assassin, yet now...

...now she had come to distrust that power, to fear it. It

was said the ancestors of the Tangata had stolen the magic of Gods—and that the magic had driven them to madness. Erika feared the same corruption had touched her soul, that perhaps her cruelty these past months came not from herself, but from that terrible power. She dared not wield the gauntlet again, dared not risk her soul for its power. Not unless—

The crunch of gravel snapped Erika back to the present. She looked around as Cara landed and folded her wings against her back. The Goddess had discarded the jacket which had covered the auburn feathers for so long—she didn't seem to need it, despite the warmth it provided. The Anahera obviously did not feel the cold as a mortal did, though whether that was a function of their divinity, or their mountain home, Erika did not know.

Certainly, Cara had been vulnerable to the poisons of man, though she seemed to have recovered now. Something had happened back in the pass when she'd confronted Yasin, the queen's assassin. Her rage had been terrifying to behold, a terrible, bestial thing promising only death. Whatever poison that had affected her had been burned away, and Yasin had died horribly. Cara's clothes were still stained with his blood.

Erika shuddered at the memory, for there had been a moment when it seemed Cara would not stop there. For the briefest of seconds, she had thought the Goddess would attack her next, that the bloodshed would not stop until every soul on the mountainside had perished.

But then Romaine had breathed his final words, and the Goddess had returned to herself, leaving only the grief they all carried now in their hearts.

Another of the Anahera touched down, carrying the third surviving member of their party. Maisie, spy to the Gemaho king, looked unusually pale as the God deposited her on the open ground before the city. She staggered as they landed and almost fell. Erika stepped in to offer a hand when the God that had carried her ignored the spy's disorientation.

"You okay, Maisie?" she whispered.

Maisie nodded and tried to straighten, before deciding better of it and bending over instead. Erika leapt back as she vomited onto the stones. But a moment later the spy straightened once more, wiped her mouth with a sleeve, and forced a smile.

"That was...quite the experience," she managed, though there was still a sickly colour to her face.

Erika grinned in response. Whatever discomfort the spy had experienced, the short flight had been exhilarating. It reminded her of something Cara had mentioned a few days ago, about how she had been forbidden from leaving the mountains, from soaring beyond the range of her home. After just a taste of that magic above, of the freedom, she could understand the Goddess's desire to explore greater expanses.

Turning, she appraised the young Goddess. With long copper hair and amber eyes that seemed to pierce her soul, Cara appeared no older than Erika's own twenty-five years of age—though she'd confessed in the last days to being closer to fifty. Yet despite that, she often acted with the exuberance of an adolescent, and was innocent to the workings of humankind.

Now though, her usual smile was absent, and the sadness in her eyes couldn't help but remind Erika of the comrade they'd been forced to leave behind. Romaine. A lump rose in her throat as she thought of the old warrior, of his struggle to protect those he'd loved. Finally, he had saved one.

A third Anahera landed behind Cara, the one she had

called her brother. His wings were a dark emerald, his hair a short-cropped black that reminded Erika of the soldiers in Flumeer. Eyes stained scarlet made her shiver, though there was no animosity in his face. In fact, concern showed in his gaze whenever he glanced in Cara's direction.

"So you have returned."

A voice, hard and without emotion, cut through Erika's thoughts. She looked around to find the speaker—a new God that had emerged unnoticed from the city. Wings of pure white stretched wide to either side of him, while his dark hair was cropped short, a match to Cara's brother. His amber eyes did not lack anger as he looked upon the intruders in his valley.

Standing alongside the humans, Cara lowered her head in supplication. Erika's heart twisted at the sight of the fiery Goddess bowed low, and silently she reached out to grip her friend's hand. Cara flinched at the touch, glancing at Erika. Her lips tugged upwards, though she didn't quite manage a smile, before returning to the newcomer.

"Hello, Father."

The God said nothing. He stood staring at Cara, seeming to appraise her, taking in the torn and blood-soaked clothing, her filthy feathers and downturned eyes, until finally he blinked, seeming to notice Erika and Maisie for the first time. His lips drew tight as he shook his head.

"I see your recklessness has finally born fruit," he said, his voice like gravel. "Have you doomed us all, my daughter?"

# THE HERO

Lukys sprinted along the shore, gravel slipping beneath his boots, the others racing alongside him, desperate to reach the line of ships before the Tangata noticed their approach. Spear grasped firmly in hand, he kept his eyes on the village as he ran, watching for the first signs of movement. Dale drew slightly ahead, Kloe and Warren just a step behind, the four of them leading the charge.

Then they were beneath the broad hull of the chosen ship. It was smaller than the ships that had been an ever-present feature of the harbour in Ashura, with only a single hull and no cabin atop the deck. They would be exposed to the elements on the long journey north. Lukys hoped the twin masts would at least make for a faster journey.

Grunting from the exertion, Travis rushed past and splashed into the water with hardly a care for the sound he made. Speed was more important than stealth now. So close to the village, the Tangata could not miss their presence on the beach...

Lukys's heart clenched as a figure appeared between the wooden huts. Despite his time living amongst the Tangata in New Nihelm, he couldn't help but feel a familiar terror as the Tangata emerged from the shadows. The reaction was almost innate, beaten into his psyche through his years at the academy, and even before, in those shadowy memories of bedtime tales told by his parents.

Shifting his feet into a fighting stance, he nodded his satisfaction to see Dale and the others readying themselves. Above, more of the creatures had emerged from the village, half a dozen and still growing. Lukys felt a cold breeze upon his neck. Too many. Even the weaker amongst the Tangata were the equivalent of three soldiers on the battlefield.

A shame Sophia and her brethren would not fight, but they had sworn not to go against their own kind. The very idea was anathema to them. And Sophia had told him long ago that she was tired of war, of death. That she wanted something else for her future, to create new life…

Gritting his teeth, Lukys forced the thought from his mind and risked a glance behind. Travis and his crew were already hauling themselves aboard the chosen ship and taking up oars. With the lack of wind, those oars would be needed to negotiate the estuary before they reached the ocean—especially if the Tangata decided to pursue them into the water. In the sluggish current, it would be easy for the creatures to overtake them before they reached the freedom beyond the dunes.

Those not part of Travis's crew gathered around the hull of the ship, preparing to push it into the water when Travis gave the signal. But already Lukys could see something was wrong. Travis was tugging at the ropes hanging from the mast and shaking his head. A moment later he rushed to the bow and waved at them.

"Sails are rotted," his voice carried across the sands.

Lukys cursed. Oars might help to navigate an estuary, but they would struggle in the open oceans without sails.

"Try another!" he called back, grimacing.

There was a moment's pause as the men and women with Travis exchanged glances—then they were leaping from the gunwales. Water splashed around them as they raced to another vessel. Most carried oars with them and some rope bails—hopefully they would make up for any shortages on the other vessel.

But it was obvious they would not have the ship afloat before the Tangata reached them now. Gathering himself, Lukys faced the enemy and gestured his comrades closer. Unconsciously, he reached out to them with his mind as he did with Sophia, seeking to reassure, to grant them courage. It might have been his imagination, but Dale and the others seemed to stand a little straighter.

Above them, a dozen Tangata had now gathered at the edges of the village, grey eyes locked on the Perfugians who dared intrude on their territory. A flicker of fear passed through Lukys as several started forward, but he clenched his teeth and resisted its call. He couldn't afford weakness, not now, not with the lives of his friends on the line.

*Lukys.* Sophia's voice called to him from where she stood preparing to push the ship from the shore. *Lukys, please, do not—*

Tightening his fists around the haft of his spear, Lukys pushed the words aside. He couldn't afford the distraction of Sophia just now. Just the thought of her, of her deceptions, set his anger alight. How could she have manipulated him so, betrayed his trust, convinced him of her innocence? Now she thought to repair their connection, to pretend they could be like the others. That they could be happy...

He clenched his jaw as rage filled him, set his body to trembling. Instinctively he reached out with his mind for the enemy, for a hint of what was to come. For a moment he sensed fear, confusion, then...a shudder touched Lukys, a red-hot heat, like his own rage reflected back at him. He could almost hear the snarls of their inner voices as the pair atop the beachhead started towards them. Stones crunched as they approached the four recruits aligned against them.

The pounding in Lukys's mind redoubled, his rage taking hold. Images flickered through his mind, of other battles, of the Tangata that had come against him, that had fallen to his blade, their blood staining the earth, their souls cast forever into darkness...

With a roar, the Tangata charged.

Snarling, Lukys leapt to meet them, Dale at his side. Lacking the customary shields Romaine had trained them to wield alongside their spears, they needed to work together now more than ever if they were to hold back the creatures.

Fortunately, the two leaders had drawn ahead of the rest. Stepping in unison, Lukys and Dale moved to intercept the female, while Kloe and Warren lowered their spears against the male.

Teeth bared, the first of the Tangata threw itself at Lukys, her anger reverberating from the nearby sand dunes. Lukys stabbed out with his spear, seeking to skewer her on its steel point. Rage showed in the female's stony eyes as she twisted aside, moving with deceptive speed on the soft ground. Lukys flinched as she darted past his blow, struggling to bring his weapon to bear, even as fingers extended like claws slashed for his throat.

Only a thrust from Dale's weapon saved him. Snarling her rage, the Tangata turned away from him, her forearm slamming into the haft of Dale's spear to turn aside the blow. Even so, the razor point slashed her hip, tearing through the faded tunic she wore.

The Tangata's eyes widened as she retreated, reaching down a hand to press against the wound. Her fingers came away stained red, and her brow wrinkled in surprise. Then her eyes flicked up, catching on Dale, and Lukys saw a darkness pass across them. A growl rattled from her throat and Lukys felt the familiar fear swelling in his chest.

The Tangata moved faster than Lukys would have thought possible on the loose gravel, darting around Dale's outstretched spear. Before Lukys could react, the creature slammed into Dale, hurling him back. Metal flashed as the spear spun through the air and the creature hissed. It raised a fist above the Perfugian's face, ready to crush his skull against the stones.

Roaring, Lukys threw himself at the creature. She looked up in time to brush aside his spear, but the momentum behind his charge carried him forward, and now it was his turn to slam his weight against the enemy. Despite her superior strength, the blow still staggered her, forcing her back from his friend.

A moan came from Dale as he struggled to regain his feet, but teeth bared, Lukys focused all his attention on the Tangata. Blood pounded in his skull and he felt a rage in his heart, a hatred for these creatures, for how they had manipulated his friends, how…how Sophia had tricked him, worming her way into his heart.

Across the stones, the Tangata straightened, but now she flinched away from him as though struck. Lukys snarled and advanced, taking advantage of his enemy's weakness. This time when he attacked, the Tangata's movements seemed sluggish. The gravel slipped beneath her feet and she stumbled. Lukys didn't hesitate, and leaping forward, he drove the point of his spear at her chest. Again she twisted, her fist sweeping down to deflect the blow. This time though it was not enough, and with a sickening *thud*, the spearhead slammed into her thigh.

A scream sounded in Lukys's mind as the Tangata staggered back, tearing the spear free of her leg. Blood stained the gravel as she crumpled against the shore.

Heart pounding in his ears, Lukys raised the weapon again.

*Lukys!* Sophia's voice cut through his thoughts, thrusting aside his defences. He froze. *Don't!*

Images flashed across his consciousness, of their time in New Nihelm, of the children he'd seen in the streets, of the peace he'd found in that strange city, however briefly. For a second, his rage receded, and he felt a sense of peace, of calm…

Then he saw again the Tangata Adonis, standing in the yard of their compound, felt the creature's mind pressing against his own, the terror Adonis had thrust upon him. And he saw those new emotions for the truth of what they were.

Sophia. Toying with his mind. Again.

Tightening his grip on the spear, Lukys brought it down, driving it through the heart of the Tangatan woman. A distant cry sounded in his mind, but he thrust it away and slammed the doors of his mind shut. Tearing his spear loose, he quickly looked around, and was pleased to see that Warren and Kloe had finished off the second enemy. Dale had regained his feet as well, though he looked unstable.

Still standing at the edge of the village, the other Tangata seemed to have been given pause by the death of their brethren. Sophia had been right—these individuals were not warriors. If they had been, he and the other Perfugians would never have stood a chance.

Shouts came from behind, and Lukys's heart soared as he saw that Travis and his companions had the second ship afloat. Flashing a last glance at the remaining Tangata, Lukys called the retreat. Forming up with Dale and the others, he led them from the shore, though they kept their spears to the enemy in case of another attack.

Lukys gasped as they plunged into the icy waters, though in truth the Shelman River had warmed since their desperate swim to escape New Nihelm. Carefully they waded out to where the rest of their companions waited. Ropes were thrown over the gunwales, and in moments the four of them were clambering aboard their new ship.

Water rushed from Lukys's clothing as he splashed onto the deck. Dale and the others had gone first, and he exchanged a grin with his friend, part joy at their success, part relief—that they had survived yet another encounter with the deadly enemy.

Drawing in a breath, Lukys gathered himself, taking stock of their situation. Travis was already at the tiller, and those he'd chosen as his crew were busy manning oars and preparing the sails. But none of that would matter should the Tangata decided to follow. Steeling himself, Lukys gathered his spear and moved to the gunwale.

But the Tangata had made no move towards the water. Instead, they were gathering around their fallen brethren. More than two dozen stood on the beach now. Silence fell over the shore as several of the Tangata fell to their knees and reached for the lifeless bodies, though Lukys knew they were likely communicating in the wordless way of the Tangata.

*You blocked me out.*

He looked around as Sophia appeared at the gunwale alongside him. Glimpsing anger in her eyes, he quickly faced the shore again. The ship rocked beneath them, turning slightly as Travis's recruits shifted their oars.

*You were trying to stop me,* he said finally, keeping his gaze carefully averted from the Tangata beside him.

Back on the shore, a figure moved amongst the huts.

Lukys frowned, straining his eyes as he tried to guess how many more of the creatures hid in the village. Were they planning to cut through the forest and head the Perfugians off before they could reach the outlet to the ocean?

*I wasn't trying to control you,* Sophia replied, her voice touched with emotion. *I was only trying...trying to make you see the truth. To warn you.*

*Warn me of what?* Lukys snapped, swinging on her. *Warn me that the Tangata you claimed were peaceful were trying to kill me?*

Sophia did not retreat from his anger. Instead, her grey eyes caught his, so human, and yet so eerily different, foreign.

*They attacked because you threatened them, Lukys.*

"What?" he spoke out loud, a frown crossing his face. "No—"

*You did,* she snarled. *I told you that my people cannot control you, that it is forbidden.* Her words faded and Sophia looked away. In that pause, Lukys sensed a sadness from her, before she continued. *But the same cannot be said for you.*

Lukys started. *What?*

Sophia's eyes returned to watch him. *Just as you did with the guards as we escaped New Nihelm, your mind touched those of my brethren. I told you before the dangers of broadcasting, but now...*

A sudden dread touched Lukys, a fear for this new ability he possessed. *What did I do?*

*Your rage,* Sophia whispered, anger showing in her own eyes. *Your...your hatred for us. You broadcast it to the world, Lukys, to those you see as your enemies. You drove them to attack us.*

On the shore, a lone figure emerged from the village. She was smaller than the others, only a child, but she moved with the fluid movement of the Tangata as she ran down the beach. At the last moment, the others saw her approach. Several tried to stop her, but these she evaded. The rest stepped aside, accepting this was something they could not protect her from.

Lukys watched as the child fell to her knees beside the Tangata he had slain.

And a distant cry of anguish carried across the waters.

*I told you they were not warriors,* Sophia whispered.

## ❧ 4 ❧

## THE FOLLOWER

Standing on the banks of the Shelman River in New Nihelm, Adonis watched as the blindfolded humans edged forward. With their hands bound behind their backs, they were as sheep led to the slaughter. A smile touched his face at the thought. Finally, the humans who had lived so openly amongst the Tangata had assumed their rightful place.

They numbered in the thousands, some who had been assigned Tangatan partners, others who had been born amongst them, several who had even descended from the Tangata themselves, though their eyes had lost their grey, turning to the treacherous hues of humanity. Some amongst them could even still Speak. Adonis could hear their voices in his mind, clearer than the beastly cries of the other humans, though reflecting the same desperation, the same pleas for mercy.

The joy he felt at their doom almost made the agony of his chest wound bearable. But only the capture of the human who had dealt the blow would sate that pain. For now, he would make do with these sorry souls.

Beside him stood Maya, the last of the Old Ones, the ancient ancestors of the Tangata. Her long blonde hair wavered in the breeze and her skin shone in the rising sun, pale from her eternal sleep. He had woken her from that darkness and she had rewarded him with a place at her side. Partnered in body and mind, they would lead the Tangata to a new future.

Under their watchful gaze, there would be no mercy for the humans of New Nihelm.

Only death.

The cold grey eyes of the Old One watched those below, supervising her new subjects. Her lips did not move, but he could *feel* the pounding of her thoughts, the command radiating from her, the power. It was intoxicating, irresistible.

A scream rose above the gurgling of the river, followed by a *splash*. Adonis watched as the crystal waters turned red with tainted blood. Below, the body sank beneath the racing currents and vanished. The waters cleared, returning to crystal clarity, as though the lost soul had never been.

Ready for their next victim.

*Death, death, death.*

Adonis watched as his sister Tangata staggered back from the bank. Tears streamed down her face and she only managed a few steps before falling to her knees. Throwing back her head, she howled to the rising sun. Two of Maya's guards leapt forward at once, grasping her by the arms and dragging her away. She would join the rest of her brethren, those Tangata who had already cleansed themselves of their human weakness.

*Does your wound pain you?* The pounding in his mind dimmed as Maya turned her gaze on him. A shiver ran down his spine as she touched a hand to his cheek.

Adonis quickly removed his hand from his wound. It had been stitched and bound in the hours before dawn and would heal quickly, though he'd been fortunate that the human had failed to land a mortal blow. He still could not understand how Lukys had resisted his Voice, where even his own brothers and sisters of the lesser generations had bowed before him.

*It is a reminder,* he whispered, meeting his partner's eyes. *When next we meet, the human Lukys will know my wrath.*

Maya's smile grew and she returned her gaze to the cleansing. The pounding redoubled in his mind, and his heart throbbed as the next human was led to the riverbanks. The woman was bound and blindfolded like all the others and he could hear her whimpers over the racing waters. She was whispering a name over and over, pleading with her Tangatan partner to tell her what was happening.

But her partner would not answer. There was a glazed look to the Tangata's eyes as he drew the woman forward, forcing her to her knees. Only then did he pause. Hands trembling, he glanced back, finding where Maya stood overseeing the slaughter. The thrumming in Adonis's mind rose to a fever pitch, and then the Tangata was howling, his fist lashing out...

...and another body fell dead into the waters of the Shelman.

It was a mercy, truly, Adonis found himself thinking as the woman sank into the depths. Death had come for her on silent wings, unknown, unexpected. There had been no suffering, no agony at her partner's betrayal. Only a sharp pain, then...nothing.

Not so for Adonis's brother. A howl rose above the babbling of the river as the Tangata fell to his knees. Adonis listened to his grief without pity. What had they expected, these brethren of his, when partnering with ones so weak? Despite their fallen Matriarch's belief that they could coexist, Maya saw the truth. The humans were a disease, an infection that threatened the Tangata with their very existence.

No, there could be no peace between their species. Only death. Only annihilation.

Before the banks of the Shelman, Adonis's brother made as though to leap into the racing waters, to follow his partner into death. The Old One's guards reached him first, hauling him up, dragging him away. In the end, he went without a fight, arms limp, face downcast, tears staining his stone-grey eyes.

Adonis shook his head at his brother Tangata's weakness, but soon it would be cleansed, burned away in the flames of the Old One's campaign. This pain was necessary. The Tangata could no longer turn their backs on their noble past, on the responsibilities of their species. Maya was amongst the first of them to have been born. Uncorrupted by the taint of humanity, she would renew them, guide them to a great victory.

And so Adonis stood with pride, watching as one by one, the human plague that had infected his people was exterminated.

Until finally, he stood alone on the banks of the river with Maya. Watching the Old One beside him, he couldn't help but wonder what thoughts passed through the mind of one so ancient. Maya had lived through the time of their birth, had lived to see the world Fall, before being locked into an eternal sleep. Had she dreamed through those countless centuries?

Her eyes flickered suddenly, turning to meet his gaze, and he felt the pressure of her mind against his. Smiling, she reached out to cup his cheek.

*Thank you, Adonis, for bringing me to my children,* she murmured. *Their rebirth will not be without pain, but a great future awaits us, a glory unlike any your Tangata have known.*

Adonis swallowed as a warmth filtered through his consciousness. He recognised the influence of another's Voice, but did not resist.

*What future?* he asked. *What glory?*

Maya's lips drew back in a grin as she turned towards the city. Her guards had led their people back within the walls, back to the great Basilica that stood at New Nihelm's centre. The wind blew between the wooden buildings, carrying with it the distant cries of grief.

*All in good time, my mate,* Maya replied, laughter on her lips. *First, we must prepare my children.*

With that, she moved towards the city, towards the distant howling. Adonis hesitated a moment, watching her as she strode towards the empty gates. Despite his wounds, the heat of desire was strong upon him, the need for her touch, for the warmth of her mind against his.

He made to start after her, but something caught his attention and he paused once again. His nose twitched and he glanced down, seeing for the first time the blood staining the grass beneath his feet. The waters had returned to clarity, but the earth still bore marks of the killings that had taken place through the night. The hackles on his neck stirred as he looked upon that blood, as he listened again to the grief of his brethren...

*Are you ready, my mate?* Maya's voice intruded upon his thoughts, and when he looked up, Adonis saw that she still stood in the entrance to the city. Her grey eyes watched him, far darker than his own, than any Tangata that had been born in decades. *Come, they wait for us.*

Adonis's blood stirred at the heat of her mind and all thought of the dead humans turned to dust in the breeze. Smiling, he strode after her and together they entered the city. Within, the citizens of New Nihelm awaited their new masters.

## 5

# THE EMISSARY

"I see your recklessness has finally born fruit," the God said. "Have you doomed us all, my daughter?"

Erika couldn't help but flinch at the accusation in the God's tone. She found herself shrinking away from the anger in his eyes, even as Cara shrivelled beside her, eyes on the stones at their feet. Erika glanced at the Goddess, waiting for her to reply, to refute the accusation. But the rebellious woman she had come to know had vanished. A submissive Cara stood in her place now, head bowed low, as though waiting for a blade to fall.

Swallowing her own fear, Erika faced the God again. Cara's father towered over the others, stood taller than most humans, in fact. He made no move to conceal his wings. With their broad white feathers stretched wide, they must have spanned at least twenty feet.

Finding his gaze on her, Erika shuddered and dropped her eyes back to the ground.

"Your…Divinity," she stuttered, her training in the queen's court abandoning her. "We…have travelled through war-torn regions and endless mountains to find you, to beg for your aid. The Tangata ravage the earth, bringing destruction—"

"Was it worth it, I wonder?" Cara's father interrupted suddenly. Erika's head jerked up, and she saw that the God's eyes were locked on his daughter. "To corrupt your soul? To bring shame upon your family?" He drew in a breath, and in his words, Erika sensed something beneath the anger. "To betray your people."

"Father…" Cara said, her voice barely rising above a squeak. "Please, they have committed no crimes—"

"And what of your crimes, daughter?" her father snarled. He made a wild gesture at Cara. "Your corruption lies exposed before us all."

Cara shrank before his rage. Erika's stomach twisted at her friend's distress and she glanced around, seeking someone, anyone that would stand up for the youthful Goddess. But Maisie was doing her best to appear invisible, and the other Gods present made no move to intervene. Finally she swallowed, and gathering her courage, Erika stepped between father and daughter.

"Sir, Your Divinity, please," she said, managing to place more force behind her words now.

But her tongue stumbled as those terrible eyes turned upon her once again, fear raising the hackles on her neck. She found herself squeezing her fist, and was surprised when the warmth of her magic did not materialise. Over the past months, she had grown so used to the gauntlet that its power had become second nature. It felt as though a part of her was missing now.

Still, Erika would not back down, and finally she managed to continue: "Your daughter speaks the truth: we mean you no harm. My people would never betray you as the Tangata once did. We seek only your aid against their darkness."

"The Tangata?" the God snorted. "What do we care for those creatures?" He shook his head, his attention returning to Cara. "It is my wayward daughter that concerns the Elders."

Behind Erika, the Goddess seemed to shrink even further, her wings lifting a fraction, as though she might hide beneath their feathers. The God shook his head.

"Your mother was disobedient, but even she in all her recklessness never brought such darkness to our doors. Even she did not break our most basic laws, did not place her own people in danger."

Erika glimpsed a shine to Cara's eyes as a tear spilt down her cheek, but still the Goddess said nothing to refute the reprimand. Anger touched Erika then, that this being could be so cruel, could condemn his daughter for some imagined crime.

"Your Divinity, my friend and I would both be dead if not for—"

"Hugo," the God interrupted, speaking in a tone that brooked no argument. He gestured to Cara's brother and the Anahera immediately stepped forward. "Take Cara to her quarters. The Elders will convene shortly to judge her crimes."

Cara's brother nodded, and flicking them both an apologetic look, he took Cara's hand. She flinched at his touch, looking at him in surprise, but then her shoulders slumped again. She did not speak as Hugo lead her away, but as she walked past Erika, their eyes met.

Erika shivered as she glimpsed the terror in her friend's gaze. She reached for the young Goddess, but already Hugo was leading her away, back towards the building rising from the barren slopes. Then they were gone, disappeared into the City of the Gods.

Erika allowed her hand to fall back to her side. Icy fear

slid down her back as she turned to the God, realising she and Maisie were now alone in his presence. He towered above them, his massive frame and wings dwarfing the two humans, and suddenly she wondered if they might be in danger after all. Cara had confessed to them that the Anahera did not kill, but then…the young Goddess *had* killed Yasin. If her father decided to make an exception…

Swallowing, Erika decided to try another tactic. "I—"

"Come," Cara's father said abruptly, then turned and strode towards the door through which Cara had vanished.

Erika and Maisie remained fixed to the spot, staring after the God's departing back. It was a moment before they threw off the shock of the Anahera's abrupt invitation and scurried after him. The walls of the city rose above, taller than Erika had thought when she'd first looked down from the mountain pass above. Though the lack of windows made it difficult to gauge, she guessed the interior must have at least two storeys. The entire building was the size of a small town.

Cara's father was the only God in sight now, and Erika supposed in such a remote location, there was little reason for the Anahera to venture outside. Certainly there was no sign of water or edible vegetation in the rugged valley. Idly, she found herself wondering where they found their food. Her people believed that the strange Guanaco—the long-necked, woolly mammals that wandered these mountains— were the flock of the Gods, but she could not see any of them now, nor a trail in or out of the valley, for that matter. But then with wings to aid them, what need did the Gods have for roads or trails?

It meant that she and Maisie were trapped here, though. There would be no leaving this place without the Gods' permission, even if they could have survived alone and without supplies in the harsh wilderness.

Shivering, she tried to shake the feeling of being trapped, returning her attention to the city. Drawing closer to the entrance, she saw that her first impression had been right, that the entire structure was shaped from the same strange stone she had encountered in the other ancient sites she had uncovered. But the corrosion was worse than she'd first thought, the outer walls pitted and spotted with patches of stone a different colour from the rest. Repair work, she realised…though why had they not used the same material?

The hackles rose on her neck as they neared the entrance. There was something wrong about this place, this old, almost broken structure. Surely the magic of the Gods should have protected their city, should have preserved it as with those other ancient places.

"So this is the City of the Gods?" Maisie mused as they drew to a stop before a pair of metallic doors. "I have to admit, Archivist, I'm a little disappointed."

Erika nudged her, flicking a nervous glance at their chaperon, but Cara's father was already stepping up to the entrance and did not seem to hear the spy's words. She shook her head at Maisie and offered an irritated frown.

The spy replied with a fleeting smile. She still looked pale, and glimpsing a bloodstain on her sleeve, Erika belatedly remembered that she had taken a wound in combat with Yasin. Still, it couldn't be too serious, or the Gemaho woman would not be on her feet. Though…perhaps it explained her pale colour.

A *screech* came from the entrance as Cara's father pushed open the double doors. Erika winced at the noise, and couldn't help but pause after they stepped inside. The doors were shaped from some unknown metal—the same one they had discovered in the ancient caverns. Her people had been unable to even dent it, and indeed here the metal remained untouched by the elements. The doors themselves slid into cavities in the walls rather than swinging on hinges, but here the wear of nature had taken its toll. Dust and stones from the mountain environment had gathered within, inhibiting the opening of the doors.

"Erika," Maisie called from ahead. The spy seemed to have recovered her composure and gestured for Erika to hurry. "Come on, our hosts don't seem the patient sort. You do recall how humans entering these mountains have a habit of never returning, right?"

Erika's heart lurched at the thought and she jogged to catch up. Every kingdom of humanity had learnt to avoid the Mountains of the Gods. Gemaho such as Maisie might disbelieve in the Gods themselves, but even they weren't so foolish as to defy the prohibition.

Within the structure, Erika was greeted by a familiar sight. A corridor of grey stone stretched away from the entrance. Glowing orbs placed in the walls lit its length, though their light was fainter than the other sites in which she had found the magic active. Protected from the elements, the cracks in the stone were fewer than outside, though farther along the corridor, they discovered other features that had not been present in the ancient sites.

Decorations hung from the plain stone: weavings of plants and twine and flowers, and small mosaics created from coloured pebbles, even several carvings of red wood, though there were no forests in these mountains. Did that mean some of the Anahera were permitted to leave their territory, or did such rules only apply to their youths, such as Cara?

They followed Cara's father through the twists and turns in the corridors, and while Erika tried to keep track of the pattern, she was soon lost in the great structure. The pattern of branching corridors and rooms might have been the same as the other sites Erika had visited, but without her map she could not say.

Only the occasional side chamber was barred by a door. The rest stood open, and Erika took the opportunity to glance into each as they passed. A few appeared to be simple sleeping chambers, but Erika was disappointed to find that most were empty.

Finally the God came to a stop in front of one of the few chambers with a door. Pulling it open, he indicated for them to enter. Erika and Maisie exchanged a look, but there was little opportunity to argue. Cara's father had already made his displeasure at their presence evident.

Hesitantly, they stepped inside, and Erika breathed a sigh of relief as they found themselves in a sparsely adorned sleeping chamber. Barely ten feet by ten feet, it contained two beds pressed up against either wall. Each was little more than blankets stuffed with straw or feathers, but at least they would be preferable to sleeping on the rocky ground as she had done the last few weeks.

The room held little else, but even so, Erika turned and bowed to the God.

"Thank you," she said, pleased that her voice was steady now. "Your daughter tells us your people are called the Anahera. What might we call you, Your Divinity?"

A frown wrinkled the God's face as he glared at the two of them, and for a moment Erika thought he would not answer. Then abruptly he waved a hand.

"I am called Farhan, human," he growled.

"I am the Archivist, Erika, and this is Maisie of the Gemaho," Erika replied, keeping a respectful tone. "Might I ask, what do you plan to do with us, Farhan?"

The God's frown deepened. "You should not be here, human," he said. "You will stay in these quarters until the Elders have decided what to do with you."

"And what of your daughter?" Erika pressed, then hesitated. "She…did not lead us here. I discovered a map that revealed the location of your city. Do not blame her for my crime."

Farhan said nothing in response to her words, only stood staring at her, amber eyes burning.

"The Elders will decide my daughter's fate," he said at last.

Then he was gone, the door slamming shut behind him. This one only used a simple hinge, and while the door was of the same strange metal as the outer ones, the hinge appeared to be of normal iron. As it clicked closed, Erika looked at Maisie.

"What now?" she asked.

The spy snorted and fell back onto one of the beds. A cloud of dust billowed out of the pile of blankets and she immediately started to sneeze. By the time she managed to regain control, Erika had hidden her grin.

"What now indeed," Maisie coughed, her eyes still watering. She shook her head and sighed. "Some mess you've gotten us into, Archivist."

Erika frowned. "I thought this was your king's idea."

Maisie laughed. "Monarchs only have good ideas, Erika," she replied. "Didn't your queen teach you that? No, judging by our reception here, this little venture was entirely your doing." She paused. "So, what do we do now?"

## ❦ 6 ❦

## THE HERO

Standing at the railings of the fishing ship, Lukys looked out across the open ocean and tried to pretend his worries did not exist. That the strife he faced, the fear and danger, even the hatred that infected him, all of it might simply float away on the salt-tanged winds. For a while, he almost manged to convince himself there was only the endless water, only the rolling waves and the soft creaking of the ship, the flapping of the hastily-patched sails and the shouts of his comrades as they struggled to recall lessons long since forgotten.

Travis's voice rose occasionally above the others as he shouted out instructions. Lukys was impressed by the way his friend had stepped up since they'd taken control of the vessel. Watching him, he couldn't help but think Travis should have been the one to lead them. The role of sea captain seemed to come naturally to the man.

It was more than Lukys could say for himself. Again, he found himself recalling the Tangata charging down the shore towards him, saw the rage in the female's eyes as she attacked—and her fear as Lukys raised his spear. Heard the child's scream.

Travis would not have lost control, would not have driven the creatures into a frenzy. Travis would not have slain a child's mother.

He screwed his eyes closed, but there was no hiding from the memory. His guilt kept summoning the scene, and each time that cry cut a little deeper. He recalled the look Sophia had given him as they stood at the gunwale, the anger, the hurt in her eyes. Humanity had regarded her kind as monsters for as long as history had been written—yet it was Sophia who wanted to stop the killing, who craved peace, to bring life into the world.

Instead, Lukys had given her only more death.

A shudder shook Lukys and he swung away from the ocean. He would find no lasting peace in those endless depths. Across the little ship, he watched instead as his companions worked. Human and Tangatan pairs toiled side by side, united in hearts and minds, though they could not even truly communicate.

United because the Tangata had manipulated their human assignments into feeling affection, into feeling love for their captors.

Or had they?

Lukys found himself suddenly doubting everything, and he swallowed, seeking out a glimpse of Sophia. He found her near the bow with Keria, Dale's partner, helping to set up a piece of canvas to catch rainwater. The ship had no supplies and though they had some limited food, lack of water would soon force them back to land. With hundreds of miles of Tangatan territory between themselves and their island homeland, every visit ashore would put them at risk. Even an encounter with their own side might prove risky, given they were likely to be accused of desertion, or worse, treason.

As he watched, Sophia finished tying the rope that would hold the canvas in a concave shape. Her head lifted and their eyes met. Her face hardened and she quickly looked away.

"The two of you should talk."

Lukys started as Dale appeared beside him and leaned against the gunwale.

"What?" Lukys frowned at the man.

Dale gestured in Sophia's direction. "It's obvious something's wrong between you," he said, then hesitated before adding: "We can't afford to be divided, Lukys, not when we get to Perfugia. I know it hurt to kill those people on the beach, but we did what we had to. She will understand. Keria does."

Guilt lodged in Lukys's throat—not for the Tangata he had slain now, but for his companions. After New Nihelm, he had delayed telling Dale and the others the truth, about how the Tangata had manipulated them. In the rush of the escape, of fleeing the hunters, there hadn't been time, but now…

"It's…complicated, Dale," he said finally, swallowing hard.

"Love always is," the soldier replied.

Lukys looked sharply in the man's direction. This was his opportunity, his chance to finally reveal the Tangata's deception. Dale had been his enemy once, but over the course of the war he had earned the man's respect, even his friendship. Dale, Travis, all the others, they deserved to know what had been done to them.

"Is it really love we feel?" he whispered.

Dale said nothing, though his eyes drifted to where Sophia stood. Keria had joined her at the gunwale.

"They're not what they say they are," Lukys whispered, the words leaving his lips before he could hold them back.

"I know." Dale smiled.

"No," Lukys said quickly. He shook his head, though his eyes remained on Sophia. "You don't understand. They... the things they can do, what *I* can do, speaking into our minds, it's more than what you think."

"Lukys, *I know*," Dale said softly. Lukys looked at him sharply, and the soldier raised his eyebrows. "You think the rest of us haven't realised there was something strange about how we met, about how we fell for our partners?"

"They're manipulating your emotions," Lukys hissed.

"Yes," Dale replied, "and no." He glanced at Lukys out of the corners of his eyes. "It's strange, our emotions are... heightened around them, enhanced. But I trust her, Keria. Around her, even the bad, even when we fight and I feel anger...even then, I can still feel the good beneath."

"And you don't have a problem with that?"

Dale shrugged, turning his eyes to the distant shore. "Do you remember what it was like at the academy, Lukys? Every moment of our lives was controlled, planned, scheduled. So much pressure, to be better, to excel, to pass." He paused. "Or maybe it was different for you?"

"No," Lukys murmured, memories of sleepless nights flickering through his mind. He might not have been noble born like Dale and Travis, but the pressure had been the same. "I remember."

Dale nodded. "Then we arrived in Fogmore, and I thought things might finally change, that there I could earn myself some respect. Instead, they threw us to the wolves. Even when we survived, we were barely fed, given the most rundown, filthy, cold lodging in town." He sighed. "I was close to giving up. We all were. Except for you. Only you stood up, went looking for help, for someone to train us. You and Romaine, you gave us something to fight for, Lukys. Even if for me that was only saving face."

Lukys shrugged, uncomfortable with the praise, but thankfully Dale went on.

"Then in the dungeons beneath New Nihelm, the despair came for me again. The pain, the hunger. I thought nothing could keep the darkness at bay." A smile touched his lips as he looked over his shoulder at Keria. "Instead, I found happiness, found her. Maybe she pushed on my emotions, but…it was still her kindness that lifted me from the despair."

Lukys swallowed but said nothing. Dale's words echoed his own thoughts during those dark days in the dungeons. He'd come to realise that even as their prisoner, the Tangata had treated him far better than his own kind ever had.

That *Sophia* had treated him far better than anyone else in his life.

He cursed beneath his breath. Beside him, Dale laughed and clapped him on the shoulder. "There we go," he said, flashing a final smile before he moved away to join Travis at the tiller.

Letting out a long sigh, Lukys stepped away from the gunwales and weaved his way across the crowded deck. Sophia was still looking across the waters to the distant horizon. Moving alongside her, he couldn't help but think how tiny they all were, how insignificant their petty squabbles beside the endless expanse of that ocean.

Sophia did not react to his presence, didn't even glance in his direction. Lukys bit his lip, wondering how to begin. She wasn't going to make this easy on him. Struggling for the words he needed, Lukys ran a hand through his hair, watching her out of the corner of his eye. Her figure had narrowed since their escape—the Tangata insisted that the humans eat before they did, and there wasn't always enough to go around. There was a softness to her face beneath the battle-worn edge she showed the world. The wind tugged at her ash-brown hair, tangled from the half-a-week they'd spent on the run. A twig from the forest had caught in one of her locks, and absently he reached out to pluck it free.

She flinched at his touch, withdrawing from him, and his hand fell back to his side.

*What do you want, Lukys?* Her voice came to him, taut with suppressed anger.

Lukys swallowed, twig still clutched between his fingers. Absently he flicked it over the side, then sank to the deck and leaned back against the gunwale.

*I should have listened to you,* he whispered to her. *I should have found a way to make peace with those...people.*

He could feel Sophia's eyes on him, but Lukys did not risk a glance, only pulled his knees to his chest and watched as Travis gestured wildly from the tiller, shouting for one of his crew to trim the sails—whatever that meant. He really should have paid more attention to their maritime classes.

There was movement beside him as Sophia joined him, though she left space between them.

*And now a child's mother is dead.*

Lukys closed his eyes as that awful scream echoed through his mind again. He clenched his jaw, seeing again the fear in the Tangata's eyes as he lifted the spear, heard again Sophia's plea for him to stop.

*I'm sorry,* he said, though he knew it was not enough.

Silence answered his words. He did not speak again, only leaned his head back against the gunwale and watched as one of the crew struggled to scale the mast, presumably for a better view of the ocean around them. They were trying to keep close to the coast, though not so close they drew the attention of every Tangata in the area.

*There has been so much death, Lukys,* Sophia's words finally came to him. *You are not the only one who has shed innocent blood. I thought...I thought finding you, with our union, that I might finally leave the nightmares behind. But...*

*All I know is death,* Lukys finished for her, his voice bitter.

It was true. His assignment to the frontlines had proven his inadequacy in every other facet of life. The Sovereigns of Perfugia had judged him unworthy to even clean the privy of his betters. Only in battle had he excelled, had he found his worth.

*No,* Sophia replied with surprising force. Lukys started as her hand touched his shoulder. *No, Lukys. You are capable of so much more.* She turned her gaze on the Perfugians and their Tangatan partners. *You united them, lifted them up when they lacked the strength to stand. You ask why Travis does not lead, but you cannot see that he draws his courage from your own.*

Tears stung Lukys's eyes and he shook his head, refuting her words. "My rage will leave them dead, just like that child's mother."

*There is a rage in all of us, Lukys,* Sophia replied, *in the Tangata. It is the curse of my people.*

*Then...how do you control it, keep it from influencing others?* He hesitated, thinking of the times he had seen the Tangata enraged, the way they changed, attacking without hesitation or constraint. *From controlling you?*

It was a moment before Sophia replied. *We learn to keep that part of us suppressed,* she said at last, *mostly. During battle, there are some who uncage the beast, but...I dream of a world where such violence is no longer needed.*

*And your powers?* Lukys added.

*Powers...* Sophia spoke the word as though she found it strange. *Such an unusual term, for an ability we have from birth. It is much like breathing for us, Lukys, to sense the emotions of others.*

*And to influence them?*

Sophia hesitated. *You are as a child, Lukys, unschooled. And...*

*your ability is far stronger than any human has a right to—even had you a recent Tangatan forefather.*

Her words brought a frown to Lukys's face. Sophia had said his ability meant there was Tangatan blood in his line, but the claim still rung hollow. How could that be possible, when he came from Perfugia, the one foothold of land the Tangata had never reached? At least, not so far as their history stretched.

Perhaps they would find the answer to that question in Perfugia, though he was not hopeful. Just convincing his fellow Perfugians not to slaughter them on the spot when they discovered the Tangata onboard would be nigh impossible. He couldn't bring himself to think beyond that trial. Though perhaps if he could master this ability…

"Will you teach me?" he whispered, turning to Sophia.

She still sat away from him, but leaning against the gunwale, their faces were close. Her eyes shimmered in the noonday sun, still the strange solid grey of the Tangata, so dark they seemed to absorb the light, though in doing so they grew just a little lighter, more human. Without thinking, he leaned towards her, reaching up to cup her cheek. Her eyelids flickered as his fingers caressed her cheek and silently he moved to kiss her—

*No!*

Before their lips could meet, Sophia jerked away from him, rearing back. Lukys started, shocked by her rejection as she scrambled to her feet. Now he glimpsed the anger simmering in those grey eyes. Heart pounding, he reached out with his mind, desperate to understand, to know what he had done.

*Sophia…* he whispered.

Her anger crashed over him like a wave, pounding against his consciousness, and for a second he felt as those Tangata on the beach must have. Then he broke beneath the surface, and an icy cold touched his mind, a freezing sadness…and even deeper, a terrible hurt, pain at his betrayal.

Standing over him, Sophia shrieked, and suddenly Lukys found himself hurtled backwards, torn free of her mind. He gasped, staring up at her, still struggling to process what he had seen, what he had felt. His mouth parted, but her words forced their way into his mind before he could speak.

*So arrogant,* she spat. *You think you can ignore me, treat me like vermin, and I will simply forgive you?*

*I'm sorry!* Lukys gasped, coming to his feet and reaching for her. She twisted away from him.

*Sorry?* Sophia hissed, baring her teeth. A heavy silence stretched out as they faced one another, and reluctantly Lukys allowed his hand to fall. Sophia drew her lips tight, and when she spoke again the anger was gone from her voice. Only sadness remained.

*You don't think of us as people, Lukys,* she murmured, still watching him with those haunting eyes. *The way you've looked at me these past days…it was like I was some animal that had bitten you.* She swallowed, and he watched as a tear spilt down her cheek. *We're not perfect, Lukys. I should have…should have told you the truth. But…you didn't even give me a chance to explain. Now you ask for my help, try to…try to kiss me?*

He opened his mouth, then closed it again, seeking the words he needed, the ones that would make things right, that would prove his remorse. He could not find them.

*We're human, Lukys,* she said at last. *Just as human as you or Dale or Travis. Until you realise that…* She trailed off.

With a shake of her head, Sophia turned and walked away.

## THE EMISSARY

Erika paced up and down between the beds, reaching the wall only to spin on her heel and stride the half-a-dozen steps to the door before turning again. The way she was going, she would wear a groove in the stone floor before they ever saw another of the Anahera. But what else was she meant to do? Farhan had left them here, alone, without a single hint about what was to become of them.

"Gah, how can you just sit there?" she burst out, swinging suddenly on Maisie.

The Gemaho spy lay reclining in the bed she'd claimed, a crystal globe rolling back and forth between her fingers. The orb could have been mistaken for the crystal balls used by fortune tellers at the markets in Mildeth, but Erika knew from experience there was far more to it than met the eye. It was another of the artefacts recovered from the time before the Fall, an item of power like her own disused gauntlet. Contained within was the magic to make them invisible to the eyes of others. Little good that would do them here though, locked in the unadorned room.

Pocketing the orb, Maisie entwined her fingers and looked at Erika. She said nothing, only raised her eyebrows.

Erika growled and did another lap across the room. "What do you think they're going to do with us?"

On her bed, Maisie shrugged. "That probably depends on what they're going to do with Cara."

Erika paused mid-stride. "What do you mean?"

Even as she spoke, she recalled that last look Cara had flashed her when confronted by her father—broken, defeated, terrified. A shiver ran down her spine and she stared at Maisie, waiting for the other woman to reply.

"Well…" Maisie mused. "If she's sentenced to death, chances are we won't be long in following."

Erika started, shocked by the spy's words. She'd thought themselves in danger, trespassing in the forbidden mountains, but Cara? This was her home. Whatever rules she'd broken, surely her father couldn't condone such an extreme recourse.

"No," she said finally, shaking her head. "The Anahera do not kill. Cara said as much, in the mountains…" She trailed off beneath Maisie's unwavering gaze.

The spy raised her eyebrows into her mop of curly black hair, as though to ask whether Erika could really be so naïve.

"I must have knocked my head harder than I thought, back in that canyon," Maisie said finally, her eyes unblinking. "Because I could have *sworn* the 'good Goddess' *tore a man's limbs from his body.*"

Erika shuddered at the reminder of that brutal scene. There had been little left of Yasin by the time Cara had been done with him. Quickly she forced the memory aside. She should be thankful—the man had planned to deliver her to the queen, and the Gods only knew what Amina had planned for her treacherous Archivist.

"You don't think...you don't think that's what Farhan meant, when he accused her of corruption?"

Maisie rolled her eyes. "You know, for someone who dedicated her entire life to studying these Gods of yours, you don't seem to know much about them."

Erika's cheeks grew warm. "I got us here, didn't I?"

"Yes, though personally I prefer to avoid being imprisoned by Divine beings." She paused. "So...do you have a plan yet?"

Erika gritted her teeth and swung away, struggling to recall everything Cara had told her about her people. Two facts stood out stark in her memory—that the Anahera did not kill, and that they did not lie. Yet she had only Cara's word on each—had the Goddess been lying even then?

No, she had seemed sincere when they'd spoken. Erika had put her faith in the youthful Goddess when she'd released her from her bindings. Cara might have betrayed them then, could have torn them apart with her bare hands had she wished.

That meant...

"We need to get out of here," Erika said abruptly.

If Cara had been telling the truth, it meant that what she'd done to Yasin was forbidden in the eyes of her father and the Anaheran Elders.

"About time!" Maisie exclaimed.

Levering herself off the bed, Maisie grabbed her knapsack and moved to the door, where she took something from the bag. Erika frowned, shifting closer to try and decipher what she was doing. But Maisie said nothing, only placed her eye to the keyhole, then lifted her hands. A sliver of metal shone between her fingers and Erika realised what she was planning.

"You think Gods would make a lock a mortal could pick?" she asked, leaning against the wall beside the spy.

Maisie grunted. "Gods? No. Anahera, maybe," was all she said.

Erika rolled her eyes at the woman's casual blasphemy. How Maisie could still disbelieve when the evidence was all around her, Erika couldn't understand. But at this moment, a theological debate seemed the least of their worries, so she kept her silence.

Minutes slipped past, punctuated by the occasional curse from Maisie. The spy had a colourful vocabulary and Erika learned several new words over the next half hour. Absently, she recalled the woman's story of how she'd come to be in the king's employ.

"Did you learn to pick locks on the streets of Mildeth?" she asked, trying to make conversation.

Maisie snorted. There were now three slivers of steel sticking from the lock. "What, they didn't teach you how to pick locks in Archivist school?"

Erika rolled her eyes. "We preferred black powder," she said, then: "Actually, we didn't even *have* locks at the school. What do students have to steal from one another…"

She trailed off as an idea came to her. Maisie didn't appear to be listening anyway. Frowning, Erika thought again of everything Cara had told her, then reaching out, she twisted the door handle. A soft *click* followed as the door to their room swung open. Outside, the corridor was empty. Farhan hadn't even posted a guard.

Still on her knees in the now open doorway, Maisie scowled. "Well that takes the fun out of this."

Erika chuckled. "What purpose would a society that only ever tells the truth have for locks?"

"I'd say it makes them easy picking for a species that lies," Maisie commented, regaining her feet and tucking her tools away.

A smile twitched on Erika's lips and she extended a hand towards the corridor. "Ladies first?"

Maisie's scowl deepened but she took the lead. She kept her magic orb out of sight, and Erika guessed the narrow corridors would make it difficult to evade the Anahera, whether they were invisible or not. The magic created a bubble around its users that concealed everything within, but anyone who stepped into the bubble would immediately see the truth.

And besides, it wouldn't hurt to keep a few secrets of their own. Her hand drifted to her bag and the gauntlet within. She knew its magic could bring down a God—she had used it on Cara herself. Perhaps it was best it remained hidden, at least for now.

Thankfully, the corridors around their rooms appeared empty, and Erika wondered again at the strangeness of the place. Without any clue where to go, they headed in the opposite direction from which they'd entered. They moved slowly at first, taking time to inspect the rooms they passed and to pause before branches in the corridor, wary of Anahera who might be wandering the place.

But all they found were chambers and corridors empty of their inhabitants. As they drew deeper into the building, more and more of the chambers appeared as living quarters. These rooms were warmly decorated, mostly with objects found in nature and shaped by Anaheran hands. The larger of the chambers held as many as half a dozen beds, and Erika found herself imagining entire families sharing a single space together. It was stranger still to find each chamber open, without even doors to provide the inhabitants privacy to those without.

Though she supposed it followed with what Cara had told them, of a people without secrets, with no fear of death or crime. A paradise, just as human records spoke of the days before the Fall, when humans had lived side by side with the Gods. Little wonder humanity's corruption had driven them to these distant mountains. With the power they wielded, the Anahera must have feared humanity would betray them again, would try to steal their magic as the Tangata once had.

Such deliberations did not bode well for Erika and Maisie. She quickly swallowed the lump in her throat. King Nguyen's plan had relied on Cara being welcomed home with open arms—not put to trial for murder…

Quickly Erika forced the thought aside. This was the City of the Gods, a place of wonder and miracles. Whatever their reluctance, when the Anahera learned of the state of the world, of the Tangata rampaging across the land, burning villages and driving humanity to the brink of destruction, surely they would not stand idly by. Surely they would aid the kingdoms—

*Bang!*

Erika cursed as she walked headlong into Maisie. The Gemaho spy had come to an abrupt halt and was staring at the wall beside them. Erika frowned, but her mouth dropped as she followed the spy's gaze. A painting covered the wall from floor to ceiling, its details perfectly preserved beneath a pane of glass. Glass of such size alone would have been something to wonder at back in Flumeer.

But it was the painting itself that had drawn Maisie's attention. The detail of the image was something to behold —so fine that Erika could not even begin to make out the individual brushstrokes. It didn't seem possible that a human could have the skill to create such a masterpiece, but then, this was the City of the Gods…

…and the image depicted was a scene beyond her wildest imagination. A blue harbour stretched away from the artist's viewpoint, a bridge of deepest red rising from the raging waters, so grand, so enormous it would have put the greatest of human citadels to shame. Beyond the scarlet bridge, brilliant towers of glass rose from rolling hills, far taller than even the greatest works constructed from Perfugian marble, such that only the awesome power of magic could have held them aloft.

A shiver ran down Erika's spine as she stared at the image, as she beheld the true City of the Gods. *This* was what she had expected to find in these lonely peaks, some spectacle of wonder, of impossibility.

"It must be one of the cities lost in the Fall," Erika mused, "but…why have the Gods not built themselves a new heaven here?"

Maisie flashed her a glance and looked like she was about to speak, but then the distant murmur of voices carried to their ears. They hesitated for half a moment before setting off in the direction of the whispers. Erika shivered as they passed more empty chambers, though her mind remained on the image of the city.

They slowed as the voices grew clearer, and Erika sensed they were coming from the next doorway. They approached cautiously, aware they were violating the Anahera's trust, but knowing they could not stand idly by while Cara's fate, and their own, was decided.

They paused a moment outside the room and Erika felt a cold breeze blowing from the opening. She frowned, sharing a glance with Maisie. Voices echoed from beyond the doorway, but they seemed muted, obscured, as though the sound came from a great space.

Erika drew in a breath, then flashing a final glance at the spy, she stepped through the doorway…

…and into an open yard. She blinked at the brightness of the outdoors, and for a moment she did not notice the sudden silence that had fallen. Eyes watering, she struggled as her vision adjusted to the light.

When it finally cleared, she found herself staring across an open space enclosed within the walls of the city. An enormous yard had been left open in the centre of the great building. Around the edges, glass houses stood at intervals. Erika glimpsed vegetation through the great panes, and guessed these must be where the Anahera grew their food.

Otherwise the yard held only dirt and rocks and the occasional snowdrift—and a tall structure of stone rising from its centre. It was there the voices had come from.

At least a hundred of the Anahera were gathered in the centre of the yard and now stood staring in their direction. Each bore wings of every hue and colour, some lifted in fright, others folded neatly against their backs.

Silence had fallen across the yard and Erika couldn't help but shudder as she felt the gaze of the Divine upon her. She swallowed, but there was no chance to turn back now. Flicking one last glance at Maisie, she strode forward in search of Cara and the Elders who would judge them.

The Anahera parted without a word and more of the structure rising from their midst came into view. An enormous altar of granite lay in the centre of the yard, stone monoliths rising from each of its corners, stretching some fifteen feet high. Unlike the rest of the city, the rock for the structure appeared to have come from the surrounding mountains.

As they neared the centre of the yard, Erika finally caught sight of Cara. She knelt in the mud beneath the strange monoliths, her auburn wings drooped low, suffering under the gaze of five Anahera. Each bore the marks of age —lines that wrinkled their faces and hair bleached white, withered limbs, and tired eyes. Even their wings, so glorious in all the Anahera who had gathered in the yard, had lost their lustre, with patches of naked skin showing in the place of feathers.

All, that was, except for the looming figure of Farhan in their centre.

The hackles stood on Erika's neck as she looked from Cara to the Elders, to her father standing amongst them. Outside the city, Farhan had spoken of the Elders as though they were apart from him. Now her blood ran cold as she realised the weight his anger carried. How could Cara have neglected to mention that her own father was amongst the rulers of her people?

Farhan showed no emotion as he watched their approach, and she wondered again at this God. Surely, whatever his anger at Cara's defiance, he could not condemn his own daughter.

"Humans," Farhan growled, stepping from the other Elders to confront them. "You are not welcome here."

A lump lodged in Erika's throat as her heart began to pound. She fought the urge to run, to flee from the power she glimpsed in Farhan's amber eyes, from the towering God before her. Even Maisie beside her took a step back.

But then Erika's gaze was drawn beyond the God to where Cara still knelt in the mud. She had looked up at their approach and her eyes were wide as she stared at the pair of them. A smile touched Erika's lips at the open surprise on her friend's face, and she offered a reassuring nod, before turning to face Farhan.

"We humans have names, Farhan," she said, managing to add iron to her voice. "I am called Erika, as I informed you in our quarters."

For the first time, a frown wrinkled the God's face. She caught a flicker in his eyes as he appraised them, but whatever doubt she had caused, it was quickly replaced by irritation.

"You have trespassed on our lands, corrupted my daughter." He took a step closer to them, his wings lifting to cast the two humans in shade. "Now you come here, uninvited to our private assembly, and demand our attention?" He raised a fist, and Erika couldn't help but imagine an iron hand closing around her throat. "Even our youngest fledglings know to show more respect."

Erika shuddered, trying to still her racing heart, to suppress the sudden desire to throw herself at the feet of this being and beg his forgiveness. Farhan was Divine, God to her people, to herself. What right did she have to stand here and question him?

But that would mean abandoning Cara to her fate, and looking at the terrified Goddess, Erika knew that was something she could not do. Lifting her shoulders, she met Farhan's glare.

"And...what corruption do you speak of?"

The God stood in silence for a long moment, eyes fixed to hers, as though expecting her to melt before his power. But summoning every inch of her court training, Erika resisted the urge to squirm, to subjugate herself before his Divinity. Cara's fate, even their own, might rest in her hands. She would not back down.

"My daughter has spilt the blood of a mortal, an act condemned by the Sacred Founders of the Anahera."

Ice spread through Erika's veins at the coldness of Farhan's words for his daughter. Could he truly be so callous, so heartless? She swallowed, drawing her own mask of nobility about herself, of defiance.

"Very well," she said, advancing a step. "Then I would speak on behalf of my friend."

## ❧ 8 ☙

## THE FOLLOWER

*ear me, my children!*

H Adonis's heart swelled as Maya's voice rose above the cries of the Tangata gathered in the square before the Basilica. There was a serenity to her Voice when she spoke, a power far beyond that of their fallen Matriarch. She stood on the steps of the Basilica, arms outstretched towards her children, her mental Voice ringing through the minds of those gathered before her.

*Fear not, the darkness has passed,* she continued, the inner notes of her Voice swelling to a crescendo, lifting her people, banishing their despair. *No longer will we stand idle. The time of the Tangata has come.*

Thousands had gathered at her command, torn loose from their obligations to their humans. Men and women, old and young packed the streets, and all of them looked to Maya, hanging upon her Voice.

*The corruption has been cut from our midst,* Maya continued, and for a moment darkness filled Adonis's mind, a hatred, an anger for the creatures that had walked so blatantly amongst them. Rumblings came from the crowd, and he sensed their questions, their confusion, that they had ever allowed such monsters to pretend to be their equals, to be honoured alongside their Tangatan betters.

*The future belongs to us, my children,* Maya whispered. *Our enemies have grown weak. They war amongst themselves, have grown isolated, divided. They will fall like leaves before the flames. This world, it is ours for the taking.*

Blood pounded in Adonis's ears as she spoke. Long had he petitioned the Matriarch to expand their warrior forces, to lead greater attacks against the human lines, to drive them back into the oceans. She had resisted, believing peace might yet be achieved, that the humans would finally come to see them as equals.

It had been a foolish hope. Humanity in its arrogance could never see another species as peers. But what did it matter now? Adonis had seen the Old One in all her glory, her devastating power. All the armies of humanity could not stand against her, not with the Tangata at her back.

The sobbing had stopped now, as the Tangata of New Nihelm stood and watched their new Matriarch, as they felt her Voice wash over them, calming their minds, sweeping away the grief. A great calm came over the square as every soul waited for her next words.

*Today, the Tangata stand united. Today, we all march upon our enemies!*

Adonis's head jerked up at the words. Surely Maya could not mean they would leave the city today. Even the Tangata would need time to prepare for a campaign of such size, to gather supplies for the march and survey the enemy formations, even to hunt down what scouts the humans had stolen across the great river.

Nor could all the Tangata of New Nihelm march, however much Adonis might long to see that sight. There were hundreds of aged members amongst their numbers, and as much again children. Those of the lesser generations would struggle with the cold of the northern territories, where winter had yet to release its grip.

But even as he looked from Maya to those gathered in the square, he felt again the pounding in his mind, the desire for vengeance, to finally bring death to the enemies of his people. They had waited long enough, had delayed and obfuscated. No longer. Humanity would finally face retribution for the genocide they had launched against the Tangata all those years ago.

Below him, the Tangata surged from the square, their voices raised in harmony, minds united in a single thought, a single cause.

*Death, death, death.*

Smiling, Adonis turned to Maya. *What of those who escaped?* he murmured. *The traitors who fled with their humans.*

Maya's eyes danced as she regarded him. Smiling, she stepped closer and placed a hand on his bandage. Adonis struggled to keep the pain from his mind as the muscles of his chest spasmed. Her smile grew and he sensed her consciousness prodding against his.

*You desire revenge, my mate?* she asked.

Adonis swallowed as the pressure from her hand increased. *Yes, my Matriarch,* he replied, bowing his head. *The human...my pain will not be sated until his body lies dead at my feet.*

*Yes...I can feel your rage,* Maya replied, stepping closer now, leaving only an inch separating them. Leaning in, she pressed her lips gently to his, and for a moment Adonis's pain was forgotten.

*You will have your revenge, my mate,* her voice came again, and he felt a rush of ecstasy, *but for now, it must wait. My children, their future, must come first.*

Adonis's heart twisted at her words but then her body was pressing hard against him, her hands shifting their attention, and his concerns were swept away in a surge of lust. A groan hissed from his lips.

*Where will you lead us, my Matriarch?* he growled, desire burning in his stomach.

For just a second, Maya broke away from him, and he glimpsed a flame burning in her own eyes, a desperate desire, the rage of lost centuries. A sudden chill touched Adonis, though a moment later it was swept away, drowned by the emotions rushing from his mate. Only as they fell to the stone steps did he hear the Old One's reply, the faintest of whispers, a promise of what was to come:

*To war.*

## ❦ 9 ❦

## THE HERO

Lukys watched in silence as the black clouds raced towards them. The ocean seemed to rise to meet that darkness, white caps bubbling, thrashing, until it seemed they might consume the sky itself. Thunder clapped and for a moment all was turned to a brilliant white.

When the glow faded, Lukys turned from the storm. Onboard the ship, all was chaos. His comrades ran to and fro, clutching at oars and dragging sails into the sky, anything to eke another knot of speed from the little fishing ship.

Lukys already knew it was futile. Even as he caught a glimpse of land in the distance, the oceans rose around them, waves churning the depths to white and cutting off that faint hope. Screams came from the Perfugians as the deck rocked violently beneath them, hurling several from their feet.

The wind followed. Howling down from the sky, it struck the sails with a *boom*. Fabric shrieked and the masts groaned, and for a moment Lukys thought the strength of the storm would plunge them straight to the bottom of the ocean. He staggered towards where Travis stood at the tiller as rain began to fall. Driven by the wind, it slashed at his face like knives, biting where it struck.

"We're not going to make it!" Lukys shouted as he reached Travis.

Fear showed in Travis's eyes as he tore his gaze from the waters ahead. "What do we do?"

Lukys gritted his teeth. What wisdom did he possess that could answer such a question? He forced the doubts aside.

"Whatever we have to," he growled, gesturing to the waters. "Take what shelter we can, ride it out. It's our only chance now."

Travis's face grew pale, but after a moment his jaw hardened and he nodded. Isabella moved alongside him, and they shared a glance. It seemed to Lukys that some unspoken words passed between them, though he knew Travis did not possess his ability. Then Isabella reached out a hand to grip the tiller alongside Travis.

"We'll do our best to see us through," Travis's voice rang through a crash of thunder.

Lukys opened his mouth to order them to take shelter with everyone else before thinking better of it. Instead, he gripped each of them by the shoulder, offering his silent thanks.

Then he turned away and started across the deck, shouting for his comrades to drop oars and take shelter with their Tangatan partners. The storm roared, threatening to steal his words, but some heard and the cry was taken up by others. In moments the Perfugians had released their oars and dropped what ropes still remained in the rigging. They staggered for the bow and gunwales, desperate for something, anything upon which to cling. The Tangata went with them, even their inhuman agility struggling on the sharply-pitching ship.

Lukys cried out as a wave broke over the gunwale. Icy water gushed across the deck, carrying discarded oars and spears with it. Around them, the ocean surged, pitching the tiny vessel back and forth, each wave threatening to finally be the one that drove them into the unknown depths.

As Lukys watched, another wave broke across the railings. Instinctively, he threw himself at the mast, gripping it tight as the water crashed into him. Even so, it almost tore him loose. Drenched to the skin, he clung on as the storm hurled its rage upon them.

A cry carried to his ears. Squinting through the water lashing his face, Lukys caught a glimpse of Warren's face as he was washed across the deck by the waters. There was a crash as he slammed into the gunwale, followed by a sharp *crack*. Before anyone could react, the wooden piles gave way, and the recruit vanished into the swirling currents.

Screams carried across the deck, and a moment later a Tangata plunged after him, hurling herself into the depths. Whether she reached the Perfugian, Lukys would never know. They were gone, and the fishing ship rushed on, another wave looming above.

Glimpsing a rope lying strewn across the deck, Lukys threw himself on a coil and pulled it to him. Gathering it in a loop, he made to tie it around his waist, then hesitated. His eyes were drawn back to the tiller, where Travis and Isabella alone stood against the storm. He sensed those two were the only hope any of them had, that only by their efforts would the ship remain afloat. Looping the rope over his shoulder, Lukys staggered back towards the stern.

He reached his friend just before the next wave struck. It rose above, a mountain upon the ocean. Together they clung to the tiller as Travis directed the little ship towards the peak, defiant. The deck pitched beneath their feet, carrying them up, up, up…

The wave broke as they were halfway up the slope. White water crashed over the ship, engulfing them. For a moment, Lukys knew only darkness, as they were swallowed by the raging waters. Then the chaos receded once more, and he found they were somehow still upright.

With no time to spare, he tied the rope about Travis's waist, then to the tiller. With luck it might save him from being swept away should he fall. He reached for Isabella next, but she waved him away, face taut as she watched the next wave approaching. Nodding, Lukys returned to his friend. Travis's face was grim as he battled the ocean. Lukys could see the terror in his friend's eyes, but thinking of Isabella's warning on the shore, he couldn't help but smile. Whatever Lukys's private doubts, Travis had more than proven himself aboard the ship.

He swung around, surveying the damage the storm had wrought. His remaining countrymen still sheltered beneath the gunwales, but there was no hiding from the storm. Salt stung Lukys's eyes, but he knew he could not rest. These were his people. They had followed him on this mad path, had trusted him to lead them to safety. He would not fail them now, could not.

A cry came from the bow as water broke across the prow. Lukys's heart lurched as he saw Dale torn from the mast he clung to, the power of the ocean hurling him across the deck. White water surged around him, sweeping towards the hole in the railings left by Warren's fall. Desperately, Dale clutched at the wooden planks—and somehow managed to halt his momentum.

Roaring his fury into the storm's rage, Lukys started across the ship towards his friend. Not a single soul more would be lost to this tempest, not while he lived. He staggered as the ship crashed down the other side of a wave, but managed to keep upright. Dale was not so lucky, the movement dislodging his grip and throwing him sideways, thankfully away from the gaping hole in the railings.

Unfortunately, the mast brought him to an abrupt halt. Lukys winced at the audible *thud* of the impact, and watched as his friend slumped to the deck. Pain showed on Dale's face as he tried to rise, but the blow had damaged something, and he slumped back to the wooden planks.

Lukys continued, even as he searched the ship for Keria. He found Dale's partner at the bow, eyes wide with fear, locked to Dale's slumped form. He knew that expression all too well. It was one of unspeakable terror, one beyond reasoning, the kind that could freeze a soul in place, rendering one unable to move, to act. Adonis had given them all a taste of such fear, back in New Nihelm, but that had been his power. Keria's terror now was real. She would be of no help to Dale, not in that state.

Another wave built beyond the prow and Lukys darted forward. Dale would not survive without aid. The ship pitched beneath them, throwing him off-balance, and he fell to one knee. Desperate, he righted himself, but it was already too late. The wave rushed towards them, thundering down upon the keel...

...in a flash of grey, Sophia crashed into Dale, one arm hugging him tight. Waters surging around them, her other reached for the mast. Her fingers scraped against the heavy oak...

...and missed!

Lukys's heart lurched into his throat as the deck tilted sharpy. Caught in the swirling waters, the two were swept beyond reach of the mast—and towards the gaping hole in the railing.

Without thinking, Lukys dived after them, arm outstretched. Somehow, his hand found Sophia's. Her fingers locked around his in a crushing grip and he felt a rush of elation—then the weight of his friends yanked him forward, dragging them all towards the raging ocean. In terror, Lukys scrambled for purchase, some hold that would save them from the waters, but there was nothing. The three of them were swept on towards the hole.

Just before they went over, his eyes met Sophia's. In that moment, he saw her panic, her fear. His stomach twisted and in desperation he slammed his fingers into the deck. Their weight tore his nails as they scraped the wood, but it made no difference.

Then suddenly iron fingers were closing around his wrist, jerking him to a stop. The weight of Sophia and Dale almost tore his arm from its socket, but screaming, he clung on to Sophia, to their unknown saviour he couldn't quite glimpse through the raging storm, until finally the last of the water drained away and the ship drew level again.

Coughing, Lukys released Sophia and dragged himself to hands and knees, struggling to catch his breath. Finally he looked up and saw Keria standing over them. Her face was so pale she might have been a spirit, sent by the Gods above to save them.

But no, she was only mortal, only a Tangata, and Lukys watched as she crouched alongside Dale, cradling his injured head in her hands. His eyes were closed and Lukys prayed he was only unconscious. Shaking off his own pain, he forced himself to inspect their surroundings. His stomach lurched as he saw how close they'd come to tumbling through the broken gunwale. Dale's legs were already hanging over the edge. Another second...

"Come on," he rasped, drawing Sophia and Keria's attention. His throat was raw from the salt in the air, but he forced himself to speak out loud. It helped to keep his thoughts focused. The storm still raged around them and any moment now another wave could break across the deck. "We need to get him to safety."

Together they dragged Dale back to the mast, and using another rope torn from the rigging, they bound him in place. There was no time to inspect his injuries, but when Lukys checked his pulse it was strong. That would have to be enough for now. Keria crouched alongside her partner after they'd secured him, holding the man tight. The Tangata still carried the haunted look in her eyes and Lukys couldn't help but wonder what secret strength she'd drawn on to save them. He wished there was something he could do to reassure her, to take away her fear, but all he could do was nod his thanks.

Then, exhausted, barely able to keep himself alert, Lukys crawled his way to where Sophia crouched against the second mast. Her skin was pale from the cold, her clothes soaked, her hair pasted against her scalp. She watched him come, seemingly unable to move, to speak, and Lukys wondered if she'd been injured in the fall.

"Are you okay?" he cried, reaching out to lay a hand on her arm.

Sophia did not move, only tightened her grip around the mast. A shudder shook her, and he saw that her eyes were not focused on him. Their grey depths were fixed on the hole in the railing, on the swirling, icy depths beyond.

Swallowing, Lukys looked around, wondering what to do, but there was no one else. The rest of the Perfugians seemed secure, while at the tiller Travis roared his defiance to the storm, the sound like mad laughter beneath the ringing of thunder. Turning back to Sophia, Lukys swallowed his hesitation and wrapped his arms around her, seeking to warm her, to grant some small comfort amidst the tempest.

There they knelt as the storm raged on, as mother

nature hurled all her strength against them, as they waited for the end to come.

And there the sun finally found them as it broke through the clouds. The storm vanished at its appearance, as though banished by its light, by its warmth. The sea grew calm and the wind died away, leaving them to drift at peace.

Lukys found himself blinking, his body stiff, aching with a dozen fresh bruises. Carefully he detached himself from Sophia. As the sun touched her face, she shuddered and the light returned to her eyes. She looked around, frowning to see him so close, as though she had not noticed his presence until that moment. He felt a soft probing upon his mind, a questioning, as though she wasn't quite sure what he was doing. He offered a smile, too exhausted to talk. Then he rose to inspect the aftermath of the storm.

The main mast was now slightly off-kilter, its sail hanging in tatters, while the mast he and Sophia had clung too did not even have remnants. A single oar had been left to them, wedged against the gunwale in the bow.

He was surprised to find Travis still standing, though his friend was sagging against the tiller, though not even that had survived the storm's wrath. At some point the rudder had been torn free from its bracket, leaving only the wooden handle to which Travis clung. Isabella stood alongside him, her arm around his waist, offering her strength. Her eyes met Lukys's, and she nodded.

Lukys swallowed, his throat raw from the salt and the screaming. Bracing himself, he staggered across the deck to where Dale was still bound to the second mast. Keria had remained at his side. She was fumbling desperately at the ropes as Lukys approached, and for a moment he thought the worst. Then an answering moan came from Dale. His head lifted a fraction, words slipping from his lips, too soft for Lukys to hear. Keria cried out and threw herself at Dale, sobbing into his shoulder.

In his mind, Lukys heard her gushing apologies. He helped her with the last of the ropes, then placed a hand on her shoulder.

*It's alright,* he said softly. *You're both alright.*

Others had not been so lucky. Despite his oath, he could see that some had not survived the disaster. Perhaps twelve Perfugians remained alongside their Tangatan partners. So few. He couldn't help but think back to that first day when they'd arrived in Fogmore, how many faces that had vanished, forever lost.

Anger touched him, at his commanders, his Sovereigns. They had done this to them, had cast aside their lives as though they had no worth, as though they were nothing. Yet he had seen the true strength of these men and women, their courage. They deserved so much more.

The anger faded, though, as he looked beyond the wreckage of their ship, his eyes sweeping the horizons. His heart sank as he took in the endless ocean in all directions and he tried to keep his fear in check, to keep it from broadcasting, from infecting the other Tangata.

They sensed it anyway, and he felt their gazes upon him, heard their unspoken questions. He closed his eyes, not wanting to speak, to tell them the source of his fear.

But there was no hiding the truth now, not from the Tangata.

They were stranded in the middle of the ocean, with no sails or oars or supplies, and no help in sight. He had led them to their doom.

## THE EMISSARY

The Gods were all looking at her—every one of them. Even Cara seemed shocked, as though she couldn't quite believe a human would name her a friend. Sadness touched Erika at the thought. How poorly she had treated Cara over these past months, even after the Goddess had saved her life.

It was finally time to repay that debt.

"As I was saying," Erika managed to say into the silence that had followed her pronouncement. "I would speak for my friend." She cursed inwardly as a tremor betrayed her nerves, but she refused to break from Farhan's stare.

"My daughter has committed an unforgivable crime," the God growled, his words sending a chill down Erika's spine. "There is no need to compound my family's shame by having a human speak on her behalf."

Behind him, Cara's eyes returned to the ground and she slumped where she knelt, her wings draped across the dirt. The sight of the Goddess so subdued lit a fire in Erika's stomach and she bared her teeth.

"Regardless of the shame it might bring you, Farhan, I

would defend my friend," she snapped.

Farhan said nothing, only stared at her as though what she had just said was some absurdity.

Taking his silence for permission, Erika pressed on. "Your daughter only killed Yasin in self-defence, in defence of all of us," she argued. "If not for Cara, I would not stand here before you."

"It matters not," Farhan replied, his voice untouched by her plea. "The taking of life is forbidden."

"Even in defence of another? Even if doing nothing means someone you love will die?" She paused, staring up at the towering God, wondering whether to press on. She drew in a breath, knowing it must be said. "Even if it means hundreds of thousands, even millions of lives, will be lost?"

The God did not reply, yet...Erika could see the answer in the coldness of his eyes. Yes, not even to save another could this law of theirs be broken. Not even to save humanity. She swallowed, struggling to comprehend the enormity of what stood before her, to keep the despair from her soul. Balling her fists, she began to shake, to feel herself coming apart.

"All my life," she gasped, her voice close to breaking. "I have been praying for your return. I studied the legends of the past, searched out the secrets of your people, the ruins you left behind, the artefacts, the magic. All in preparation for this day, when I might finally speak with you, might beseech you to return, to save my people. All so that others would not have to go without their fathers, as I have."

She exhaled slowly and her emotion went with it, leaving only an emptiness, a dark despair, devoid of hope.

"Please," she said, unable to summon anything more elegant than the simple plea.

Silence met her words. Farhan stared at her, and Erika couldn't help but think herself as a bug before this being, that at any moment he might decide to crush her beneath his boot. Again she felt a pang of longing for the gauntlet, but she squashed it down and met the God's eyes.

"So naïve," he said quietly. "You know nothing of the Anahera, human. We shaped this world, have already saved it from destruction once. The price was too great. That is why our Sacred Founders forbid interference in your affairs." Slowly he turned to look at his daughter. "That is why we do not kill." For an instant, Erika thought she glimpsed pain in the face of the God, but a second later it was gone, and he continued in the same cold, unyielding tone. "Under threat of de-winging."

"*No!*"

Still knelt in the mud, Cara's head snapped up at her father's words. Terror showed in her amber eyes and her wings lifted from the dirt as she leapt to her feet, as though only now did she think to flee.

The other Anahera were faster. Several that had approached unnoticed darted forward to catch her arms and wings, locking them in grips of iron. Cara screamed and struggled against them, but she fought now against her own kind, and her strength was evenly matched by each of her captors.

Finally she slumped into their grasp, defeated. Tears streamed down the Goddess's face as she looked at her father.

"Father," she rasped in a tone that tore at Erika's heart. "Father, I beg you, don't do this."

"The Elders are in agreement," Farhan said, ignoring his daughter's pleas. Behind him, the elderly Anahera inclined their heads. "All your life, you have ignored the commands of the Founders. No longer can we ignore your wilfulness." He paused then, and again Erika glimpsed a flicker of something in his eyes. "This is for your own good, daughter," he continued finally. "Lest you follow your mother's path."

"No, no, no!" Cara was sobbing, trying to tear her wings from the grasp of her captors. Suddenly the Goddess swung on Erika, and she saw the desperation in her friend's eyes. "Please, Erika, don't let them!"

Erika's heart pounded in her ears as she looked from Cara to her father. "I…" She struggled to find the words to argue, to defy the God before her.

How could he be so callous, so heartless, to stand there and order the mutilation of his own daughter? Yet she saw no give in Farhan's eyes, only a cold determination, an inevitability like the ocean tides to see his sentence passed.

"Please, spare her," she finally managed.

"I have tolerated her dalliances for too long," he said dismissively. "I would not expect your kind to understand." He turned to face his daughter once more. "The guillotine will be prepared over the coming days. The Elders have granted you a week to ready yourself, daughter. Until then, you will be confined to your quarters. Take her there, now," he finished, gesturing to those who held Cara.

Erika watched as Cara was led away through the ranks of Anahera, unable to speak, to so much as move. A knot tied itself around her insides as Erika realised the depth of her failure.

She couldn't help Cara, couldn't save her people. She couldn't even save herself.

"What…what are you going to do with us?" she croaked, no longer able to meet Farhan's eyes.

Silence answered Erika's question. Beside her, Maisie shifted closer, her entire body taut. But after a moment Farhan only shook his head.

"Come with me."

Turning on his heel, he strode through the ranks of the

Anahera. They were already beginning to filter from the yard, disappearing into any number of doors lining the walls. Erika frowned as a thought came to her—there were no children present. In fact, Cara would have been one of the youngest.

The squeal of a door opening brought her attention back to Farhan and she drew herself up as he led them from the yard, prepared to make her arguments anew. The Elders had already departed, but they were followed by another of the Anahera this time. Erika drew to a stop as she recognised Hugo, Cara's brother. Before they could speak, though, Farhan reappeared in the doorway. The look in his eyes brooked no disobedience and she hurried forward.

Hugo closed the door behind them as Erika and Maisie found themselves in another antechamber, this one some kind of workplace rather than a living quarters. A bookcase had been placed in one corner, but it was the desk that drew Erika's attention. Made from the same metallic substance as the outer doors, it was covered in an array of unfamiliar objects. Erika's heart started to race at the sight and she thought again of the artefacts discovered in other secret sites, her gauntlet and Maisie's orb. What fresh magic might these objects hold?

Farhan must have seen the look in her eyes, for he stepped between her and the desk, his wings stretching to hide the objects from view. Erika swallowed as she found his gaze upon her and quickly lowered her gaze.

"I...you didn't answer my question, outside," she said lamely.

"My daughter should never have brought you here," he rumbled, as though that was an answer. Erika stared at him, waiting for the rest, and to her surprise, the God turned away. "Now that you have seen our city, you cannot be permitted to leave."

Erika's heart lurched in her chest. She opened her mouth to denounce him, but suddenly her throat was parched and all she could manage was a strange rasping. A shudder shook her as she stared at the God.

"You...you can't," she finally said lamely.

"I am sorry," he replied, and this time he seemed sincere. "You are not the first humans to have reached our haven these last centuries, though you are the first to have been brought by one of our own. But the Elders have made their minds clear. There will be no exceptions."

Words abandoned Erika then and she stood staring at the God, struggling to comprehend the ramifications of his words. They could never leave, were condemned to remain forever in the City of the Gods, locked away high in the mountains, away from civilisation, from their own kind. They would never return to their kingdoms, would never bring word of their discovery back to the realm of man.

She found herself staring at Maisie, wondering what they would do, how they would survive in this inhospitable place for the rest of their lives. There would be no escape. Even if they slipped from the city, there was only barren rock and ice for a hundred miles. The Gods would track them down within a day—if they did not freeze to death first.

"Come on," Maisie said finally, her voice soft, without judgement. She touched a hand to Erika's shoulder. "There's nothing more we can do here. Let's go back to the room."

Erika nodded dumbly, but Farhan spoke before either could move.

"My son, Hugo, will be your guide, until you have... adjusted to our customs."

Erika took that as a reprimand for their breakout. Hugo flashed them what could have been an apologetic look as he held out a hand for them to enter into the corridor. Erika hesitated, looking again at Farhan. Surely there was still something she could say to save them, some plea that might melt his cold heart. But Maisie was already stepping from the room, and realising she had been defeated, Erika followed.

Hugo led them back to their quarters in silence. That suited Erika. In the face of her failure, she was in no mood for conversation. When they reached the room, he gestured them inside and closed the door behind them. Erika didn't need to ask to know he would be waiting outside should they attempt any further excursions.

Slumping to the bed, she looked at Maisie. "I'm sorry," she croaked. "This...this is all my fault."

To her surprise, the spy only shrugged. "Probably." Seating herself across from Erika, she rustled in her bag for a moment, before coming up with a leather-bound book. "Still," she continued, tossing the book to Erika. "We might as well use the time productively."

Erika frowned as she caught the book. It was obviously old, its cover cracked and the papers within so dry they had become brittle. Opening it with caution, she found herself looking upon pages of handwritten script. She looked back at Maisie.

"Where did you get this?"

A smile touched the spy's lips. "I told you they would be easy picking," she replied.

Erika's frown deepened and she looked again at the words on the page. They had faded with the passage of time and had obviously been placed upon the page by someone unused to writing script. The size of the words changed constantly and the author hadn't even kept his lines straight. She flicked to the beginning and read the first line:

*What hath we become?*

# II

# THE HERO

They drifted for days without a glimpse of land. Occasionally gulls hovered overhead, circling the empty masts before disappearing back into the endless skies. Travis said that was a good sign. It meant they were still close to the coast—but without any way to navigate or propel the ship, it mattered little.

So they drifted on, carried by the gentle lapping of waves against the hull, by the soft breath of the ocean. No more storms appeared, but exposed on the open deck, the sun beat down upon the Perfugians. The storm had torn through most of their canvas and the little freshwater that remained was quickly consumed. They did their best to ration the food, but even that quickly dwindled. A few of the recruits were now trying to string together fishing lines from the scraps of the sails.

Without water and exposed to the unrelenting sun, Lukys's mouth became as dry as straw, his skin scorched red like a lobster thrown in a pot to boil. An ache began at the base of his skull and grew with each passing day. His eyes throbbed with the constant, unbearable light—yet when the night came, the temperatures would plummet and the sorry crew would find themselves huddling together, desperate for warmth.

And still there was no sign of salvation.

On the fourth day after the storm, Lukys found himself alone in the hull of the ship, curled up against the gunwale, desperately trying to hug a sliver of shade. A terrible silence hung over the ship. Not a soul spoke, not even the Tangata, as each suffered their trial alone. Most remained in pairs, though Lukys didn't know how they could stay so close to one another. His skin was so raw from the sun and salt, it hurt just to brush against the wooden railings.

He looked up as a shadow fell across his legs, finding Sophia standing above him. They had not spoken since the storm, since their argument.

*You saved me,* she whispered. *Why?*

Lukys frowned at her. *Why would I not?*

She shook her head, glancing away from him. *Because I manipulated you, lied to you.* She paused, and when she went on, he heard the pain in her voice. *Because I'm a monster.*

He jerked at the word, so visceral, and finally he realised the truth, the pain she felt. The way he had treated her, the things he'd said, his anger, his rage, all of it had only served to confirm her own doubts, her own fears. Just as Lukys loathed his own past, that the only thing he'd ever achieved was death, Sophia feared the monster within herself.

Perhaps they were a better match than either of them had realised.

Rising to his feet, Lukys reached out and wrapped his hands around her fingers. *You're not a monster, Sophia,* he said gently. *I never thought that.*

*I sensed your hatred, Lukys.* She did not meet his eyes, but neither did she pull away from him.

He swallowed. His throat was so raw, he was glad he did not need to speak out loud.

*I was angry,* he whispered. *I felt betrayed. I didn't know what to think, who to believe.*

He hesitated, turning to stare across the ship, taking in the Perfugians and Tangata huddled together. More hardy than the Perfugians, Sophia's brethren had refused to eat or drink, gifting their rations to their partners. His eyes found Keria seated near the tiller, wrapped in Dale's embrace. He recalled the terror in her eyes as the storm had raged about them. Yet she had come for them, had saved Dale and Sophia and Lukys himself when all else was lost.

Dale was right. Sophia and her brethren were as human as any of them.

*But I know now,* he said, turning back to Sophia. *You ask why I saved you—but it was you who saved me first, back in that clearing, when Adonis would have killed me.*

For the first time, Sophia's eyes met his. There was surprise there, but Lukys went on before she could respond, fearful of what she might say.

*You saw through the nervous recruit, saw past the worst of our species, the terrors in my mind, and still you wanted to know me, to protect me. I...I never thanked you for that.*

He thought he glimpsed a hint of red in Sophia's cheeks now as she watched him. For a long while, she said nothing, though her head tilted to the side, as though inspecting him for something. Finally she shrugged and turned away.

Lukys's heart sank, and exhaling, he slid back to the deck of the ship and leaned against the gunwale. His stomach panged, sending a bolt of pain through his side. Dark spots danced across his vision. Like the Tangata, he had set aside his rations for others.

*You need to eat, Lukys,* Sophia's voice came to him.

He looked up as she crouched alongside him and offered

her hand. A piece of jerky lay in her palm. A frown creased his forehead and gently he pushed the food aside.

*You eat it,* he whispered.

*You need it more than me, Lukys,* Sophia insisted, *and they need you. It is the responsibility of the strong to protect the weak amongst us.*

Lukys glanced at her. *That is not what Adonis believed,* he replied, remembering how the Tangatan leader had tried to control them, calling them weak.

He'd tried to forget that day, the trembling terror that had come so close to unmanning him. Stronger than all of them, Adonis had pushed the fear upon them, used it to control them. A shudder went through him as he recalled what it had taken to resist, to fight back.

*How did he do it?* he asked suddenly. *How did he control all of us so easily?*

*All of us but you,* Sophia replied softly.

Lukys's head jerked up at that, and he saw she was watching him again.

*All of us but me,* he agreed, then frowned. *How is that possible?*

A sigh slipped from the Tangata's lips and suddenly she was sitting before him, legs crossed, fingers drumming on her knees.

*As I said, even untrained, you are stronger than you have any right to be, Lukys.*

Lukys swallowed as he was trapped in Sophia's grey eyes. *Then I must learn to control it.*

*You must,* Sophia agreed.

With a struggle, Lukys tore his gaze from her, looking across the deck instead. *I will ask Isabella to teach me.*

*Why?*

His head snapped back to where Sophia still sat, unmoving. *What do you mean?*

She rolled her eyes as though the answer were obvious. *I*

*will teach you, Lukys,* she said as though the matter had been decided long ago.

*But I thought...*

Sophia's brow hardened and Lukys trailed off, swallowing the words. Clearly she had no desire to rehash the past. Instead, he nodded his accord, and a faint smile returned to her lips.

*How...how do we begin?* he asked after nothing had been said between them for a while.

*How should I know?* Sophia replied, and her smile grew. *This is like breathing for us, Lukys, the sense of another mind, reading the colours of emotions—*

*Wait, the colours of what?* Lukys interrupted.

*Emotions,* Sophia said. *When you look closely, you can see they each have a colour. They are constantly changing, mixing.*

Lukys frowned, thinking back to the bridge in New Nihelm, when he had touched the minds of the Tangatan guards. In his desperation, he had been able to influence them, convince them there was nothing to concern them in the dark waters of the river. Then again in the village, he'd inadvertently broadcast his anger, his rage, into the minds of the Tangata they faced. But he'd never realised there was a colour to those emotions.

*Can I...can I see?* he asked hesitantly.

After a moment, Sophia inclined her head in agreement. Closing his eyes, Lukys reached out with his consciousness to brush against her mind. Silence fell between them as he concentrated, listening, watching, trying to glimpse the colours she had spoken of. A tingle began in the back of his neck, the hackles lifting as he sensed...something from Sophia, a shimmer of colour amidst the swirling of her thoughts.

He hesitated, lingering, trying to pierce the cloud about her, and slowly colours took shape from the ether. A swirling grey amidst black, hints of pink, but stronger than all that, a deep sapphire, darker even than the ocean that surrounded them. Lukys frowned as he took in the colours, trying to decipher their meaning. They were chaotic, constantly changing, just as Sophia had said, but the blue appeared the most stable. He reached for it with his consciousness, and felt a shudder go through him.

*You're afraid,* he said softly, his eyes flickering open, *but of what?*

She glanced away from him, and before he could speak again, she rose to her feet. He followed as she leaned against the railing, eyes on the open ocean. Hesitantly, he reached out again, touching his consciousness to hers.

*I'm sorry,* he spoke with caution, *I did not mean to intrude.*

*No,* Sophia said, biting her lip. *It's not that. It's...* She glanced sidelong at him, wrinkles creasing her forehead. *I have never...never been on a ship before. At first it was something...different. Now though, after the storm...* She trailed off, and now Lukys glimpsed the fear she had hidden so well in her grey eyes.

*You're afraid of the ocean?*

Sophia did not reply, only inclined her head.

*But...you can swim.* Lukys frowned. *Better than any human ever could. Why would you fear it?*

*It's endless,* her response came sharply, *immense. I could swim—but how far? If I had fallen in that storm...fallen as my sister Tangata did...how long until my strength gave out? I would be...powerless.*

Lukys found himself smiling. Somehow, the fear made Sophia more human, all the more real to him. He wanted to lean in and kiss her, but resisted, knowing that was not what she wanted. Sadness touched him, that he might have ruined something real, but...

*We all feel powerless at times,* he said softly. He glanced over his shoulder at the rest of their companions. *All of them, they're looking to me to protect them, to save them. It hurts, to know I can do nothing. But...that's what it is to be human—to be helpless before the greater powers in this world.*

*I don't like it,* Sophia said after a while. *It is not a...sensation that we are familiar with.* She hesitated. *It makes me think of our forgotten ancestors, those who lost their grey eyes, who were sent away on the ocean in exile. What they must have felt, lost on these endless waters, the powerlessness...*

Lukys chuckled despite himself. *I guess being superhuman hasn't put you at too many disadvantages in life.*

A smile flickered on Sophia's face. *I suppose that's true,* she replied, then hesitated, *or it was—until I met you.*

*Oh?*

Sophia laughed. The sound surprised Lukys—gone was the fear. Instead, he glimpsed a light in her eyes. Reaching out, he caught a glimpse of the swirling colours again. The blue remained, but it had receded, other colours rising to the surface, purples and pinks. Abruptly they vanished and he frowned.

*You know, it's rude to pry, Lukys,* Sophia said, raising an eyebrow.

Lukys felt his cheeks grow warm at the admonishment, but the Tangata only chuckled and continued with her story:

*Yes, none of this is how things were meant to go. Right from that first day in the cells of New Nihelm, I have felt a helplessness I have never known before. While my brothers and sisters found happiness with their assignments, I was forced to sit with you in silence, to suffer your anger, your hatred—when all I wanted was to make you happy. It was...galling.*

*Strange,* Lukys replied with a smile. *I was completely within your power in that cell, yet you were the one who felt helpless?*

Sophia shrugged. *As I've told you, we cannot create emotions that are not already there. I had to wait...* She finished abruptly.

Lukys frowned as she glanced in his direction. *What?*

For a moment, Sophia said nothing. Then she leaned in, her head lifting to meet his, and suddenly she was kissing him. Lukys was so surprised that he almost pulled away. Hadn't she just rejected him, made it clear she could not forgive him for how he had treated her after their escape?

Then Sophia's lips parted and their tongues met, and his worries were washed away by the taste of her, by the feel of her body pressed against his, by the sweetness of her scent. For a moment his senses were overwhelmed, and he found himself carried back to the kiss they had shared all those nights ago in New Nihelm, as they danced to the music of the Calafe. It seemed a hundred years had passed since that night now. Then, Lukys hadn't known yet the true secrets of the Tangata, the power they could wield. He'd been naïve, distrusting. He hadn't known the treasure he held, the sweetness of the creature before him.

Now...now he pulled Sophia tight and breathed her in, savouring every moment. He realised now what his friends had seen so quickly, saw Sophia for the unique individual she was—not Tangata, nor human, but everything in between, with her earnest emotions and a strength all of her own. A person who had dared to dream of something other than death in the midst of a decade long war, a woman who wanted nothing more than an ordinary life. So as the sun dipped towards the horizon, he kissed the strange, wonderful woman that had come to him in the darkness.

And she kissed him back.

Amidst their passion, it was a moment before the two heard the cries from the others. Finally they broke apart, and Lukys spun, thinking the worst had happened, that another storm had finally come upon them, that the winds and waves would soon swallow them up, plunging them to the bottom of the ocean.

Instead, great sails of blue rose from the ocean, marring the horizon. A ship, bearing the colours of Perfugia. Of home.

## ❦ 12 ❦

## THE FOLLOWER

The storm raged around Adonis, the heavy sleet cutting across his vision, the fog closing in. He staggered on, teeth clenched, determined. He would not fail Maya now, would not fall behind. Others marched around him, his brothers and sisters struggling through the storm. Their voices thrummed in his mind, some still strong, urging their comrades to keep faith.

But others were fading, growing weaker as the endless miles ate their strength, as the thick snowbanks and icy chill drained the life from them. Not all possessed the strength of Adonis and the cleaner generations, and these struggled to keep pace against the violence of the spring storm.

It had come upon them with the full fury of the mountains above, its winds howling down through the valley, tearing at the simple clothing of the Tangata with its icy breath, until even the strongest amongst them had begun to struggle.

Except Maya.

With the power of the Old Ones flowing through her veins, she had laughed in the face of the storm. Amidst the grey tempest, her grey eyes had fixed upon the Tangata and bid them to follow.

*Fear not, my children*, her voice had rasped into their minds, momentarily drowning out the storm. *The raging of this world cannot stop us, will not bow us low. We are... Tangata. We will prevail.*

And so they had continued into the teeth of the tempest. Young and old, strong and weak, every one of the Tangata had followed their Matriarch onwards, clinging to the pounding of her voice in their minds, to the touch of her power, her spirit.

But that had been long hours ago, and now even Adonis could barely sense her mind. She and her guard had drawn ahead and while Adonis longed to follow, he'd found himself lagging instead, held back by the pain radiating from his brethren. They each suffered in silence, but that did not change their aura, the dark greys and blacks of their despair. As the Old One's Voice faded, that darkness only grew.

He tried to encourage them in Maya's place, using his own Voice to lift them, to stir the embers of their rage, their courage, their love for the Matriarch. But even strength was lagging, sapped by the leaching cold, and for once he found his power insufficient.

Soon they began to fall. He found the first lying across his path, her body draped across a snowdrift. Adonis reached for her with his mind, to seek the life within, but death had already claimed her. The snow was beginning to cover her face, and after a moment he turned away, continuing his endless march.

They came more often after that, one after another lying dead where they had fallen, left behind by brethren too weak to offer anything but gentle goodbyes. Despair rang through the forest, the voices of the Tangata crying out for their lost brothers and sisters, even fear for their own lives grew within.

Adonis renewed his efforts to lift them, to add flames to the dying embers of their souls. The few others of his generation had drawn far ahead now; even those of the fourth and fifth were out of sight. It was the youth that lagged, those born in recent decades, the sixth and seventh generations, more human than Tangata.

Yet weak as they might be, their eyes remained grey, and their Voices still rang in his head. They were Tangata still, his people. Their former Matriarch had preached that the responsibility of the strong was to protect the weak. Adonis had scoffed at her philosophies, fuming at the humans that had come to live amongst them. Surely if such weakness was allowed to thrive, they would soon outnumber the strong. What would become of his people once there was no one left to defend them?

Now though, watching his people die one by one, he found himself doubting his own convictions. Those who fell were weak, and yet...what might be lost with each of the fallen, what knowledge and skills?

Soon he began to find the dead in groups. They had tried to huddle together, to unite in order to preserve the whole, just as the Tangata had since the calamity of the Fall. Yet against the power of the storm, not even that had been enough.

Then he saw the first of the children.

She lay with one of the fallen groups. They had placed her in the centre, using their own bodies to shelter her, to protect that precious gift that was the life of his people. Ice clung to the child's face and her skin had long since turned blue, her life stolen away by the cold, just as it had her parents.

Adonis crouched alongside the group for a long time,

listening to the screaming of the wind. Its icy breath tore at his flesh, seeking the warmth at his core, to snuff it out as it had that of the precious child.

But it would not take him. It could not. He was Tangata, strong, enduring. The raging of the storm would not be the end of him as it had been for these sorry souls.

Finally Adonis found himself rising to his feet. There was something wrong about this, about all of this. Something had changed, ever since the day he had woken the Old One from her slumber. Yet his mind was a tangled web and he could not pierce the mystery, could not place the pieces of this puzzle together.

His gaze travelled back to the child, to her ghostly face. Driven by the wind, the snow was already beginning to cover her body. He closed his eyes, taking a moment to memorize her features, to remember what had become of the child in the snow.

## 13

## THE EMISSARY

*T he Guanaco did doth appear this present day. It doest outdoith goat, and tis wool might preserve us. But death cometh upon the land. May those houses of glass provide this winter, or I feareth we might starve…o how didst it cometh to this?*

Erika sighed and started flicking forward through the journal. It had been written in some old dialect, by someone she assumed was one of the Anahera—perhaps even one of the Sacred Founders that Farhan had spoken of. It was a struggle just to read, though some of the older works from the library of Archivists had been written in a similar manner.

But the early pages at least spoke of little and less: of empty days and long nights, of dark winters and burning summers. She wondered if the writer was describing The Fall from the perspective of the Gods. If so, his experience had been altogether different from what few legends humanity kept from that time, of ages lost to darkness and destruction.

Finding a fresh entry, she began to read again.

*I didst see those folk this present day, creeping from a cave. The*

*Fall didst not taketh all. I should be'est relieved, but I findeth mine own despair only swells with the rising of the sun. Those folk we did doth warn, could hath changed. After all those folk didst commit, the hand wast forced. Though, perhaps there wast another path...*

Exhausted, Erika let the diary slip from her fingers and fall to the covers of her bed. Two days had crept past in the cold confines of the city and reading the ancient text was draining. She couldn't help but think there was an irony to her situation, that she had spent most of her life dreaming of this day, when she might stand amongst the Gods and learn their secrets. But now that she was here, she found herself bored.

What was the point of new knowledge, of fresh discoveries, if they could never be shared? So instead she found herself reading the old journal to pass her time. A shame there hadn't been much to write about in these mountains, even during the Fall.

The rest of her time she'd spent exploring the city. Its upper levels had been forbidden to them, but with Hugo as her shadow, she had criss-crossed the lower corridors. The few living quarters she'd found on the ground floor were situated near her and Maisie's room, but the rest of the Anahera she assumed lived above. They seemed to be avoiding the two humans in their midst, and otherwise the lower levels of the City were empty. In her endless hours of investigation, Erika had only found a handful of workrooms like Farhan's, and these were empty.

She made other discoveries though, mostly in the darker nooks, in antechambers barely large enough to fit a single human, let alone the Gods and their wings. Most were empty like the rest of the city, but in a few she found strange boxes filled with orbs of dark glass, like the relics her mother had once collected from old dig sites. As a child she had once managed to make a similar orb emit a flash of light, and so she pocketed one when Hugo was not looking—although the Anahera didn't seem too concerned by her explorations.

Her excitement had been short-lived when she returned to their room, however, as despite her best efforts, she failed to unlock whatever secret power the orb might contain. Not that Erika was sure she wanted to. She still hadn't taken the gauntlet from her knapsack.

Erika's only other discovery was what looked like a prison block deep within the city. She didn't stay long, only enough to see it was empty, the bars and floors dusty with disuse. Even so, the sight sent a tremor down her spine, and from then on she was sure to be thankful for the simple room they had been granted.

While Erika was in their room, Maisie spent much of her time in the corridor with Hugo. Whether the spy had taken a liking to the young Anahera, or she was just seeking another advantage in their trusting nature, Erika hadn't asked. At least she had managed to weasel a few parcels of information from the youth. Hugo had confessed he was only Cara's half-brother—the two shared Farhan as a father—though he would not speak of Cara's mother.

At other times, Erika found herself standing in the corridor studying the painting of the City of the Gods. The owner of the diary had made no mention of that ancient city, nor the incredible powers that had helped raise it. So instead she whittled away the hours by looking upon its likeness. The closer she stared, the more she saw amongst those towering spires. The sleek ships that sailed the raging waters, the shimmering objects that had been caught upon the bridge by the painter—frozen, yet from the circular wheels, Erika guessed they must have been some type of carriage. What magic had driven them without horses?

More than anything though, there was one question that

came to burn within her mind, to keep her awake at night. If this was the ancient City of the Gods, then where were the Gods themselves? The skies above the bridge were empty, and what use did beings with wings have for ships and wagons, even ones that moved without horses?

Back in their room, Erika let out a sigh and picked up the journal once more. Perhaps the answers lay somewhere within its pages, though she feared the ancient text might blind her before it gave up its secrets...

"Sleeping well?"

Erika jerked awake as Maisie appeared in the doorway. Hugo stood behind her, and Erika quickly tucked the journal beneath her pillow. The Anahera had not questioned over its absence and Hugo didn't seem overly bothered by her explorations so far, but Erika was quite sure stealing from his father would be against at least one of the commandments left by their Sacred Founders.

"I..." Erika trailed off when she saw the amusement in the spy's eyes.

The door clicked closed on their Anaheran guard, before Maisie threw herself onto her own bed.

"Never thought I'd see you sleeping on the job," she said with a smirk.

"What job?" Erika scowled, then gestured to the room. "This *is* the job, this is everything we'll ever have. Maybe I should ask Hugo if I can have some twine—may as well learn to start knitting now, if this is my retirement."

Maisie said nothing in reply and Erika looked across at her, wondering what the spy was plotting behind those brown eyes. What was she playing at with Hugo? Surely she couldn't hope to turn him against his own people. He might not share the same fanatic beliefs of the Elders, but his loyalty was without question. He had practically hopped to obey every instruction his father had given him.

"Are you done?" Maisie said finally. "As much as I enjoy watching you mope, we're running out of time, Archivist."

"Running out of time? Haven't you been listening—we have all the time in the world!"

"*We* might," Maisie replied, "but *she* doesn't."

Erika's stomach tied itself in a knot at Maisie's words and she quickly looked away. She had spent the last two days trying to forget her disastrous failure, the look Cara had given as she was led away. The despair in her friend's eyes, the terror, had struck Erika to her very core. But...

"There's nothing we can do for her," she whispered.

Again there was silence as Maisie sat staring at her. Then abruptly she shrugged. "Okay," she said, then lay back on the bed and closed her eyes.

Frowning, Erika watched Maisie's chest rise and fall. For all the world she seemed to have fallen straight to sleep. Anger touched Erika as she watched the spy. How could she be so calm, so dismissive of their friend? Cara had saved both their lives back in the valley with Yasin.

"Well, did *you* have a better plan?" she said shortly.

Without moving her head from the pillow, Maisie cracked an eye open. "Why don't you go talk to Hugo?" she replied. "You might find more answers from him than that crumbling book."

Erika scowled. If that was the best advice the spy could offer, Cara was doomed. But Maisie's eye only slid closed again, and after a moment, Erika cursed. She rose from the bed, then crossed to the door and yanked it open.

Outside, Hugo leaned against the wall, his emerald wings drooping to either side of him. His head jerked up at her appearance, and she caught a flicker of excitement in his eyes. It faded though when he realised it was only Erika in place of the Gemaho spy.

"Archivist," he said respectfully. He'd begun to call Erika

by her former title after hearing Maisie do so. "Was there something you needed?"

Erika said nothing, only closed the door behind her and leaned against the wall opposite the Anahera. He was one of the few she'd noticed around the city who was younger than Cara, as he was the child of Farhan's new partner. Erika's heart twisted as she recalled Farhan's words about Cara's mother. What had happened, that Farhan should be so fearful of his daughter following in her footsteps? Was that why he was so harsh, why he sought to rob his daughter of her…freedom?

A sob started in Erika's throat at the thought of the young Goddess without her wings. She might have first met Cara as a strange young woman of Calafe, but much had transpired since that day. Erika had come to know Cara the Goddess, who soared through the skies on wings of auburn, who exalted in her life, in her freedom. The thought of what her friend might soon lose…

"Archivist, are you okay?" Hugo asked, his voice hesitant.

Erika looked at him through a mist of tears. The young God shifted on his feet, clearly uncomfortable with her grief. Swallowing, she managed a nod.

"I am sorry, Hugo," she said softly. "I did not mean to impose upon you."

"Why…do you cry?"

"It's just…how is your sister?" she asked.

Hugo frowned and eyed her closely, as though confused or expecting a trap. It was strange how the Gods looked at them, almost as though they were waiting for something terrible to happen. Was that their memory of the human thieves who had stolen their magic all those centuries ago, giving birth to the Tangata?

"Cara is well," Hugo said at last.

"So you've seen her?" Cara said, and her voice cracked. She quickly looked away, wiping a tear from her eye. "Sorry," she whispered. "It's just...I worry for her. She is important to me. She has saved my life more times than I can count these last months. I just want to help her."

"You cannot," Hugo replied in a serious voice, as though she'd just announced a plan to break his sister out of prison. Then he looked away, and when he spoke again, Erika heard a new softness to his voice. "As much as any of us might like to help my poor sister, she...she has written her own fate."

"I know, Farhan has made that clear," Erika said. She had learned enough of Hugo these last days to know he would not go against his father. "But...surely she does not have to face it alone?"

A frown crinkled Hugo's forehead. "What do you mean?"

Erika's eyes returned to the floor. "Nothing..." she said, then: "Only...it seems cruel, to leave her alone, with nothing but her own thoughts for company. Would it not be more...humane to grant her a visit from a friend?"

Hugo hesitated at her words. "For what purpose?"

"So that she would not be alone," Erika replied. She swallowed. "And...perhaps I could help...prepare her for... for a life without her wings. Or has your father forbidden this?"

"No..." Hugo said hesitantly. "Cara is permitted visitors, only...it is not the way of the Anahera to visit the condemned. Only Father has visited her since the assembly."

"Farhan is the one who condemns her," Erika replied. Hesitantly, she reached out and touched a hand to Hugo's. "It is the way of my people to comfort our friends when they face something terrible. Please, would you take me to her?"

"Very well."

Erika was so surprised by his agreement that she already had her next argument half-formed on her lips. Her heart began to race as she swallowed it back and said instead:

"Now?"

He nodded and without further word, he started off down the corridor. Erika glanced at their door, wondering about Maisie, but…this was something she wanted to do herself. Turning, she hurried after the Anahera.

He led her quickly through the twists and turns of the city, passing empty chambers and a few of his fellow Gods. Thankfully none stopped to talk with them, for despite Hugo's assurances, she wasn't certain Farhan would be pleased to learn of her visit with his daughter. Finally they turned up a corridor Erika did not know, where a narrow spiral staircase waited.

Hugo went first and Erika followed close behind, gripping hard to the steel railings. Her heart started to pound as she realised he was leading her into the forbidden second storey of the city. Surely here would be where the Gods hid their secrets, where they kept the magics that had once lifted entire towers of glass into the sky.

But when they emerged onto the second level, Erika was only greeted by another plain grey corridor. Hugo wasted little time leading her through several more hallways, before coming to a stop outside an open entrance. Erika paused beside him. Glancing inside, she was surprised to find a chamber much larger than the others she'd seen below.

Hugo indicated she should enter first, and she stepped hesitantly inside. In the dim light of the magic orbs, she could make out only shadows of the decorations dotting the walls. As she stepped farther into the chamber, she noticed rough patches of stone on the ceiling, stretching in a line from one wall to another. It took her a moment to realise it marked where another wall had once stood.

Other than its size though, the chamber appeared much alike the living quarters she'd seen below, with blankets piled high on a handful of straw beds. They were alone in the room, but Erika guessed this must be the chambers of Hugo's family. Only, where was Cara?

It was a moment before she noticed the door in the far wall. It was the first she'd seen on this level, and as she stepped closer, Erika thought it seemed out of place, its hinges untouched by corrosion.

She turned to Hugo in silent question and he nodded. Swallowing her hesitation, Erika crossed the room and reached for the handle. The mechanism within ground as it twisted, but finally it gave a click as the lock released. The hinges let out a sharp shriek as the door swung open.

Within, a room was revealed unlike any she had seen within the city. Pink paint transformed the plain stone walls, and purple drapes of silk hung from the corners, as though windows hid beyond. The magic orbs still let out the same half-light as the rest of the city, but a lantern had been left lit on a stand in the corner. A pile of books that looked far too modern for a city that had been kept remote from human civilization lay stacked on a bedside table.

Sitting cross-legged on the bed itself, twin amber eyes looked up from an open book.

"Why is it, Erika," Cara said softly as their gaze met, "that ever since I met you, I seem to keep finding myself a prisoner?"

## ❧ 14 ❧

## THE HERO

S tanding aboard the *Brereton*, Lukys watched as the rocky cliffs drew closer. They rose from the waters of the harbour and grew up into mountains, soaring high above. The city of Ashura, capital of Perfugia, lay amongst the narrow foothills between water and sky. Carved from marble dug from the island's bottomless mines, the academy taught it was the most glorious of all the cities of humanity. That was the claim, at least. Having seen New Nihelm and the Flumeeren capital of Mildeth, Lukys now knew such teachings to be false.

There was no snow on the rocky peaks above Ashura, not at this time of year, but that didn't keep Lukys from shivering as a breeze blew across his neck. They were a long way north now, and gone were the long days and warm winds.

This was Perfugia, home. Lukys didn't remember it being so cold.

Watching the cliffs approach, Lukys couldn't help but think this was no longer truly his home, if it ever had been. Ashura might be the city of his childhood, the familiar corridors and classrooms of the academy his upbringing, but he found that memories of this place were entirely lacking joy.

Strange as it seemed, he'd felt more at home for the short time he'd lived in New Nihelm than he ever had in the towering spires of the academy. Sophia's kindness, despite his resistance, was more than his teachers and professors had ever shown him. And his parents...well, he'd been taken from them at eight, as was tradition amongst Perfugians.

He could barely recall their faces now. Had they been told the same lie as Lukys, when he'd been sent south, that their son had been chosen to lay down his life for their nation? Or did they know the truth, that he'd been a failure, banished to die because he could serve no other purpose?

Shivering, he forced his attention to the present, glancing sidelong to where the *Brereton's* captain stood at the tiller. They'd been fortunate that the ship was only another fishing vessel and not a warship to take them back to the frontlines. The captain had been suspicious at first of the broken Calafe ship filled with Perfugians. There'd been no point trying to claim they were fishermen, and so Lukys had spun a tale closer to the truth. He'd told the man they were a company of Perfugian soldiers who'd been separated from the rest of their cohort during an expedition south of the Illmoor River. That much was true—but instead of revealing their capture by the Tangata, he'd spoken of their retreat across Calafe until they'd finally reached the coast, where they had managed to steal a ship. Only a sudden storm had kept them from navigating back to a Flumeeren port to re-join the battle.

Thankfully, the man seemed to accept the story.

The identity of Sophia and the other Tangata had been more difficult to conceal. Some quick thinking from Travis had saved them. As the *Brereton* had swept towards their mangled ship, he'd begun grabbing up discarded pieces of sail and handing them out amongst the Tangata. Only when Lukys saw Isabella tying the sash across her eyes did Lukys realise his plan.

When the fishing ship had finally reached them, the sailors found half the ship's passengers lying injured, their eyes burned by the harsh sun, covered now to protect them from further damage. A simple ruse that probably would not have worked, if not for the reputation of the Tangata. Afterall, who would think the mindless beasts who fought against humanity would have the guile to sneak into Perfugia by pretending to be blinded?

At the thought, Lukys glanced at Sophia, unable to conceal a smile. She sat on a stool beside the gunwale, eyes still covered to "protect" against the midday sun. How poorly humanity had treated her kind. If they'd just been willing to talk with their enemies, a decade of war could have been avoided. Instead, they'd treated the Tangata like animals, as monsters to be destroyed, eradicated.

*I can't believe,* Sophia's voice came to him in the silence of his mind, as though she'd sensed his inspection, *that I finally get to visit Perfugia—and now I don't even get to see it.*

Lukys found himself smiling and he recalled how she'd asked after his homeland, during those first days in New Nihelm.

*Don't worry,* he whispered back to her, *this is only temporary…*

He trailed off, not wanting to betray his concerns. In truth, when they'd first set off from New Nihelm and he'd chosen Perfugia as their destination, he hadn't expected them to get this far. Reaching the island nation had seemed such an impossible task, and he'd been so angry with Sophia and the Tangata, he hadn't paused to wonder how they would be received. Even aboard their little fishing ship, there'd been greater concerns.

Now though, his negligence was endangering all their lives. Even without the Tangata, Lukys and the others were at risk, should the Sovereigns decide to name them deserters.

*No,* he said to himself, glancing again at Sophia.

The others were gathered around her, Perfugian recruits and Tangata both. They were all relying on him. He would not fail them now, not when they were so close. One final hurdle, and they would be safe.

He straightened, gripping the railings so tightly his knuckles turned white. He must call on the mercy of the Sovereigns, convince them that the Tangata were not the monsters they'd been led to believe, that they could be allies. Maybe he could present Sophia and her brethren as refugees…

An image flickered into his mind, and he imagined the Royal Guard of Plorsea rushing towards him, spears glistening in the sunlight as they drove them through Isabella's heart, as they impaled Keria, as Sophia cried out for mercy…

*No,* Lukys growled to himself again.

He would not allow it. He would demand an urgent audience before the Sovereigns. Such a request was far beneath his rank as a recruit, but maybe with his fledgeling powers, he might persuade his betters. He'd spent much of the remaining journey practicing with Sophia, though he had not attempted to push upon any emotions again, not since the disaster at the Tangatan village.

First though, he needed to get Sophia and the others off the ship without being discovered. If the guards on the dock caught even a whiff of the Tangata, a thousand soldiers would descend upon them before he saw the first of the Sovereign's servants.

The city was growing near now, the stone docks stretching out into the harbour, beckoning them home. Gulls cawed overhead and hundreds of ships of all sizes sat docked, sails furled, sleek hulls rising from the calm waters. Perfugia boasted the greatest navy in the world. The fleet had been raised over generations, the envy of the other kingdoms. Successive Sovereigns had each built a dozen ships from the great redwoods that covered the island. Their removal was considered a solemn affair, and they could only be used for the construction of ships. Not for the Perfugians the haphazard wooden constructions they had called 'buildings' in Fogmore.

The sailors of the *Brereton* raced to lower their sails, then quickly extended oars to manoeuvre the final yards to their docking on the jetty. A man leapt from the railings as they drew near, carrying a rope that he quickly looped around a wooden pile. Others followed, and within minutes the *Brereton* was safely berthed.

Lukys drew in a breath. Now came the moment of truth. Fists clenched, he started towards the gangplank being lowered to the pier, but before he could take two steps, the captain intercepted him. The antithesis of the sea captains Lukys had seen elsewhere, the man was tidy and cleanshaven, and so thin Lukys might have knocked him down with a tap.

"Hold it there, lad," the man said as he barred Lukys's path. "Where might you be going?"

"The citadel," Lukys said hesitantly. "I have news of the war for the Sovereigns."

"Might be you do, lad," the captain replied, "but can't let you go ashore without the proper processes." A broad grin split his face, though Lukys read the mistrust behind the man's eyes. Perhaps his story had not been as convincing as he'd thought. "I'm sure your news can wait a few hours yet."

With that, he turned and bounded across the gangplank. Lukys made to follow him, but several of the crew moved between them. Arms bulging with the muscle required to haul fishing nets from the ocean's depths, these were closer to what Lukys had come to expect from seamen. Their stance made it obvious they would not allow Lukys passage without a fight.

Grinding his teeth, he turned from them, mind racing. The Tangata's disguises would not survive detailed inspection. One look at those grey eyes and every man and woman in the harbour would turn against them. He shared a glance with Dale and Travis as he re-joined the others.

"Where's he going in such a hurry?" Travis asked.

"Up to no good, by the looks," Dale answered.

Lukys only grunted his agreement. His eyes were on the shore, where already he could see the captain returning. Only he was no longer alone. Two figures garbed in steel marched at his back, each bearing shining spears of silver and kite shields worn on their backs. Red plumes sprouted from their half-helms, marking them as officers.

But it was the blue armour that made Lukys's blood run cold. These were no ordinary soldiers, but members of the Perfugian Royal Guard, servants to the Sovereigns.

"That's not good," Dale hissed from behind him.

"Get everyone together," Lukys said softly. "I'll do my best to divert their attention from our friends. But...be ready."

He did not elaborate, though he could sense the tension in his friends as they turned to gather the others. At least the sailors had allowed them to keep their weapons, though they both knew that if it came to a fight, their little gang didn't stand a chance. They might no longer be the raw recruits who'd marched south all those months ago, but neither could they fight an entire army.

As the captain approached with the royal guards, the sailors at the gangplank stepped aside. Lukys moved quickly and sprung across, landing on the docks just as the captain marched up. The man stumbled at Lukys's appearance, quickly glancing behind him, as though afraid the guards might have abandoned him.

"Captain!" Lukys exclaimed, forcing a cheery tone to his voice. "I just wanted to say thank you again for your aid. I don't know what might have become of us if not for your valour."

The man frowned, apparently taken aback by his appearance. Lukys took advantage of his hesitation to turn from the man and address the guards.

"Sirs," he said, drawing himself up and offering a salute. "Cadet Lukys of the Fogmore regiment, at your service."

"I...I..." Beside Lukys, the sea captain stammered, head whipping from Lukys to the guards before he finally recovered his wits. "This is the one who calls himself their leader, sirs."

Ignoring the man, the royal guards moved closer, eyes on Lukys. One a man, the other a woman, both stood a good foot above Lukys and carried about them the aura of a warrior. Unlike those chosen for the frontlines, the royal guard were true soldiers, appointed for their skills in battle. They had positions all across the nation, representing the Sovereigns in all martial matters. But the best of them were selected to defend the Sovereigns themselves; a great honour, considering most Perfugians would never so much as glimpse the faces of those who ruled them.

"You are a long way from your station, recruit," the man said, his voice hard. "What are you doing here?"

Lukys opened his mouth to respond, but the words died on his lips as he looked into the man's eyes and saw the suspicion there. The woman seemed softer, but there was still an edge about her, a glint of danger. He sensed then that simple falsehoods would not convince these two, not unless…

Swallowing his doubt, Lukys squared his shoulders and clasped his hands firmly behind his back. "We were in the battle for the Illmoor, sirs, several months back now. In the chaos, we were separated from our unit and pursued to the coast. There we found a ship and crossed the sea…"

He trailed off as the woman took a step towards him. Suddenly there was only an inch separating them, and he found himself caught in eyes of chestnut. Swallowing, he tried to regain his train of thought, but the woman spoke first.

"An impressive feat," she said, voice quiet despite the noise of the docks. "To have stood against the Tangata, to survive the wild oceans of the west…"

As she trailed off, Lukys caught the glimmer in her eyes and sensed there was a trap to her admiration. Lowering his eyes, he gave the slightest shake of his head.

"I cannot accept such high praise, sir. Our efforts were but the least of what our Sovereigns might have expected of us. I fear had some of your royal guards been present, the enemy would have fallen on the waters of the Illmoor."

The hint of a smile crossed the woman's lips, but beside her, the man only snorted. "Do not think to lick our boots with pretty words, recruit," he growled, stepping past Lukys to survey the ship. "Should your tale prove less than true, I'll not hesitate to see the lot of you strung up as deserters."

"Though if you *are* telling the truth," the woman cut in, "the intelligence you bring of the enemy could prove invaluable. The captain tells us you were stranded on the *Calafe* side of the Illmoor?"

Lukys hesitated before nodding. "Yes, sir."

"And you were pursued?" the woman asked. She stepped past Lukys and the sea captain to join her companion's inspection of those still aboard the vessel. "The sea captain tells us you have injured?"

"Yes," he said quickly, flashing the captain a look. What else had he told these two? "Though their injuries were from the voyage. Those injured by the Tangata…we lost," he finished lamely.

"Ha!" the man replied. "I doubt that pitiable lot ever saw a Tangata in their lives. Look at 'em, bunch of deserters if ever I saw one."

The woman laughed and shared a look with Lukys. "You'll have to forgive Cleo," she said, resting a mailed hand on her colleague's shoulder. "Been stuck on port duty for years—he's spoiling for a promotion."

"Doesn't change facts, Tasha," the guard she'd called Cleo growled. "Something's fishy about this lot."

"Might be the fishing ship," a voice called from above.

Lukys stifled a curse as Travis leaned against the gunwales and waved to them. The last thing he needed just now was the recruit angering the two guards who would decide their fates. Beside him, Cleo scowled while the woman Tasha laughed. A growl rumbling from his throat, the man crossed the dock and thumped up the gangplank. Lukys raced after him.

"What did you say, recruit?" the guard snapped as he came to a stop before Travis.

Eyes wide, the young recruit held up his hands in peace, and Lukys darted forward to intervene.

"This is Travis, our very own sea captain," he said quickly. "It was only by his skill that we navigated the storm.

Though, I'll admit, he wrecked just about every inch of sail we had on our little ship."

"Impressive," Tasha said as she joined them. "I didn't realise we sent sailors to the south."

A hint of red tinged Travis's cheeks at her praise, but there was obvious relief in his eyes at the opportunity to change the topic.

"It was nothing, sir," he replied, waving to where Dale had gathered the other members of their group. "I had a good crew."

"Must have been difficult with half of them bloody blind," Cleo snapped.

"Ay, it sounds as you have been through quite the journey, soldier," Tasha said softly, an edge creeping into her voice.

Lukys shifted on his feet, though he thought her tone might have been for Cleo, rather than his companions. The guard seemed to realise it too, for he rolled his eyes and made a dismissive gesture.

"Fine," he muttered, facing Lukys, "let's say I believe your little story. What news do you bring of the foul enemy?"

From across the deck, Lukys sensed a fluttering of emotion from Sophia, quickly stifled. Thankful the royal guards could not sense the Tangatan language, Lukys inclined his head to Cleo.

"The last we saw of them was on the coast, at the village we stole the ship from," he replied.

Cleo nodded, but alongside him, Tasha seemed to lose interest in the conversation. She wandered across to where Travis stood with the others, and Lukys caught the murmur of question, something about compasses and navigation.

"What about the battle?" Cleo growled, leaning closer. "Did you slay many of the Tangata?

"Our company was caught south of the river," he replied, drawing himself up. "The line held, protecting the river, but we were separated from the body of the army." He hesitated. "There is more though, intelligence of grave import we discovered while in enemy territory."

"Well, out with it, recruit," Cleo said, and Lukys caught a glimpse of greed in the man's eyes.

Lukys shook his head. "No," he replied shortly. "This information is too important. I will report to the Sovereigns themselves."

For a moment, the royal guard stared down at Lukys, disbelief twisting his bearded face. Finally he shook his head. "Has the sun addled your wits, recruit?" he growled, advancing a step, so that he towered over Lukys. "I am a soldier of the royal guard, your superior in every way—"

A cry from behind them interrupted Cleo's speech. Lukys spun as a commotion broke out amongst his friends and the disguised Tangata. They scattered away from a blue-garbed figure standing in their midst—Tasha. She held a fist triumphantly above her head, a scrap of cloth grasped between her fingers.

Still struggling to understand what was happening, Lukys saw Sophia next. She stood beside Tasha, struggling to free her arm from the guard's iron grip. Eyes wide, a snarl slipped from her lips as she twisted and finally broke loose. Gasps echoed from around the ship as the attention of the sailors was drawn towards the commotion.

Screams soon followed.

Only then did Lukys realise that Sophia's face was no longer covered. Tasha had torn the cloth loose. Her grey eyes swept the deck and found Lukys, wide with fear.

"*Tangata!*" Tasha cried, and others immediately took up the call. "Treachery! All arms to the docks!"

# 15

## THE EMISSARY

A lump lodged in Erika's throat as she looked down at the Goddess, at her friend.

Cara had seen better days. Her face was a pallid grey and red stained her eyes, as though she'd spent much of the last few days crying. Her auburn wings hung limp, her feathers ruffled and missing in patches. Erika noted several lying scattered about the room.

Swallowing, Erika stepped into the room and allowed the door to swing closed behind her, locking them both in, and Hugo out.

"Cara, I'm so sorry…"

She trailed off as the Goddess looked away, locks of copper hair falling across her face. "What do you want, Erika?" Cara said shortly.

"I…I was worried about you," Erika croaked, eyes watering at her friend's dejection.

"Sure," Cara replied. "Because you've always been *so* worried about me." Her voice was tainted with bitterness now. She snorted in derision. "Tell the truth, Erika. What's got you so bothered? Are there some more of the Old Ones that need slaying? Or have the Tangata returned? Maybe it's another mysterious assassin from your past who needs taking care of?"

Erika flinched as she saw the accusation in Cara's eyes. Guilt twisted her stomach into knots as she recalled all the things the young Goddess had done for her. She had repaid those kindnesses with mistrust and betrayal. Cara was right to be angry, to hate her. But…

"I swear to you, Cara," she said, taking a step closer to the Goddess. "I'm going to get you out of this."

Cara shook her head, a tear streaking her cheek. "Enough with your lies, Erika," she whispered. Her words no longer held the same bite, as despair replaced anger. "Enough with your false promises. You cannot defy the Elders, cannot deny my father…" Her shoulders slumped and a shudder racked her, as though she were about to shatter right there in front of Erika.

Erika crossed quickly to the bed and sat alongside Cara. "*I will*," she said, determined, insistent.

Placing her hands on Cara's shoulders, she tried to turn the Goddess towards her. For a moment Cara resisted, but Erika's will was the greater, and eventually she allowed herself to meet Erika's eyes.

"Cara, I swear on my father's memory, *I will not let them take your wings,*" Erika whispered.

Cara stared back, anger in her red-stained eyes. But Erika refused to back down, to look away. She watched as Cara's lip began to tremble, felt the shaking in her friend's body, saw the sheen to her eyes. Then suddenly the damn broke and the Goddess threw her arms around Erika, her sobs vibrating from the walls, her tears hot on Erika's shoulder.

"Please don't let him take them," Cara gasped, her words muffled. "Please, please, please."

Her throat clogged with emotion, Erika said nothing, only held her friend tight, offering her silent comfort. It was a struggle seeing the Goddess in such a state, her will, her courage, broken. This was a being who had stood against Tangata and assassins alike with hardly a flicker of fear.

Finally they broke apart and Cara wiped her eyes, scooting back on the bed to make room for Erika. They sat there in silence for a while, each of them lost in thought, minds wandering from past to future. Erika couldn't begin to imagine how to help her friend, but neither would she turn her back now.

"That man, Yasin, he killed your father."

Erika's head jerked up as Cara spoke into the silence. She opened her mouth, then closed it again, considering her words carefully. Finally she nodded.

"Yes, but it was Queen Amina who was behind the plot to see him dead."

The Goddess said nothing at that, only sat leaning against the wall of her room. With her knees drawn up to her chest, she might have been any other human adolescent, but for the splendour of her wings. That, and the fact she was fifty years of age.

"We never knew what happened to my mother," Cara said finally, her eyes downcast, fixed on the tangled blankets beneath her. "One day she just…didn't come back."

"Your father said she was…like you?" Erika questioned, trying not to probe too much.

Cara shrugged. "It happened when I was young." Her eyes flickered to Erika before returning to the sheets. "When I was just five, I think, still a fledgling."

"Fledgling?"

"We cannot fly until our teens," Cara replied softly. "When we gain our primary feathers. Until then…well, my people are overprotective of our fledglings. My father and the Elders, they would do anything to protect them."

"Is that why there were no children at the assembly?" Erika asked. When Cara only nodded, she went on. "She just disappeared one day?"

"Father says she went out to scavenge beyond our borders," the Goddess replied. "Even then it was forbidden, but...I guess my mother was strong-willed."

"Like her daughter," Erika added. Cara said nothing, but Erika thought she glimpsed the hint of a smile on her friend's face. Swallowing her doubt, she pressed on. "Maybe your mother was right to explore, to go beyond the limits placed on you by these Sacred Founders. The world has changed since their day, grown darker. It could use the Anahera, could use the balance of the Gods."

To her surprise, Cara shook her head. "You don't understand, Erika," she murmured. "None of you do, the darkness inside us..." Cara trailed off, as though she had said too much.

But a memory had flickered into life at the Goddess's words, and Erika shivered as she recalled what had happened back in the canyon. Romaine's death had driven the Goddess into a frenzy, changed her, transformed her into something...else. A vicious, deadly killer. She had slaughtered the Flumeeren assassin, butchered him. And then there had been her eyes...how they had changed, darkened to become almost...the grey of the Tangata.

"What happened, Cara?" she whispered at last. "Back in the canyon, you changed, didn't you?"

The Goddess quickly looked away, though not before Erika glimpsed the pain on her face. "That was...a flaw," she whispered.

"What do you mean?" Erika pressed.

Cara's eyes slid closed. "A mistake in the makeup of the Anahera."

"A mistake?"

"It makes us dangerous," Cara confirmed. "That's why...that's why we're forbidden from interfering, from killing: the fear we might lose ourselves, that we will succumb to our inner nature, become like...like the Old Ones."

"The Old Ones?" Erika questioned, before connecting the facts. "Those creatures we...discovered in the tunnels?" Cara gave the slightest nod of her head, and Erika swallowed. "What were those things?"

"They were meant to all be gone," Cara whispered, her eyes seeming to stare into some far-off place. "That's what the Founders told us..." She trailed off, her eyes flicking to Erika. "They *are* the ancestors of the Tangata, but unlike their descendants, the Old Ones were mad, deranged. They wanted nothing more than the destruction of humanity."

Erika frowned. "That does not sound so different from the Tangata of today."

"That is because you cannot hear them," Cara replied absently.

"*What?*" Erika asked.

"Oh, right," Cara murmured, shaking her head. "You humans cannot Hear with your minds." She smiled, and Erika glimpsed some of her friend's old mirth. "The Tangata are not monsters, Erika. I tried to tell you before, but you would not listen. They Speak with their minds. Only those with the same ability can hear them."

Erika sat back in her chair with an *oomph*, struggling to process the new information. The Tangata were not simple beasts? How was that possible? All the legends, all the stories, the research by her fellow academics, all of it described them as mindless creatures, driven mad by the powers they had stolen from the Gods. So much of the world relied on that fact, that the enemy were monsters. Surely they could not have been wrong…

But…what if a mistake had been made? Her Archivist's mind began to race at the possibilities created by Cara's revelations. What if the tales had only been true for those ancient ancestors of the past, the Old Ones? What if the Tangata could be reasoned with. Peace between their species might be possible after all…

Then a shiver struck Erika as she recalled the Tangata that had been held captive in the queen's court. It seemed an age ago now, but Erika could still see the look it had given her, before she'd unleashed her magic. There had been despair in its eyes—and hatred. She had not imagined that.

No, humanity could not pretend the atrocities they had committed against the Tangata had never been. Nor would they forgive so easily the excesses of the enemy, the villages destroyed, the innocents of Calafe driven from their land. They had gone too far to find peace now.

Guilt lodged in Erika's throat as she recalled her own part in that darkness, how she had used the gauntlet's magic on the helpless Tangata. She shuddered, clenching the empty fist that had once wielded its power. What terrible things it had made her do…

"You're not wearing the gauntlet," Cara said abruptly.

Erika flinched at her words and looked up, seeing the Goddess's eyes on her empty fist. "I didn't like what it did to me."

"Did to you?" A frown creased Cara's face. "What do you mean?"

"There was a…darkness to that thing, to its power," she said finally. "I could feel it corrupting me, robbing me of something…of my humanity." Casting her eyes to the floor, she slowly unclenched her fist. "I am...afraid that its God magic will change me as it did the Old Ones, that it will make me a monster."

Silence answered her words, and finally Erika looked up. The Goddess sat staring at her, eyes wide, a puzzled look on her face.

Abruptly she burst into laughter.

Erika started, shocked by her friend's reaction. "What?" she snapped angrily. "Your God magic corrupted—"

Cara's laughter rose in pitch and she fell back on the bed, holding her stomach, gasping for air.

"*Oh by the Fall!*" she finally managed.

Erika gritted her teeth, wishing in that instant she had the gauntlet to hand, if only to silence the young Anahera's laughter. Cara shouldn't be laughing at her, not when she was working so hard—

There it was again, the anger. Exhaling, Erika shook her head. "Cara, I know you cannot understand," she said carefully. "You are a God, after all. It is your magic. But there is something about that artefact, it *was* changing me."

A long silence answered Erika's words, and she watched as the laughter died in Cara's eyes. The Anahera sat in silence for a long moment, staring at Erika, as though weighing what she was about to say.

"Erika, it's not our magic," Cara said softly.

"What?" Erika frowned. "What are you talking about, of course—"

"That thing is not of the Anahera," Cara interrupted, then paused, drawing in a breath. "That gauntlet you hold, it is human magic, Erika. It never belonged to us."

## 16

# THE FOLLOWER

By the time Adonis finally reached the cave, most of the Tangata were asleep. Or at least those who had survived the storm, who'd had the strength to reach shelter for the night. The rest...

He shivered, recalling the face of the child, frozen in the snow, in death.

Anger touched him. It was one thing for the weak to obey their betters, to bow before the older generations. But for the strong to march them to their deaths, to leave precious children dying in the snow...what was the purpose of such madness, this headlong race through the storm?

Inside the cave, silence prevailed as his brothers and sisters slept fitfully. He found himself counting their number as he crept through their ranks, trying to learn how many they had lost. Yet even those who had reached this simple shelter might not yet wake to see the morrow. Those within lay shivering in groups, their clothing damp, faces pale in the darkness. Not a single fire had been lit.

Thousands had set out from New Nihelm, a host grand

enough to sweep away even the largest of humanity's armies. They numbered in the thousands still, Adonis thought, but hundreds had fallen on the way. And the children…

*Adonis.*

He flinched as her Voice spoke suddenly into his mind, loud, imperious, drowning out his own thoughts. Looking around, he searched for the Old One and found her lounging at the rear of the cave, attended as always by her guards. They were like him, other Tangata of the third generation, those who had once been assigned to protect the old Matriarch.

Like him, they had seen the truth that Maya had shown them: that the Tangata had decayed beneath her rule, becoming subservient, bowing to the whims of their lessers. Unlike Adonis though, they had not lagged during the long journey, had not lingered with the weak and dying.

*Adonis, my mate, what became of you?* Adonis swallowed as Maya's consciousness pricked at his mind, probing. *Does your wound bother you?*

Adonis reached unconsciously for his chest, but in truth he had hardly noticed its pain during the long trek. Several days had passed now since the humans' escape and despite the damage done by the spear, the wound was healing well. And besides, his pain had been nothing compared to the misery of his brethren around him, to the children…

A sudden warmth swept over Adonis as he found himself looking into the grey depths of Maya's eyes. Fresh energy pulsed in his veins, as though a magic hand had reached out and plucked the exhaustion from him. He knew it was Maya's doing, knew the ecstasy was only an illusion, a spell cast so that his mind would forget his ails, but…he let out a sigh, embracing the warmth, the relief from his grief.

Adonis bowed his head as he approached her, ignoring the eyes of her guards. He wondered if they suspected him of some treachery, *he*, the one who had brought the Old One to them, who had helped to strike down the Matriarch. Or perhaps they thought him weak. He had already allowed the human to strike him, for the traitors to escape. And now he had lagged with those too weak to follow their new leader.

No matter. They were not his Matriarch, not his mate. Only Maya mattered, only her touch, only her power…

Coming to a stop before the Old One, Adonis bowed his head. *I was delayed by our people, my mate,* he said. *By those who had fallen behind.*

Her grey eyes regarded him, her inner thoughts concealed, but after a moment a smile touched her lips.

*Your kindness is to be commended, Adonis,* she said, stepping forward and placing a hand on his chest. He felt her heat, even through the dampness of his shirt. *But…another might consider this weakness. Why do you waste your strength on those too feeble to serve their Matriarch?*

*I…* Adonis trailed off beneath her cold gaze. He sensed no anger from her, only a confusion, that he could truly have risked his own strength for those who had fallen behind. *It is not their fault.*

*Perhaps.* Maya stroked his cheek, her words whispering in his mind. *Neither is it the fault of the parasite, the life it drains from its host. Still, it must be cut out, before its disease threatens the whole.*

Adonis's stomach twisted at her words and the vision came to him once more, of the child in the snow. *There… there were children amongst them.*

*Not my children,* the Old One replied. She stroked his cheek now, her face close, her breath hot upon his flesh. *Not our children.*

The words reverberated through Adonis as her fingers trailed down his throat, tingling, burning. Suddenly the images in his mind had vanished and he saw only the Old One before him, the power in her eyes, the desire. She had made him her mate the first night after her awakening, but...

...always before, his pairings had ended in disappointment. He had not allowed himself to believe it might be different with Maya. But...he swallowed.

*Our...children?*

A smile touched the lips of the Old One. It seemed to him there was a danger in that smile, though he could not think why. Her fingers entwined with his as she drew his hand to her stomach.

*Their fire burns within me already,* she murmured, her eyes locked with his, her mind entwined in his own consciousness. *New children, strong enough to survive this world, to resist even the call of death.*

Now the warmth that swept through Adonis's mind was real, an ecstasy that burned away all his fears, all his doubts. Hope swelled within, a fierce, awesome thing—not just for himself, but for the future of all his people. Their children would be the first born of his generation in decades without the aid of human blood.

A new generation, one revitalised by the power of the Old Ones, a fresh hope for his people.

A growl rumbled from Adonis's chest as he gripped Maya tight, pulling her to him. Heat swept through him as their lips met, banishing the last of the cold. They fell together to the floor of the cave, to the unyielding rock. Cloth tore as they grasped at one another, desperate for the press of flesh, for the heat of one another's bodies.

Adonis gasped when they finally came together, as Maya pushed him down, her strength taking control, a thousandfold his own. His being shuddered as he felt her mind, so vast, so powerful, mingling with his own. Their eyes locked and they moved as one, the last of his doubts burned to ash, until there was only the promise of their future, only the fiery heat of his desire.

Until there was only the Old One.

# 17

# THE HERO

"*Tangata! Traitors!*"

The screams echoed across the deck of the *Brereton* as the sailors picked up Tasha's call—followed by the soft hiss of steel on leather as swords were drawn. Lukys's comrades cried out as the royal guard levelled her silver spear, and several darted forward to place themselves between Sophia and the blade.

A growl came from Cleo and Lukys leapt aside as the guard swung at him with a spear, narrowly avoiding the blow. Heart pounding in his chest, Lukys retreated with his comrades. Sailors bearing paddles and rusted blades advanced on them, joining the royal guards.

*No, no, no.* Lukys shook his head, raising his hands in a desperate sign of peace. This was all wrong. "Please—" he tried, but Cleo thrust out with his spear in a blow that would have disembowelled him had he not leapt aside.

"Enough of your lies, traitor," the man spat as he retreated from a counterattack launched by Dale.

Fists clenched, Lukys swung on the woman, Tasha. "We're not traitors, I swear," he cried. "The Tangata are not the monsters we thought. These with us, they seek only sanctuary!"

"These?" the guard hissed, her blade coming up. "How many of the murderous creatures have you brought upon our peaceful shores?"

Movement came from amongst the ranks of Lukys's friends as Sophia pushed forward, Isabella and Keria at her side, the others too. One by one they removed their blindfolds, revealing eyes as grey as the granite cliffs above. The hiss of inhaled breath came from across the ship as the sailors drew back, and even Cleo shifted closer to Tasha, the sight of a dozen Tangata apparently enough to give even the giant guard pause.

"They won't hurt you!" Lukys said. Drawing on his courage, he took a step towards the guards, hands still raised.

As he spoke, he reached out with his mind, seeking the swirling of their emotions as he had with Sophia. Each was a vortex of rainbow light, but strongest of all was the pulsing yellow, the tang of fear. The fiery red of anger was almost as great, and in desperation he reached for those colours, seeking to sooth them, to lift their other emotions, the purples and blues and pinks, though he could not pause to know their significance.

"They are Tangata," Tasha replied, though there was a pause as her eyes flickered to Cleo, as though in sudden doubt.

Lukys latched onto the opening. "They are just as human as you or I."

For a moment, he thought his words might convince Tasha. Her spear wavered, the tip lowering a fraction as she eyed them, and he sensed a flickering of something— doubt? She looked again at Cleo, though the giant guard wore only the same twisted sneer he'd had since their appearance at the docks.

"Do you know how many of your comrades those creatures have killed?" the man spat, gesturing with his spear at Sophia in a way that left no doubt what he would like to do to her. There was loathing in his eyes as he looked again at Lukys. "And you brought them to our shores."

"Since when do the Sovereigns care for the lives of my comrades?" Lukys bristled, angered despite himself. "They sent us to die, knowing we were untrained, unprepared. If not for the mercy of these Tangata, we *would* be dead. But then, what would you know, sitting here safe in our homeland? Have you ever even *seen* combat?"

Cleo's face turned a mottled red at Lukys's words and gripping his spear with both hands, he started towards Lukys. "By the Fall, I'll show you—"

"Wait," Tasha spoke over the two of them, her voice sharp, barely controlled. Cleo froze, and Tasha fixed her eyes on Lukys. "Why should we believe what you say, when all you have presented us with so far has been lies and deceptions? No…" Her face grew grim as she looked from Lukys to the Tangata. "I think you meant to bring death to our Sovereigns, in vengeance for your perceived mistreatment."

"No, that's not—"

"*Enough!*" Tasha silenced him with a glare.

She turned her eyes to the crew of the *Brereton*. Still armed with their scattering of weapons, they shifted nervously on their feet. Lukys could see their fear. They knew there were not enough of them to defeat so many of the Tangata. But…

…the hairs on Lukys's neck lifted as he saw that seamen from the other ships were gathering on the docks. Many were better armed, having raced to grab weapons when the call of Tangata went out. And farther along the docks, a squadron of soldiers was racing towards them.

"Citizens of Perfugia!" Tasha's voice lifted so that those on the jetty could hear. "These men and women before you have brought peril to our homes, a threat to the lives of our Sovereigns. We must stand against them, must defend our kingdom at all costs. I call on you now to lend me your strength, that we might push these evil creatures back into the oceans from which they have crept."

The rumble of voices spread across the deck of the *Brereton* as the sailors clutched weapons tighter, while others began to leap the narrow gap between the docks and the ship. Grinning, Cleo nodded to his companion and lifted shield and spear.

Lukys allowed his hands to fall to his side as Dale pulled him back into the safety of his friends. Without a spear, he would only get in the way. He found himself standing next to Sophia. Looking into her grey eyes, he sensed her fear, her sadness, but beyond that…acceptance.

*It's okay, Lukys*, she whispered, reaching out to place a hand on his shoulder. *You tried your best.*

His stomach tied itself into knots. Beyond the lines of his friends, he heard Cleo bellow a curse, even as Dale closed with him. The shriek of spear striking shield followed, then grunts as Dale leapt back. Without shield or armour, he was badly outmatched by the royal guard.

Lukys found himself clenching his fists as others joined the guard to attack his friends, a rage sweeping over him. Who were these men and women to judge them, to call Lukys and his friends traitors, while they hid on their distant island, untouched by the horrors of war?

Without thinking, he reached out again with his mind, searching for the swirling colours, the pulsing emotions of those who surrounded them. They radiated from the guards and sailors, mixing and mingling, the reds and yellows almost feeding off one another. Watching that vortex of light, Lukys focused on the yellow, gripping their fear tight with his mind.

This time, he sought not to suppress it, not to remove the terror of his enemies. Instead, he fed the sickly yellow, nurtured its glow, until it swelled and grew amongst the men and women facing them, surpassing the red, suppressing all other emotion, until even the yellow succumbed, giving way to pure white, to absolute terror.

Screams rang across the waters of the harbour as men and women fell to their knees, oars and swords and other makeshift weapons clattering to the deck. Several of the sailors turned and threw themselves over the side of the ship, while others simply crumpled, too terrified to even run. Even Cleo, for all his boasting, staggered away from them, face bleached white. None could stand before the terror Lukys had inspired…

…none, that is, except for Tasha.

A frown crossed Lukys face as he saw her standing straight amidst the fallen sailors. Her eyes flickered to her comrade and her lips twitched.

"Get a hold of yourself, Cleo," she said.

"I…I…" the big man struggled, but his tongue could not seem to form words. He staggered back, coming perilously close to the gunwale. In his armour, he would sink like a stone.

"Oh for Fall's sake," she snapped, reaching out and dragging him away from the edge. He struggled against her, until she slapped him hard across the face. Only then did the effects of Lukys's terror seem to lessen. "He's a Melder like us, you idiot," she growled. "Didn't you sense him earlier?"

"I…" A frown creased Cleo's face, and suddenly the

colours of his emotions vanished. The rage on the man's face as he swung on Lukys was all too visible though. "The little bastard—"

Tasha struck him again. Cursing, Cleo raised a hand to fend off further blows. "I already locked him out!"

"I know," the guard replied shortly. "Calm yourself." Then she turned towards Lukys and leaned her head to the side.

*You're a Melder.*

For half a moment, Lukys struggled to process what he'd just heard. Or rather, where the words that had appeared in his head had come from. He stared at the woman, mind whirring as he opened his mouth, then closed it again. She had *Spoken* to him. In his mind. That wasn't possible. The only people who could Speak were the Tangata. Well, the Tangata, and himself…

*What did you say?* he finally managed, projecting the words recklessly, too shocked for subtlety.

Cleo's head snapped towards him and a scowl twisted his face. *Don't play stupid, traitor. You'll die slowly for what you just did.*

But he made no move towards Lukys, and beside him, Tasha's frown only deepened. Lukys felt a fluttering against his mind, as though a feather were brushing up against his consciousness. Quickly he tried to contain his emotions, to keep her from his secrets.

*An untrained Melder,* Tasha said at last. *That is…impossible. Why would one of your talent be sent to the frontlines?*

"What does it matter?" Cleo growled, speaking out loud again. "The traitor has chosen his allegiance."

Lukys shook his head, barely able to comprehend what was happening. A human—a *Perfugian Royal Guard*—had spoken to him in his mind. It was one thing to witness

Tangata with such power...but hearing the thoughts of his own people, that was something else entirely.

Lukys's influence was beginning to fade from the sailors now and Lukys, Cleo, and Tasha stood in silence as the men and women slowly crawled to their feet. Some regained their weapons, while others simply stood there, staring at the Tangata as though expecting the creatures to tear them apart at any moment.

Forcing his confusion to the rear of his mind, Lukys took a step towards Tasha. Her spear came up, pointing for his throat, but she did not strike. He could still see the anger in her eyes, but there was more there now. Her mind remained closed to him, but it seemed to him that she was as curious about his nature as he was of theirs.

*Why have you come here, truly?* Her voice came to him again.

Lukys swallowed. *I swear before the Gods above, I am no traitor,* he replied, keeping his voice soft. *These Tangata, they are refugees. Something has happened...sir, something that could mean disaster for our people. These Tangata, they're on our side. They want to help us.*

"Want to eat us, more like," Cleo snorted.

*We do not eat humans.*

If Lukys's ability had surprised the pair, Sophia Speaking shocked them so greatly that Cleo almost dropped his spear again. Their eyes snapped to the Tangata as Sophia approached cautiously, coming to a stop alongside Lukys. He held his breath as their knuckles whitened upon spear hilts, but neither attacked.

*Lukys speaks the truth,* Sophia continued, inclining her head in what Lukys had come to recognise as a gesture of respect amongst the Tangata. *My people come under a flag of truce.*

The guards' spear tips wavered as Sophia spoke again,

as though her Voice meant she might suddenly launch herself at them. A tension hung in the air, as both sides waited for the other to attack, to be the first to draw blood.

Finally Tasha shook her head. *You can Speak*, she said.

*Yes,* Sophia replied patiently. *As can all my people.* She gestured to the others, and they stepped forward hesitantly. *We have come to you seeking refuge.*

Tasha frowned. *What refuge could Perfugia possibly provide the Tangata...?*

Her words trailed off as she suddenly tensed, and her eyes took on a distant look. Lukys frowned, recognising the look of someone conducting a conversation in their mind. But who? Cleo still stood glaring at them, eyes alert. Silently, he reached out with his mind for some hint of Tasha's intentions, but a second later her eyes flickered back into focus. The tension drained from her and reaching out, she placed a hand on Cleo's spear arm.

"Lower your weapons," she said softly, looking from the big guard to Lukys's company. "It seems you have won yourselves a reprieve."

## ❦ 18 ❦

## THE EMISSARY

*he lady hath gone. The others searcheth, but I know those gents shalt not find her. The children mourn, but we didst teacheth them to be stout. There is nay other choice, in this world we didst maketh.*

Erika groaned and set the diary down to rest her weary eyes. Turning, she looked out through the window. During her exploration over the last few days, she had finally managed to find what must be one of the only windows in the city. The glass was cracked and somewhat frosted, with fine wires within the panel holding it together, even after all these years. Another remarkable feat of the Gods' magic…

Or was it?

*It is human magic, Erika. It never belonged to us…*

Erika shuddered as she recalled Cara's words: that the greatest discovery of her lifetime, the weapon she had wielded with ecstasy these past months, the artefact of the Gods she had displayed so proudly in Flumeer…was not of the Gods at all.

It was human.

Swallowing, she returned her attention to the diary,

flicking forward through several months' worth of notes. The answers to her questions had to lie somewhere within these pages. She had gotten nothing more out of Cara, even less from Hugo or his father. But this diary, there was a truth here, a detail she was still missing, one that might finally fill in the blank spaces of human history.

*Mine own muscles groweth weary, mine own bones frail. I shouldst hath passed from this world long ago. I longeth for yond release, but the power holdeth me to this world. The others hath did find peace, but I remain. Mayhaps I shouldst speak the truth, that others might putteth right mine own crimes...*

Erika cursed. The diary's author seemed to grow more cryptic with the passage of each year, his words made all the more unintelligible by the ancient version of their language.

A shiver shook Erika as her gaze was drawn to the gauntlet. It lay on the table beside her, glinting in the magical lights shining overhead, dangerous, threatening...

...or was that all in her imagination?

Cara had explained it was but a tool, that its magic had nothing to do with her anger, or the madness manifested in her kind. Somehow, the Anahera's words rang true, spoke to a reality Erika had suspected all along, however much she might want to resist it.

Because if the gauntlet was human, if it was only a tool, a weapon created to fight the Old Ones, then that meant...

...it meant everything she'd done, her crimes against Cara and those around her, they were of her own doing.

Tearing her eyes from the gauntlet, Erika looked out the window again. Through the tainted glass, she could just make out the great yard in the centre of the city. A storm was raging outside, and every so often a whisper would sneak through the cracked glass, carrying with it the soft breath of ice. Snowdrifts were building quickly against the walls and glass houses. She could barely make out the structure rising from the centre, the four monoliths of stone.

She clenched her fist as a tremor slid down her spine. Today was the day. Hugo had not said how it would be done. He'd been less responsive to their questions since Farhan had learned of her visit with Cara. If calling on his daughter had not been forbidden then, it was now. They had even had a second guard assigned to watch them.

*Bang.*

Erika jumped as the door to the room flew open and Maisie strode inside. Outside she glimpsed Hugo with a strange look on his face, before Maisie swung the door closed again.

"*There* you are," the spy exclaimed, clearly exasperated.

"Here I am," Erika agreed, irritated despite herself. She'd been trapped in the same quarters with the woman for a week now, and had come to this room to enjoy some peace, however brief. "Were you looking for me?"

The spy slumped into the opposite chair and glanced out the window. "I was," she said, then sighed. "Though I suppose it wouldn't work today, in this weather."

"Huh?" Erika asked.

"You know, I've been thinking, the borders of Calafe can't be *that* far from here. These Gods of yours probably wouldn't expect us to go that way—not towards the Tangata. We could skirt the foothills back to the Illmoor Fortress, avoid any Tangata in the area. We'd be back in the safety of Nguyen's protection in a matter of weeks…"

"What about Cara?" Erika murmured, her eyes on the storm. She had spent all week with the spy brainstorming ways of breaking the young Anahera from her room, but with the two guards watching their every move…

Maisie let out a sigh, and when Erika looked at her, the

Gemaho woman did not meet her eyes. "I know I said we should rescue her, but…" she began.

"No," Erika interrupted, coming to her feet.

"Archivist," Maisie said softly, looking up from her seat. "I know how much you care about her, but…" She trailed off, then shook her head. "It's not us they care about, Erika," she continued finally. "Farhan, the Elders, we're a nuisance to them, an inconvenience. It's Cara they're concerned about, the rules she broke. They need to make an example of her, but us…how hard do you think they're really going to search if we disappear?"

"They said we've seen too much…"

"Hundreds of people have seen Cara—the Elders know their existence is no longer secret. It's only a matter of time before others come looking for the City," Maisie replied. Her eyes met Erika's. "We only came here to ask for their aid. If we leave, carry the tale of what we found here, how they have abandoned us…then there is no reason for others to seek them out. Humanity has more pressing concerns to bother themselves with than these mountains."

Erika shook her head. "I can't believe you," she hissed. "What about Cara? We can't just abandon her!"

Maisie let out a sigh. "You know they're her people, don't you?" she asked. "Who are we to interfere in Anaheran business?"

"The Flumeerens were your people too, once," Erika snapped, recalling the spy's childhood on the streets of Mildeth. "That didn't stop Nguyen from 'interfering,' did it?"

"That's different."

"Is it?" she asked, staring the spy down. "Cara is one of *us* now, Maisie. Whether we like it or not."

For a long moment, Maisie said nothing. Then a curse slipped from her lips and she slumped back into the chair.

"What are we meant to do against *Gods?*" She muttered another curse.

"I thought you didn't believe in the Gods?"

The spy made a dismissive gesture. "Gods, Anahera, call them what you will. We cannot fight them, Erika."

A shiver shook Erika and her gaze was drawn again to where the gauntlet lay upon the table. Maisie did not miss the gesture.

"Nguyen wore it for a year, you know," she said softly. "Maybe Cara is right…"

Erika swallowed. She had shared Cara's revelation with the spy, about the true creators of the gauntlet. "Why did he give it away then?" Erika whispered. "Why did he give it to Queen Amina?"

"Always keep your enemies guessing," Maisie replied with a grim smile. "He hoped it might prove enough of a distraction to delay the queen's assault. In this case, I fear the queen had Nguyen's number, given our old pal Yasin."

"So you never noticed him growing…more violent?" Erika whispered.

Maisie hesitated before shaking her head. "No, though he did not use it often," she sighed. "Erika, you know we will need its power, if we're to stand any chance of rescuing her today."

"I know," Erika snapped, more harshly than she'd intended. Reaching out, she clenched her fingers around the fine mesh of the gauntlet. "Don't you think I know? But how…" She trailed off, not wanting to speak the words, but knowing she must. Her eyes slid closed. "If it was really made by us, if it's not what created the Tangata, the Old Ones, that means…that means it was me who did those terrible things."

"They weren't so terrible—"

"I struck down a God, my own friend," Erika interrupted.

"You were trying to escape a mad queen."

"I killed that man back in camp."

"He was a spy."

"Only because his family was threatened," Erika hissed.

"Even so," Maisie replied, and this time she looked Erika in the eye. "He made his choice. We couldn't know his motives—only that he poisoned Cara, that he led the Flumeeren soldiers after us."

Erika fell silent at that, staring out the window. She watched the snow fall, the flakes crystallising upon the glass. The shadow of the stone structure loomed through the storm.

"I abandoned them," she finally whispered, images flashing through her mind, of the refugees milling outside the walls of Mildeth, her own people, condemned to homelessness and poverty by an unforgiving queen. Their nation lost, leaderless. "I condemned them while serving the very woman who betrayed my kingdom. Who betrayed my father."

"Refusing this power will not change the past," Maisie replied. "That would only be giving in to your fear, allowing it to rule you. But perhaps if you face it, you might gain the strength to make a difference, to change the future of your kingdom."

Erika let out a sigh, slumping in her seat. "Maybe," she whispered, still holding the gauntlet in one clenched fist.

Silence fell between them, and Erika found her thoughts drifting. She looked at the journal once more. She was almost at the end now, and idly she flicked through the last few pages, until she found the final verse its author had written.

*Tis a weight upon mine own soul. Wast our victory worth the price? Mayhaps this is wherefore I still liveth, still clingeth to life. Beest a wrong to right, though I fear I doth not hast the strength.*

A shiver ran down her spine at the words, but before she could contemplate their ancient meaning, the door to the room swung open with a squeal of old hinges. Hugo appeared in the doorway, and quickly Erika slid her bag over the open diary. For a moment she feared he'd seen her stolen property, for he stood staring at them for a long while, jaw clenched, hands shaking.

"It's time," he said abruptly.

The hackles on Erika's neck stood on end and suddenly she found her mouth dry. Beside her, Maisie rose and stepped towards Hugo, placing a hand upon his arm. Erika glimpsed tears in the young Anahera's eyes, but he quickly blinked them back as he struggled to resume his normal stoicism.

"Where?" she whispered.

Hugo nodded to the window, and turning, Erika saw that other silhouettes had joined that of the effigy in the centre of the yard: the Anahera, come to witness the fall of one of their own. She swallowed, looking at Hugo again. His face was drained of colour, but he managed to keep the tears from flowing.

*His father would be proud*, Erika thought bitterly.

But there was no time for resentment now. The time had come to act. Erika clenched her fist around the gauntlet, the fine mesh digging into her flesh. Maisie was right: without its magic, they could not stand against Farhan. She would fail, and Cara would...

*No.*

Erika had made a promise.

She slipped the gauntlet over her hand.

## ✣ 19 ✣

## THE HERO

Footsteps echoed on stone floors as Lukys and his friends were led through the broad halls of the citadel, though the sound was muffled by the strange architecture of the building. While the sheer white walls of the corridor stretched up some twenty feet to either side, where the ceiling should have begun there was only open sky. He had read of the unusual design during his studies, but never had he imagined visiting himself. It seemed an impractical design in the cold northern climate, but thermal waters from a nearby spring were channelled beneath the floor, keeping the corridors warm on even the coldest of days.

Filthy and unshaven from their long journey, Lukys felt out of place amidst the grandeur of the citadel, as though he were trespassing on holy ground. Even now he was struggling to understand the shift in their circumstances. He couldn't help but think Tasha's sudden change of heart was a trap, a ploy to make them lower their guards and lure them to the slaughter.

But the soldiers of their escort were already more than enough to overwhelm them, even with the Tangata on their side. Sophia and her brethren walked in the centre of their party, their Perfugian partners forming a defensive ring to shield them from the soldiers. Whatever Tasha's assurances, it was clear that the men and women of their escort did not share her mercy—there was no missing the hatred in their eyes as they shot glances at the Tangata. Their minds remained unshielded to Lukys's probing, and he could sense their hatred, a shimmering green consuming them.

So far, only Cleo and Tasha seemed to possess the ability to Speak. Apparently, the powers of a Melder, as the guards had called him, were not so common as to be possessed by the average soldier. But…it still did not explain how *any* of the Perfugians had come to possess the ability of the Tangata.

He flicked a glance at Dale and Travis as they turned a corner and started up a flight of stairs. Neither had heard of the so-called Melders before, despite their noble births. It was clearly a closely-guarded secret, known only to a chosen few. But why?

Shaking himself, Lukys returned his mind to their surroundings. He'd glimpsed several doorways leading from the main corridor now, revealing side chambers of varying uses, most sporting low-hanging ceilings. The passageway itself wound slowly up the hill, running flat across the slope before turning up stairs that led to the next section of flat. Those chambers placed on the downhill sections of the palace displayed great windows of fine glass with glimpses of the harbour.

Finally the corridor came to an end, opening out into a massive amphitheatre. Their escort led them onto an open floor that spanned some fifty yards in diameter. Stands of granite surrounded the perimeter, rising some twenty feet on all sides.

In the direction of the ocean, the stands levelled out into

a platform that sat atop the corridor from which they'd just emerged. On the opposite side of the amphitheatre though, the giant steps reached higher, lifting some thirty feet to the balcony of the grand palace. Two thrones of gold and polished marble stood upon the balcony, but for the moment they remained empty.

A ring of statues surrounded the stands, set in pairs and placed at regular intervals. They were the Sovereigns of past generations, their likenesses carved forever in stone to be remembered here, where they had once reigned. Each had ruled as brother and sister, selected by the Sovereigns before them in a manner known only to the rulers themselves.

Lukys looked around as movement came from the edges of the amphitheatre, and a moment later dozens of guards in blue armour appeared atop the stands. His heart lurched in his chest as they levelled crossbows at the Tangata. Thinking they'd been betrayed, he swung on Tasha where she stood nearby, raising the spear he'd claimed from Travis.

"You said we had a truce!" he cried.

The woman only raised an eyebrow, her face kept carefully blank. "Consider them a precaution."

"Consider yourselves lucky we haven't ordered them to open fire," Cleo growled, his silver spear held tight at his side.

The rest of their escort had put space between themselves and Lukys's friends, leaving only the royal guards standing near. Lukys grated his teeth as he looked from the guards to the balcony, a tingling starting in the back of his neck as he imagined the crossbows aimed at his heart. Once again, his fate rested entirely in the hands of the Sovereigns. He could only pray they would not condemn him again.

"My lieges," Tasha announced, striding towards the stands beneath the palace. The balcony was empty, but Lukys could sense...something from the shadows beyond the broad doorway. "I bring you the Perfugian recruits and the Tangatan intruders, as you commanded."

Lukys lifted his eyebrows at her phrasing, but movement from the shadows beyond the balcony drew his attention to the palace. A guard in blue armour emerged, followed by three others. They marched to the edge of the balcony where the stands led down into the amphitheatre and came to a stop. There they waited, shields and spears shining in the fading light of the day.

His eyes drawn back to the shadows, Lukys held his breath. Despite their danger, despite the threat out on the waters of the harbour, he found himself strangely excited. They were about to set eyes upon the Sovereigns. It was an honour bestowed upon only the most noble of Perfugians. Though for them, that honour might yet prove their doom.

Movement came from the shadows as two figures appeared. Slipping from the darkness of the palace, they separated and moved to seat themselves in the golden thrones. The breath caught in Lukys's throat as he looked upon the Sovereigns. Clothed in purple silks and wearing silver crowns adorned with sapphires, these were the sacred rulers of Perfugia, the two who would decide whether they all lived or died.

The pair could not have been older than fifteen.

Lukys began to speak, but the words he had been preparing in his mind tripped upon his tongue. Instead, he found himself staring open-mouthed at the Sovereigns, struggling to comprehend what he was seeing. Surely some jest was being played on them. Little was known about the selection of new Sovereigns, but…how could anyone so young hold such a position of power?

Shaking off his shock, Lukys drew himself up. Their age did not matter; the Sovereigns had led Perfugia through the generations, since their people had come to the rugged shores of the northern island. Those first settlers had been refugees from the wars that had gripped humanity since the Fall, sailing the oceans in search of a better world for their children. If only he could convince the two above that Sophia and her people only sought the same, they might finally be safe.

The Sovereigns sat on their thrones for a time, staring in silence at the visitors in their grand amphitheatre. Lukys found their gaze disconcerting, as though they were already judging him. The two did not hold themselves as normal teenagers; there was an aged way to how they sat, a stature far beyond their years.

Despite himself, Lukys wilted beneath that gaze. What right did he have to stand before these two, the rightful leaders of Perfugia, saviours of his people? Who was he but a failed citizen, unworthy of even the most rudimentary position in their glorious society…?

*Lukys…* He started as Sophia's voice whispered into his mind. Glancing at her, he found her grey eyes wide. *Beware—*

Her voice cut off abruptly as the rustling of clothes carried to them from above. Lukys looked back to the balcony as the Sovereigns stood, moving to stand at the railings. Watching them, Lukys threw off the despairing thoughts. Hadn't he left those doubts behind long ago? He had proven his worth countless times over the last months, fighting across Calafe, defeating Tangata in single combat, escaping the wrath of an Old One.

No, he had no cause to feel shame standing before these two. Glancing again at Sophia, he offered a silent nod. Whatever their judgement said, he was a warrior, a soldier. And he would fight to the end for his people.

*"Where have you come from, Melder?"*

A hiss escaped from Lukys's throat as the words rang

across the courtyard—and his mind. It took a moment before he could piece together the words. The two spoke as one, out loud so that all could hear, but also into his mind, their words thundering in a way that made him shrink from them. He shared a glance with Sophia and saw his own concern reflected back. If the Sovereigns themselves were Melders, how far back did the deception stretch?

Clenching his fists, he took a step towards the balcony, though it did little to narrow the distance to the Sovereigns.

"My name is Lukys," he said, choosing to speak out loud. A gust of wind swept the words from the amphitheatre, sapping them of strength, but he kept on. "And I come from the frontier, from the lands of Calafe." He paused. "Where you sent me to die."

The Sovereigns regarded him in silence, their twin pairs of eyes shimmering in the fading sunlight.

*"Many have been sent to die at the hands of the Tangata,"* their reply came finally. *"It is an honour to give one's life for their kingdom."*

"Not when they die needlessly!" Lukys cried, a rage coming on him as he looked at the teenage Sovereigns. "Not when they are sent untrained. Not when the Tangata themselves do not desire war!"

*"The Tangata are blasphemers who betrayed the Gods, monsters who seek the destruction of humanity. All know this,"* the Sovereigns replied in unison.

Lukys clenched his teeth at their words, preparing to unleash his rage upon them, but a hand on his shoulder gave him pause. A warmth touched his heart as Sophia joined him, though her grey eyes were on the Sovereigns. Following her gaze, he saw that the pair were staring at her.

*"Is that not so, Tangata?"* They spoke again, and now the words in Lukys's mind were softer, as they directed their question at Sophia.

She bowed her head. *There are some who loathe your kind with a passion,* she replied softly, *some who would see you destroyed. But…there are many others, younger generations who see humanity as equals, as two halves of a whole, incomplete so long as we remain separate.*

"And these youth, they desire peace?" the Sovereigns questioned.

Sophia hesitated, her eyes flickering to Lukys. He faced the pair above.

"If granted the opportunity, many of the Tangata would join us, as Sophia and these others here have," he replied, then hesitated, struggling to put words to what he had seen in New Nihelm.

An image sprung into his mind, of the Old One Maya, as she stood in the basilica in New Nihelm. He blinked, but the image did not fade, and he realised this was a scene he had never seen before. Adonis stood alongside the creature, and as he watched she advanced on his viewpoint. Words were spoken—then the Old One moved in a blur. Blood followed and slowly the image faded to black.

*That was the last vision of our Matriarch,* Sophia said softly, directing her words to the Sovereigns. *Broadcast to all the Tangata who were nearby in her final moments, to reveal this treachery. Sadly, the others were already in the thrall of the Old One.*

Lukys swallowed and reached out to squeeze her fingers. He had not seen that image as they stood outside the basilica, hadn't realised the horror she had witnessed in her mind. His gaze was drawn back to the Sovereigns and now he saw the doubt that creased their faces. Slowly they retreated to their thrones and sat.

"So the Old Ones have returned," they said at last, voices grim. "This…changes everything."

"Old Ones?" came a voice from behind Lukys. "That sounds ominous."

Lukys spun as a newcomer emerged from the corridor. Dressed in a simple tunic and breeches, he appeared as a common man from the street. Yet no commoner could simply stroll into the court of the Sovereigns, and certainly not with a sword strapped to his belt. And this man carried a bearing about himself that spoke of nobility, as though he were used to others submitting to his every command.

But the royal guards stationed around the amphitheatre clearly had no intention of bowing to him. At his appearance, they sprang to alert, hefting spears and moving quickly to place themselves between the stranger and their Sovereigns.

The man came to a stop as the guards barred his path, though he did not spare them so much as a glance. His gaze remained fixed on the Sovereigns.

"My dear Sovereigns," he said, offering a short bow. "I do apologise for interrupting your court, but it's a matter of some urgency." He paused, a grimace twisting his lips. "I'm afraid Queen Amina has invaded Gemaho."

## THE EMISSARY

E rika shuddered as a gust of wind sent ice and sleet whipping sideways across the open yard. The cold bit at her exposed hand and sliced through her too-thin clothing, and hugging herself tight, she made to clench her fist, to summon the magic of her gauntlet for warmth.

Then she hesitated, glancing at the Anahera who stood gathered around her. They did not know of her power, had not noticed the gauntlet she now wore. Cara and her father were still absent; better she kept the magic secret for now, maintained the element of surprise.

Not that Erika knew what she was going to do—only that she would not stand idly by while her friend was dismembered.

The crowd of Anahera swelled as more arrived from their hidden quarters, though Erika noticed that as before, the children—fledglings, as Cara had called them—were not present. There were several like Hugo, slightly younger than Cara in appearance, but the rest were adults. She shivered to think how many years such beings had seen, if a youth such as Cara had passed fifty years of age.

Inevitably, Erika's gaze was drawn to the monoliths in the centre of the yard. The four towers of stone loomed above, great blocks of stone stretching from the corners of the altar. Their true purpose now lay revealed, as great blades of steel had been placed between each of the towers, forming two terrible guillotines on either side of the altar.

A shudder ran down Erika's spine as she looked upon the terrible device the Gods had crafted to punish their own. Chains lay across the altar, iron manacles awaiting their next victims. Now she was close, Erika could see the dark stains upon the stone, the grooves worn in the altar beneath each steel blade. Remnants of past atrocities. Her stomach twisted at the thought of Cara bound to that cold stone, her wings stretched out, the blades suspended above, waiting...

Tearing her gaze from the awful contraption, Erika focused instead on the object of her anger. Farhan stood nearby, his cold gaze fixed on one of the doorways to the city. Arms clasped behind his back, wings folded neatly behind, he waited with the other Elders, the image of a regal leader.

How Erika hated him. At least Hugo showed some semblance of emotion for his sister, some terror and shame for what was about to be done. But Farhan...Farhan's face could have been carved from stone, his eyes frozen into ice. There was no hint of sadness for the fate of his daughter, no compassion.

Erika grated her teeth, her entire being vibrating with her anger. How could any father commit such a crime against his own daughter? Erika could barely grasp the glory of wings, the freedom of the open sky, but she had seen the wonder of it in Cara's eyes, the joy. To lose that...it would destroy her—

Erika's train of thought was broken as Maisie nudged her in the side.

"What?" Erika hissed, glaring at the spy.

Maisie raised an eyebrow and flicked her eyes down-wards. Erika followed her gaze and saw the gauntlet had come to life. Thankfully its glow was muted in the near whiteout conditions of the mountain valley, and quickly she released her fist, allowing it to die. Exhaling, she nodded her thanks at Maisie, even as her own doubts rose again within her. Had the anger been her own? Or had Cara been wrong, and the gauntlet was affecting her again?

*No,* she thought, returning her eyes to Farhan, *no, this is my own rage. If ever a creature deserved to be hated, it was the parent who fails his child.*

Reassured, she drew herself up, preparing to denounce the God. Before she could act, a door across the yard slammed open. Her stomach twisted as a pair of Anaheran guards emerged, leading a forlorn figure between them. The gale caught Cara's flaming hair and sent it whipping across her face, and even her auburn feathers lifted at the power in the storm. For a moment it seemed she would be blown off the mountain.

Erika wondered why she did not flee. She had seen the Goddess in flight, knew her speed. She was young—surely she could outrun those who would come after her? But then, what was there for Cara out in the world, now that her iden-tity had been revealed? Erika, humanity, had already betrayed her, had failed her too many times. Perhaps she had come to accept her fate, that there *was* no place in this world for her, for a God who disobeyed her own family, her own laws.

*No,* Erika whispered to herself, clenching her fist. *She is my friend. I will not let them take her wings.*

Yet she did not move as Cara was led across the square to where the altar awaited. Her heart pounded in her chest as she watched them. The contraption seemed so barbaric, more a creation out of the dark days of the Fall than a tool of the Gods, of those who had created the wonders captured in paint on the walls of their city.

*It is human magic, Erika. It never belonged to us.*

Erika shuddered as her Archivist's mind began to replay Cara's words, to examine everything she had learned these past weeks, everything she had witnessed, Erika could no longer ignore the question on her mind: what were the Anahera? Yes, Cara's people were glorious, splendid, powerful. But then, so were the Tangata, in their own way. Sleek, balanced, with a grace no human could ever hope to match. They moved as the Anahera did.

Cara sobbed as the guards lay her upon the altar. Chains rattled as her captors forced down her arms and locked them in shackles. She did not fight as the constraints were fixed in place, though Erika noticed her head swinging around, searching the crowd, seeking a friend—seeking Erika.

Erika clenched her fist again, struggling with her anger, looking upon Farhan. How she loathed this God of Gods. Could she defy him, defy the Gods themselves to save her friend?

The hackles rose on Erika's neck as a scream carried across the square. She watched as the guards each took hold of one of Cara's wings, watched as they stretched them across the altar, until her auburn feathers lay exposed to the snow, so beautiful, so frail. Chains rattled as the guards bound them tight to the stone, fixing them in place.

Images flashed through Erika's mind as she imagined the blades falling, their razor-sharp edges slicing through the flesh and bone and feather of the fragile limbs beneath. Not even a God could heal from that…

…or whatever the Anahera were.

Erika found herself turning away from the anguish on

Cara's face, looking instead at Maisie. The woman stood nearby, her face a mask, though Erika could sense the tension radiating from the spy. She had never believed in the Gods. Nguyen, the Gemaho leader, had claimed Cara was something else, something like the Tangata.

Something that could be defied, defeated.

"Stop!"

Erika's call shattered the silence of the Anahera, drawing every face towards her as she stepped up to confront Farhan.

"This is wrong," she said, her voice steady now, determined.

*Wrong, wrong, wrong.*

The words carried more meaning than one. Wrong to commit such a crime. Wrong to have believed in these creatures all these years. Wrong to call them Gods. Her mind struggled to focus, to keep from pondering the implications of her decision—for if the Anahera were not Gods, if they had never been Divine…what did that mean for her life's study, for her purpose, for her people…?

Farhan said nothing, only watched her with those cold eyes. Gritting her teeth, Erika swung on the crowd, seeking someone, anyone who might help her. The Elders stared back, unyielding, but surely not all the Anahera could be so cruel, so heartless as Farhan.

Then she saw Hugo, standing alone, away from the others, his eyes shadowed.

"Hugo!" His head jerked up when she called his name, his eyes showing shock. He retreated half a step, but she would not let him flee, would not let him abandon his sister. "You know this isn't right!" she called, pointing. "That your father is wrong to do this. This cannot be what your Founders wanted for the Anahera, to be hidden away in this place, to live imprisoned by invisible chains, your lives controlled by laws that ceased to have meaning long ago."

Hugo froze, still half-turned to flee, hand raised as though to fend her off. He blinked, slowly turning back towards them, and for a moment she thought he might speak—

"Enough!" Farhan bellowed, drawing the attention of the square back to him. For once his face showed emotion as veins bulged in his forehead. "Enough of your foul temptation, human," he spat, advancing on her. "You have corrupted one of my children already, I will not allow you another!"

He raised his fist as though to strike her and Erika leapt back, her gauntlet coming up instinctively. Light shone upon the silver threads, setting the falling snow aglow. Gasps came from all around as the Anahera drew back, and before her, Farhan froze. Surprise showed in his eyes as he looked upon the gauntlet, but it was quickly masked behind red rage.

"So at last the human shows her true nature," he snarled, baring his teeth—though he did not advance. "The magic of the ancients is born again to be used against us."

Erika quickly lowered her fist, extinguishing the light. "No…" she said, turning to the crowd.

The Anahera stared back at her, fear shining in their eyes.

"You will not stop us from following the path set by our Sacred Founders," Farhan said, and now his voice was soft, implacable.

Turning, he started towards the altar where Cara lay bound. Her eyes widened as he approached and Erika caught the whisper of her voice on the wind, her desperate plea.

"Please, Father, no…"

Erika's heart pounded in her chest and she lifted her

hand to strike Farhan down, then froze. There had been something about the way the God had looked at the gauntlet, an expectation. He knew what the gauntlet was, even if he had not known it was in her possession. So why did he turn his back against her now, as though inviting her to use it?

Lowering her arm, Erika darted forward, trying to place herself between father and daughter. As she ran, she spotted Hugo, still standing nearby. He was no longer paying attention to Erika or his father, but instead to Maisie. The spy was speaking to him, but the wind whipped away her words.

Then Erika was standing before the altar, her back to Cara, facing down Farhan's advance. Open rage showed in the eyes of the Anahera as he advanced, and Erika could hear the sobs of her friend from behind, the whispers of the crowd, the hissing of wind through the glass houses.

A calm descended upon her as she clenched her fist, igniting the power of the gauntlet. There was only one option now, one last path left to save her friend, and she sighed as the warmth of the gauntlet's magic bathed her. Cries came from the other Anahera, but this time Farhan did not retreat. Wings spread wide, he bore down upon the frail Archivist.

But Erika did not shrink from him now, did not bow down to this creature of the mountains. No God of hers would commit such an atrocity against his child, against her friend. She raised her hand, clenching her fist tighter, the magic building. The soft crackling of her power sounded across the yard as Erika stood tall against her foe.

And still Farhan came on.

## ❧ 21 ❧

## THE HERO

"King Nguyen," the Sovereigns growled, rising from their thrones. "*What is the meaning of this?*"

Lukys started at their words, spinning to regard the stranger anew. He wore no crown, but his bearing...the greying hair and iron jawline, the piercing emerald eyes...yes, this man was older, more world-weary, but there was a resemblance to the sketches Lukys had studied in the academy. Yet...how had the Gemaho king come to be here, unheralded and alone in the court of the Sovereigns?

Spreading his hands, the king offered the Sovereigns a smile. As he did so, horns began to sound in the distance. Lukys frowned as all eyes turned from the king towards the unseen harbour, upon which towers kept an ever-vigilant watch for sign of attack. But no enemy had ever dared come against their remote island kingdom. Surely it could not have been...

The horn sounded again, a long, shrill note that went on and on. Lukys's blood ran cold as he recognised the signal from his learnings at the academy—the klaxon call to arms, the warning that an enemy had arrived on Perfugia's shores.

"Ah, that will be my fleet," King Nguyen announced, drawing the attention of the amphitheatre back to him. Reaching into his tunic, he drew out a glass and metal object and inspected its surface before returning it to his pocket. "And not a moment too soon!" he announced.

"*Nguyen, what is the meaning of this?*" the Sovereigns snarled again.

They advanced down the stairs from their balcony, hedged by royal guards. Their silver spears were extended towards the king, but he stood calmly beneath their threat, with far more poise than Lukys could have managed under the circumstances. The Sovereigns were practically bubbling with rage—scarlet waves rushed from them in bursts, and Lukys found his own emotions rising in response.

But Nguyen only stared them down as they joined him on the amphitheatre floor. Lukys stared at the man, drawn by the calmness of his aura. This was the king that nearly a decade ago had turned his back on the alliance between the human kingdoms, the man who had doomed Calafe by withdrawing his soldiers and leaving the allies impossibly outnumbered by the Tangata. Now he walked alone into the stronghold of an unfriendly kingdom. Lukys couldn't help but be impressed.

The Sovereigns did not feel the same. Lips drawn back in a snarl, their anger might have been terrifying but for their youthful faces. Even so, Lukys couldn't help but think the king had made a misstep coming to this place.

"My dear Sovereigns, did you not hear me?" Nguyen said with a smile as the Sovereigns reached the amphitheatre floor and came to a stop before him. Though he stood a foot above the two youths, the soldiers that surrounded him made the balance of power clear. "The Queen of Flumeer has betrayed the alliance and attacked the Fortress Illmoor. Even now I fear her armies are pillaging their way across

Gemaho. I come seeking Perfugian aid, before her greed consumes us all."

A stunned silence met his words as the Sovereigns stared at the king. Lukys swallowed, shocked at the gall of the man, to beg aid in the name of the alliance he had betrayed. And yet, if what he said was true…Queen Amina had committed an act unheard of in a generation, invading the lands of another human kingdom.

*"You dare come seeking our aid, after you abandoned Calafe in their time of need?"* the Sovereigns replied finally, clearly still struggling to come to grips with the foreign king. *"After you allowed the Tangata to rampage across our neighbour's lands, to slaughter and kill—"*

"Before we start too far down this history lesson," Nguyen interrupted, "Your Majesties do realise there are about a dozen Tangata standing in this very court, yes?"

The Sovereigns started at his words, their heads swinging towards Lukys and the others as though they'd been momentarily forgotten. Lukys might have laughed, if his own life and that of his companions had not also been on the line. He held his breath, wondering at the king's reaction. It seemed not even the sight of a dozen creatures from humanity's darkest nightmares could rattle his composure.

By contrast, for the first time, cracks had appeared in the regal aura of the Sovereigns. *"These Tangata are…exceptions,"* they hissed, eyes still fixed on Sophia and her brethren. "They bring…news of their people, of…an ancient power that threatens all of us."

"It seems this world is becoming clogged with refugees and existential threats," Nguyen replied, grey-streaked eyebrows lifting to crease his forehead as he appraised the Tangata.

Lukys wondered how he could keep so calm—when

he'd first encountered the Tangata, it had been all he could manage to keep down his breakfast.

"But then, they say that was why your people first settled on this barren rock, was it not?" he continued, swinging back to the Sovereigns. "To escape the ravages of man and beast." He paused, taking a step closer to the Sovereigns. Steel rattled as their guards moved to intercept him, but after a moment the Sovereigns waved them back. "You condemn me for refusing to participate in a war I no longer believed in, for shielding my people from, yet is that not the principle upon which your nation was founded?"

*"Do not think to turn your cowardice upon us, King Nguyen,"* the Sovereigns snarled. *"We have done our duty to the alliance this last decade. Where Gemaho fled, we have ensured Perfugian steel marched to meet the Tangata wherever they have threatened the lives of humanity."*

"Yes, yes, yes," the king replied, raising his hands in mock surrender. "I'm sure the children you sent to the slaughter were very noble, but as I said, let us not rehash the past. Alliances change, enemies become friends, and friends enemies. If the Tangata now stand amongst us in peace, we should discuss the true threat to our peoples."

*"And who, pray, would that be—if not the man who sails a fleet into our harbour?"*

Lukys shivered as the Sovereigns spoke this time, for beneath their words, their tone conveyed their growing rage. It clawed at his mind, threatening to break through his own control. The king stood on unstable ground.

Nguyen seemed to understand the precariousness of his situation, for his face suddenly became serious. "As I have said, Your Majesties, the Flumeeren queen has driven me from my lands. I come here not for conquest, but to beg your aid for my people. Even now, Gemaho burns. And it is my belief Amina will not be content with just the mainland."

There was silence for a moment as the Sovereigns stared at the king. *"We have heard of your provocations against Queen Amina. Tell us, Gemaho King, do the rumours tell it true—did an agent of yours truly creep into her kingdom and assault the personage of our Gods?"*

Lukys started at that, looking from the Sovereigns to the foreign king. "What?" he exclaimed before he could think better of it. "They can't mean...are they talking about Cara?"

The king's eyes widened as he turned towards Lukys, as though seeing him for the first time. "You knew the young Anahera?" Then his brow rose in sudden understanding. "You are Lukys, the Perfugian recruit." His gaze flickered, taking a moment to study the rest of their party. "It appears the rumours of your death were greatly exaggerated."

*"Then it's true?"* the Sovereigns interrupted, irritation prickling their mental voice. *"You committed blasphemy—"*

"It is not blasphemy to one who does not believe in the Divine," the king interrupted, returning his attention to the dual rulers. "But if you must know, the Anahera—or Goddess, if you prefer—came to no harm under my custody. I only...did what was necessary to ensure she was returned to her people. I fear the same could not have been said had she remained in the care of Amina."

Lukys's heart clenched at the mention of Cara. He hadn't seen her since that day by the river when he'd been captured by the Tangata, since she'd revealed herself as a Goddess. The sight of her soaring above the waters of the Illmoor, auburn wings spread wide, it would stay with him until the end of his days. But if Flumeer and Gemaho were now at war...could the king be believed as to her fate?

*"You offer us pretty words, Nguyen,"* the Sovereigns replied

after a moment, *"but past lies have proven the worth of such platitudes."*

The king spread his arms and dipped into a half bow. "Then I invite you to verify their truth, Your Majesties," he said with a smile. "Until such a time, might I offer myself as your humble hostage."

"And the fleet in our harbour? I suppose they will remain?"

Nguyen's eyes danced as he stared the Sovereigns down. "Just so."

Red touched the auras of the Sovereigns at his words, but Lukys realised they had little choice but to accept Nguyen's terms. If he was to be believed, a fleet of ships had just sailed into the Ashura harbour. The Perfugian might have more ships, but trapped within the narrow waters, they would be unable to bring their numbers to bear against the assailing force.

The Sovereigns turned away from the king, and for a moment Lukys thought they might throw caution to the wind after all. *"Very well, Gemaho King,"* they said abruptly. *"We will await word from the mainland. In the meantime, I trust you will surrender yourself to our guard."*

The king bowed his head. "Of course, my dear Sovereigns."

*"Then our business is concluded."*

With that the Sovereigns turned and began for the steps leading back to their balcony. A pair of guards moved to escort Nguyen from the room. Lukys and the others watched on, their fate still unknown, until finally Lukys could take it no more.

"Your Majesties!" he burst out, swinging from the king to the receding Sovereigns. They paused on the stands, glancing back at them. "What of us? What of the Tangata?"

A strained silence followed his words as the Sovereigns looked from him to Sophia and her brethren. For a moment, something flickered in their eyes, a familiar loathing, a hatred he recognised all too well. Despite his arguments and Sophia's words, despite their shared powers, the Sovereigns still despised the Tangata.

The expression vanished, though it lingered in the faces of the royal guards, like an echo of the Sovereigns' own hidden emotions. Lukys clenched his jaw and balled his hands into fists, preparing himself for their decree. The pair were only a few steps up the stairs towards their balcony—if he was quick, he might reach them before the nearest guard...

*"We will grant you your reprieve."*

Their response came as such a surprise that Lukys almost fell over himself, one leg already extended towards the steps on which the pair stood. Even the guards seemed surprised by the verdict. Movement came from nearby as Cleo started towards the Sovereigns.

"Your Majesties, you cannot let these animals—"

He broke off as twin pairs of eyes turned in his direction, the words abandoning him. *"Were you asked to speak, soldier?"*

"I only wished to remind—"

*"Enough!"* the Sovereigns boomed, silencing the guard.

Cleo's face turned a mottled red and his mouth opened and closed, but no more words emerged. The Sovereigns continued to glare at him for a long moment, the guard withering beneath the power of their Voice. When they finally turned away, the guard shuddered. Tasha took him by the shoulder, but as she led him away, the guard looked back towards the Tangata. Across the distance, his eyes met Lukys's.

A shudder ran down his spine. He did not need his

ability to see the man's hatred, to know it would not end with a command by the Sovereigns. Whatever happened next, he had earned an enemy today.

Then the Sovereigns were gone, leaving Lukys and his friends alone with the guards on the amphitheatre floor. Looking at those surrounding them, at the crossbowmen above, Lukys was touched with despair. He could sense their anger. The abhorrence of his people for the Tangata had been instilled through generations, through childhood tales of bloodshed and slaughter. Could even the blessing of the Sovereigns protect them from such visceral hatred?

*"You and your Tangata will be guarded, confined to your quarters. When this…other matter has been resolved, we will speak more of the Old Ones. Until then, you will have your asylum."*

The words of the Sovereigns rung from the stands of the amphitheatre, carrying with them a sense of finality, and Lukys knew they had been dismissed. Guards moved forward to escort them, as they had with the king, but Lukys could see the loathing in their eyes as they approached. Looking at the Sovereigns, he felt no relief at their verdict. Their struggle had only just begun.

## ❧ 22 ❧

## THE EMISSARY

"I knew you would betray us," Farhan said as he advanced on Erika. "It is the nature of your kind, to lie, to cheat, to kill."

Erika raised her glowing fist in warning, but the Anahera came on, inexorable, determined. She bared her teeth as the wind howled about them, the raging storm swallowing up the yard, reducing the world to just the two of them.

"No," Erika said, refuting him. "I wish the Anahera no harm. I only do what I must for Cara, to protect my friend."

"She is my daughter!" Farhan snarled, taking another step. His wings beat down, sending snow swirling and adding to the falling sleet. "You know not what you do, the doom you would bring upon us."

"Even so," Erika snarled. "I will not let you have her."

Retreating another step, she flinched as her backside came up against the stone of the altar. Quickly she risked a glance over her shoulder at Cara. The Goddess was struggling now, fighting to break free, but the chains that bound her were clearly intended to withstand the strength of the Anahera.

Erika clenched her fist as she faced Farhan once more, wondering if she could do as she had back in the camp all those nights ago, when she'd used her magic to break Cara's cuffs. If she could get close enough, a few seconds was all she needed.

Abruptly, Hugo stepped between her and Farhan, his eyes wide, wings trembling. Erika flinched, thinking for a moment he had come to stop her. But to her surprise, he raised a hand to Farhan.

"Father, please, do not harm her."

Open shock showed in the Anahera's face as he looked upon his son. Erika opened her mouth to add her words to Hugo's—then paused. The weather was closing in, reducing visibility to just a few yards. With the other Anahera lost to view and Farhan absorbed by the confrontation with his son, this was her chance. Spinning, she leapt upon the altar and scrambled across to Cara.

"Erika," Cara was babbling as Erika reached her. "Erika, I can't, please, don't let him…" She trailed off as Erika placed a hand to her cheek.

"Quiet, I'm getting you out of this, okay?" Erika whispered to the Goddess—whatever she thought of the other Anahera, Cara had long ago proven herself worthy of the title. "Just hold on."

She was surprised to find the Goddess's skin cold to the touch. Tears had streamed down her friend's face, freezing in the cold, and her eyes were red. Clenching her jaw, Erika set to work before the storm drew the last of the warmth from her friend. Through the storm, she could hear Hugo confronting his father, though the wind obscured their words. There was no sign of Maisie. Erika wondered what the spy had said to the young Anahera to convince him to confront his father.

Aware of the great blades of steel teetering above, Erika crawled to the first of the chains that bound her friend and grasped the iron manacle that held Cara's left arm. Her hand began to vibrate as she ignited the gauntlet, and a brilliant glow bathed their faces, then with a sharp *shriek* the metal tore itself apart. A moan came from Cara as she pulled her hand free and Erika's heart soared.

Then a cry came from behind them.

Spinning, Erika looked in time to see Hugo collapsed to the snow, felled by a blow from Farhan. Cursing, she returned her attention to her friend. The chains binding Cara's wings were thicker than the manacles and gritting her teeth, she clenched them tight. A wave of dizziness swept through her as the magic shone, until with another screech of twisting metal Cara's wing came free.

"Archivist!" Somewhere in the snow, Maisie's voice cried a warning.

*Thunk.*

Erika gasped as something slammed into the altar beside her. For a moment she thought the worst had come to pass, that one of the terrible blades had fallen, robbing Cara of flight forever.

Instead, she found herself staring up at Farhan, his face twisted in rage, his eyes dark…turning darker, stained with grey.

"Human," he growled. "You will pay for your defiance, for corrupting my children, turning them against me."

"I did nothing to your children." Erika bared her teeth as she rose to face him. "It was your own foulness that turned them against you, Farhan."

Before she knew what was happening, Farhan had Erika by the throat. She tried to cry out, to raise the gauntlet, but

he tossed her aside as though she were of no more consequence than a mouse before the lion. The storm swallowed
up her scream as Erika found herself soaring, the rocky
ground rising up to meet her...

*Thud.*

She struck with a force that drove the breath from her
lungs. Light flashed across her vision and for a moment,
Erika knew only white. Then the world came rushing back
and the taste of blood filled her mouth. Groaning, she
pulled herself to her knees and looked up at her foe.

Farhan stood atop the altar, wings spread, face twisted in
a mask of rage and sorrow. At his feet, Cara was still trying
to tear herself free, the wing Erika had loosed flailing. But
with a snarl, Farhan brought his boot down upon the limb,
pinning it to the stone. A gasp came from Cara as she beat
her fist upon his leg, but Farhan was far stronger,
unmovable.

Then broad arms rippling with muscle, he reached up
and took hold of one of the blades.

"I will not lose another," he cried. "The will of the
Founders will be done."

"Father, please, no!" Cara screamed. She clutched piti-
fully at his pants now, pleading, in despair.

Farhan did not look at his daughter. His eyes were fixed
on Erika, his mouth twisted in a snarl of hatred. She
flinched from that look, that rage, as the ropes holding the
blade aloft began to vibrate, their threads yielding to the
unyielding strength of the Anahera.

Struggling for breath, Erika pulled herself to her feet
and summoned her magic. She swayed as the power came.
Her strength was running low, but she would not surrender.
Farhan had hurled her beyond the range of the magic, and
teeth bared, she staggered towards him, fighting back the
pain that engulfed her body. Yet even as she moved, Erika

knew she would not be in time. The rope was already beginning to give way, the blade creeping down. In seconds it would fall, crushing her friend's freedom, breaking her soul.

Still Erika fought through the howling wind, fist raised, power gathering, desperate for one final chance. She didn't bother with words. The storm had closed in around them anyway, swallowing the watching Anahera, so that it seemed only she and Farhan remained in the square. She wondered what the others thought, why they did not interfere. Surely if Farhan commanded it, they would descend upon her? Yet the Elder Anahera seemed determined to do the deed himself...

Erika hesitated as she glimpsed movement on the altar —then abruptly, Farhan vanished. She froze, mouth falling open as a roar came from empty air. A moment later two figures reappeared, tumbling backwards from the altar. One was Farhan. His wings flailed, but he hit the ground before they could halt his fall.

The other was Maisie. Brown hair swirling, she tumbled from the altar with Farhan, but she landed awkwardly, her leg twisting beneath her. A scream sounded through the storm as she crumpled into a snowbank and lay still.

Heart pounding in her ears, Erika stared at the Gemaho spy. What madness had possessed the woman to use her magic to attack Farhan? Even hidden by the magic of her artefact, surely Maisie couldn't have thought to overcome the Anahera by herself?

A roar sounded from nearby as Farhan surged back to his feet. Wings spread, teeth bared, he started towards the spy, the snarl on his lips promising violence...then froze.

A frown crossed Farhan's face and for a second his eyes took on a distant look. Turning, he looked away from them, up into the swirling storm, as though even now he could see the peaks surrounding the city. His frown deepened.

"What…"

Erika followed his gaze, trying to find what had distracted him, even as she sensed the rumble of other Anaheran voices, raised against the wind and sleet. Something was happening, something the humans could not discern.

Then Erika heard it: a distant reverberation above the wind and snow, already growing louder, more insistent, until she knew it for what it was.

The roar of a thousand voices raised in unison.

"What the Fall…"

"*Tangata*," Farhan snarled.

## ❀ 23 ❀

## THE FOLLOWER

Adonis drew in a breath, savouring the crispness of the morning air, the chill of winter's breath. It tugged at his clothing, seeking to steal his warmth…but not even the falling snow could touch the fire at his core, the strength granted to him by hope. There would be a future for his people, a new legacy set by his own children.

That legacy would begin today, with the conquest of their ancient enemy.

The pounding began again in his mind, a dull throbbing, a call to battle. Around him he could sense his fellow Tangata, brothers and sisters all, their minds united. Forgotten were the weak who had fallen behind, lost forever to the sands of time. Each who still remained knew their place, their task for the conflict to come.

Adonis balled his hands into fists as he glanced at his companions, those others who had been honoured by the Old One. Theirs was the assignment of greatest importance, the task upon which Tangatan victory or defeat would rest. If they failed, the sacrifice of his brothers and sisters would be for naught.

*Are you ready, my mate?*

Adonis's heart pounded in his ears as Maya's call came to him, setting his blood aflame with images of their nights spent entwined, with promises of a new generation of Tangata, more powerful than any seen in centuries.

But that future would not arrive without cost, without sacrifice. Blood must be shed for new life to be born, to ensure the survival of his species.

His stomach stirred as an image flickered into his mind, of the child in the snow, lost despite her parent's own sacrifice. He shivered, seeking to thrust the image aside, but it lingered, refusing to fade.

*We are prepared, my Matriarch,* he whispered, steeling himself for what was to come.

*Then the time has come.*

Maya's voice was followed immediately by a rush of adrenaline, by surging, burning anger. Howls rose from the mountainside around Adonis, as the Tangata gathered there responded to the same call to arms.

They had marched hard these past days and nights to reach this place. Now looking down into the valley, Adonis struggled to pierce the falling sleet and snow. Their enemy waited somewhere below, concealed by the growing storm, yet Adonis could sense their minds, buzzing softly amidst the white. Ignorant of what was to come.

The burning within him built, the howls of his brethren growing to a crescendo. Adonis resisted the call to violence. His task would require more than bloodlust, more than sheer ferocity. It would take a refined touch, would necessitate the speed and cunning of the older generations.

He shivered, looking across the slope to where his mate stood, ringed by his brethren, preparing to lead them to war. Her grey eyes were fixed on the valley, as though she could see through the raging of the storm. Perhaps she could—the powers of the Old Ones were far beyond his own, undiluted by generations of human crossings, untouched by the disaster of the Fall.

*Tangata, the time has come!* Her voice rose above the thrumming in Adonis's mind, and he knew in that moment she spoke to all of them. *Our foes wait below, weak and unaware. Let the power of the Tangata will consume them. Are you ready?*

A roar sounded in Adonis's mind, the raised voices of a thousand Tangata, distorted and unintelligible, twisted by rage.

*Then go!*

The Tangata screamed again in unison, and then they were surging down the slopes, a dark wave of movement, rushing over the uneven surface with a speed only the uncanny reflexes of the Tangata could achieve. Adonis and his fellows remained for the moment, watching as their brethren vanished into the cloud, swallowed up by the haunting grey.

But their Voices remained, hurling their fury, their hatred into the valley, to the enemy that awaited them. Adonis shivered, thinking of the terror such a call would bring upon those below, the dread. Would their foes crumble, bowed before the united Voice of the Tangata, as Maya expected? Or would they fight back? Would their terror forge them anew, forewarn them of the danger that came upon them?

It was Adonis and his companions' task to ensure that did not happen, to break the spirit of their foes before a resistance could be mounted, before they could fight back. The battle below, the fury of his brethren, was but a distraction.

Maya still stood on the hillside, watching the valley with those terrible eyes. As though sensing his gaze, she turned to him, a smile touching her lips.

*It begins,* she murmured. Her hand drifted to her stomach. *Today, we birth a new future for our children.*

Adonis's heart throbbed at her words and he inclined his head. *I will not fail you.*

*Then go,* she called back. *Crush our enemies. Bring about their despair, so that our children might know freedom.*

A fresh rush of fire wrapped about Adonis, crushing all hesitation, burning away doubt, until all that remained was the call of battle, the promise of Maya's future, and the life that would be born of her womb.

Unleashing a battlecry, Adonis leapt from his perch on the hillside and started down the crumbling rock, down towards the secret valley, the hiding place of their ancient enemy.

To bring war upon the home of the Anahera.

## ❧ 24 ❧

## THE HERO

They put Lukys in the same room as Sophia.

The decision hardly seemed significant as they stumbled into the chamber and collapsed onto the feathered bed, the days and weeks of exhaustion weighing on them. It was already dark outside, the longest day of his life at an end. His eyes flickered closed and within moments, the lure of sleep carried him away.

He woke to bright sunlight streaming into the room. Blinking, he pushed himself up from the pillow, finding an open window in the opposite wall from them. Unlike the corridors and amphitheatre, the chamber at least had a ceiling to protect them from the elements, and with the thermal waters flowing beneath the floor, it was a strange sensation to awake in Ashura to warmth. At the academy, no resources were wasted heating the dormitories of the students.

Letting out a moan, he sank back to the pillows. The bed was softer than even the luxurious one the Tangata had provided him in New Nihelm. Larger too, though he hardly needed so much space, sleeping alone…

The thought drifted away as he rolled on his side and found Sophia next to him. Her eyes were still closed, and the whisper of her breath tickled his cheek as she snored softly. She had shifted close in the night, and now her scent carried to him, a gentle earthly fragrance, despite their days at sea.

A shiver ran down his spine. Watching her sleep, Lukys was struck again by the softness of her face, the gentle curves of her lips, the occasional snort as she dreamed. How could he ever have imagined the creature beside him a monster, that she was anything but human?

Without thinking, he ran a finger across her cheek. Her eyes flickered open at his touch. A smile creased her lips when she saw him and she gave a quiet groan.

*Is it morning already?*

Lukys kissed her. It seemed to take Sophia by surprise, just as it had the first time. But she soon melted against him, her lips pressing against his, parting as a moan rasped from the back of her throat. Her tongue swept out to meet his own as he wrapped her in his arms, hugging her tight.

Warmth washed through Lukys as her fingers slid through his hair, drawing him deeper into the kiss, stealing away his breath. A groan of his own built in his soul as he felt her body against his, sensed her desire, her need.

They broke apart for a moment, each gasping for breath, but their lips soon found one another again. Lukys's hands slipped beneath her shirt, pulling it up, forcing them to separate again to lift it over her head. He tossed it aside as Sophia kissed him once more, even as her fingers began working on the buttons of his tunic. Goosebumps rose on his arms as her warm hands slid across his skin, running over his chest, his stomach, then up to his shoulders, pulling, tugging at his shirt, eager.

Taken by a sudden impatience, Lukys tore the tunic

from his shoulders. Sophia fell upon him before he could even discard it, her lips moving to his neck, kissing, licking, nibbling at his flesh. A growl rose in his throat and he grasped her by the hips, flipping her so she landed on her back before him.

Despite Sophia's enormous strength, she did not resist, only lay there looking up at him, grey eyes drinking him in, even as he feasted upon the sight of her, upon her naked flesh, lying there, waiting…

He crouched over her, kissing her again, pressing his weight against her, feeling the warmth of her breasts on his chest. Her arms wrapped around him, pulling him tight, and her moans grew more insistent. He resisted, breaking off their kiss, his lips touching her neck, moving slowly to her collar, tasting her soft skin, trailing, circling, until finally she gasped as he kissed her breast.

*Lukys!*

A smile crossed his lips as she whispered his name, even as he sucked and licked, then moved to the other. Her hands wrapped around his waist, sliding lower, slipping beneath the pants he had been too exhausted to remove the night before. A groan escaped him as her hands slipped beneath the fabric, pulling him down. He looked up from her breasts and saw her mischievous smile, the desire in her eyes.

*I want you, Sophia,* he whispered to her.

*I want you too, Lukys.*

They kissed again, hard, passionate, as though that alone would sate the flames burning within. But it was not enough, and they soon slid free of the last of their clothing, leaving them both lying naked upon the bed.

Again he found himself looking into those sweet grey eyes, sensing the warmth there, the passion. Neither moved, even breathed, as they looked upon one another, as though they were waiting for something.

*Take me, Lukys.*

And he fell upon her, their bodies entwining, minds become one...

Afterwards, they lay gasping in one another's arms, eyes on the ceiling, content to enjoy the silence, the rare peace they had found for themselves. The warmth of the chamber, even as clouds passed before the sun outside, soon had them dozing. They dreamed and woke again, snatching snippets of the sleep that had evaded them for so long—and stealing kisses as well.

Each time Lukys touched Sophia's mind, he sensed a brilliant pink about her, a radiance he wasn't yet ready to contemplate. Though he had no doubt his own mind must be coloured the same.

So far from Calafe, from the threat of the Old One and her followers, Lukys found he was finally able to breathe a little. He knew there were still battles to come, but looking at Sophia as she dozed, he could finally appreciate what he had found. Now he just had to protect it.

They might have the Sovereigns' temporary blessing, but there were other dangers in this city. Cleo was not alone in his loathing for the Tangata—the academy had sown that hatred into the people since long before the latest war. He would need to change their minds, show them the truth about the Tangata, their beauty and intelligence.

But even then, the Old One would not rest. Sooner or later, Maya would come for humanity. She would not stop until every one of their kind was exterminated, until the Tangata dominated the world. With Adonis and his followers at her side, it would take all the kingdoms united to stand against her.

Though if the Gemaho King were to be believed, even that might yet prove impossible.

*Focus on what you can change,* Sophia's words whispered into his mind as her eyes flickered open.

Lukys smiled and leaned in to kiss her. She was right, of course. They could do nothing about the warring kingdoms or what Maya might be planning in the south. Here, now, there were only the Sovereigns, only the Perfugian citizens to convince of their benevolence.

That brought a thought to his mind. *How could they speak with you?* he murmured. *How could they hear you?*

He was sure that this ability was a large part of why the Sovereigns had accepted the Tangata in the end, why they'd even been granted the honour of an audience. Even the Gemaho King had thought it more prudent to sneak into the citadel, than risk being turned away at the gates. But none of that explained how the Sovereigns and their Guard possessed the abilities of a Melder—as they called them.

*There must be Tangatan blood in your people's history,* she replied sleepily.

That had been her explanation for his own ability, but it still made little sense to Lukys. His ancestors had come to the island hundreds of years ago to escape the warring tribes of humanity, and had remained isolated ever since. Could a Tangatan ancestor have snuck onto the island unbeknownst to the people? Even then, surely one or two could not explain such a prevalence of Melders.

No, if the ability could be so easily passed on to humans, surely it would have manifested first in the kingdoms with greater proximity to the Tangata.

He shook his head. It was a mystery he intended to solve, but for the moment, he found himself restless. Rising, he crossed to the window and looked out across the city. A rumble of thunder carried across the harbour and he caught a flicker of lightning amidst dark clouds in the distance.

Ashura stretched away below, and he found himself wondering at the view he now enjoyed. It wasn't difficult to pick out the academy, its sandstone walls rising from the otherwise polished marble buildings of the city. The academy had taught duty and austerity, and had been shaped to represent those ideals.

Windowless and glum, most of his life had been spent in its dark confines. The open brightness of the citadel was its opposite in every way. To stand in a room such as this, in the vicinity of the Sovereigns themselves, was something he could never have imagined even a few short months ago.

*What are you looking at?* Sophia asked, slipping from beneath the sheets. She crossed to where he stood, her movement sensuous as always, fluid, like a cat amongst the grass.

"Just thinking about our problems," Lukys replied.

His gaze continued to where the city curved around the harbour. Half the Perfugian fleet now bobbed on the calm waters, while beyond the yellow sails of the Gemaho blockade seemed to fill the horizon. There could not have been more of them than there were Perfugians, but the other half of their fleet remained docked, unable to join their comrades for fear of collision in the crowded bay. If it came to a battle, the losses on both sides would be terrible.

Then he frowned, noticing a ship passing carefully between the others. It flew the same blue colours as the other Perfugian vessels, but by its broader hull and heavy sails, Lukys realised it was no warship. A trader, perhaps, arrived from the mainland?

Travis might have known, but they'd all been separated as they left the amphitheatre, taken to different accommodations. Lukys wondered now whether they'd been wise to allow it. Apart, there was no way to know what had become of the others. Unless...

A frown touched Lukys's lips as an idea came to him. Back in the throne room, the Sovereigns had mentioned commanding Tasha to bring them to the citadel—yet the royal guard had never left their presence. That meant the Sovereigns must have spoken their orders into Tasha's mind. Lukys hadn't realised that was possible over such a distance.

Closing his eyes, he reached out with his mind. He felt Sophia immediately, and sensed a probing question back from her. Lukys sent a burst of reassurance to her, then turned his attention further afield. Sophia had managed to see what the Matriarch had seen, back in New Nihelm. They'd been some hundred yards from the Basilica, and separated by thick stone walls.

So what were the limits of his own senses? He reached out farther, and immediately encountered another presence, an unfamiliar aura tainted with green. It was still some distance away, but already growing nearer. There was a purpose about the presence, and an image of his own self standing alongside Sophia flickered into his mind.

Shocked at the success of his experiment, Lukys opened his eyes again. For a moment, he felt disorientated, as though he'd truly been separated from his body, but it quickly cleared.

"Someone's coming," he said to Sophia.

By the time the door to their chambers swung open, they were fully clothed and standing in the window, waiting. Tasha frowned as she paused in the doorway, looking from one to the other. Lukys sensed suspicion from her, but after a moment it faded. Thankfully there was no sign of Cleo, though perhaps his absence should have been of more concern. If the boisterous guard was not with Tasha, did that mean he was supervising some of the others?

"You're wanted," Tasha said shortly.

Lukys couldn't help but notice how her face hardened when she looked at Sophia. He suppressed a sigh. If even the most reasonable of the royal guards couldn't bother to conceal their hatred, what chance did he have of winning some to their side?

"By whom?" he asked.

"King Nguyen," the guard replied, then added: "Before you ask, I don't know why. Only that we've been asked to accommodate him."

Lukys hesitated. There was bad blood between Gemaho and the other nations, but if the king wanted to talk...it meant he might be less prejudiced than the Perfugians at least. He offered Tasha a nod.

"If you're ready then..." She pushed open the door, revealing a dozen regular soldiers outside.

Lukys raised an eyebrow, but the woman ignored him. He shared a glance with Sophia, but she only shrugged and marched from the room without sparing another look at the royal guard. Lukys moved to follow, but as he passed, Tasha grasped him by the arm.

*Lukys.* He started as her voice whispered into his mind, the words meant only for him. *I have read the reports from Fogmore. You are a brave soldier, worthy of much more than the hand fate dealt you. If you are willing—*

Her words ended abruptly and Lukys glanced at her, wondering at the pause. But her attention was no longer on him. He followed the direction of her gaze, and saw the unmade bed. Their...lovemaking had left the sheets and pillows in a tangled mess. His cheeks grew warm as he realised what had distracted her.

*I am honoured...* he started, but her eyes flickered back to him and he couldn't bring himself to finish the words. Gone was the respect he'd glimpsed just a moment ago.

*So it seems,* she said shortly.

Then she was gone, striding through the open door. Lukys paused a moment, confused by her abrupt change in manner. But her inner mind remained closed to him, and shaking off his doubt, he quickly followed her before they locked him in the room alone.

# THE FOLLOWER

Adonis howled as one of the Anahera dove towards him, wings furled, feathers rustling as they dove through the hissing sleet. A wooden staff slashed for his head, but he ducked and it missed by inches, the winds sending the Anahera swirling away. Rolling through the snow, he threw a mental curse into the storm as he reared back to his feet, expecting the creature to come for him again. But with the Tangata all around, the Anahera had already picked a fresh target for his wrath.

Whirling, Adonis continued, racing across the torn ground with impossible agility, his companions right behind. Others amongst the Tangata hurled rocks into the sky, striking back against their aerial cousins as they danced in and out of the storm. Whenever one appeared a dozen rocks the size of fists would flash in their direction, though they'd yet to bring one of the Anahera down. They were far more powerful than the Tangata—Adonis remembered well his encounter with one of their kind in the lowlands.

But just as in the lowlands, the Tangata were not without advantages. The Anahera might duck and weave and evade, making them difficult to count, but it was clear the Tangata had them outnumbered. Those few of the creatures that decided to land were swarmed, forced to lay about themselves with staff and wing and foot, just to keep from being overwhelmed. And those of his brethren the Anahera struck did not stay down. They rose to come for their foes again.

The Matriarch was right—the Anahera had grown weak, if not in body, in mind. Had they attacked to kill, the Tangata would have been slaughtered.

Adonis could feel the ecstasy of his brothers and sisters, the pounding of their joy. But Adonis had other duties, and reluctantly he forced his attention from the rush of battle. He could not fail, for even as the Tangata fought valiantly, he knew this was a battle they could not win.

No, they needed something to sway the battle, a way to strike at the heart of their foe, to bring the Anahera low.

A desperate, terrible gamble.

The sounds of battle faded into the storm as Adonis and his fellows crept away from the epicentre. They did not speak, kept their minds shielded now, their emotions carefully in check. For like the Tangata, these enemies could Hear and Speak. And if those within the city were forewarned…

The storm swallowed them up, building to a renewed fury, until even Adonis began to feel its bite, as if it might tear them from the mountain itself. It amazed him, that the Anahera could fly in such chaos, but even so, he could see they were having difficulty. He continued on, senses outstretched, seeking, searching…

*There!*

From a distance, he sensed a thrumming, pulsing *white*. Fear—so powerful he could almost taste it. His companions sensed it as well, for he caught a flicker of excitement before they regained control. Without a word, they diverted their path, heading now towards the enormous building that filled the valley, towards the fear. Stones crunched beneath their feet, but the noise was swallowed up by the storm. With the world engulfed in white, they had no need to fear being seen or heard. Only sensed.

Walls of plain grey stone emerged from the snow and they paused, scanning the terrain, seeking an entrance. The source of the terror was close now, so potent that the air was practically awash with it.

Adonis wondered at such ill-discipline. Even the youngest of the Tangata learned to control their emotions, to keep from broadcasting to the minds around them. For a moment he was reminded of the human, Lukys, and how his mind had lain open for the world to read. He had drawn the Tangata to him like flies to a corpse.

Maya was right: the Anahera had more in common with their human enemies than the Tangata now. They would have never chosen to ally with his people, never have supported them, helped them. They would see only an enemy to be disposed of. It was better this way, attacking before they could ally with the humans.

Moving along the wall, they finally found a door, heavy and of steel, barring the world without. And unlocked. It opened with a squeal. Adonis could have laughed. Whatever instincts these creatures had once possessed, they had long since succumbed to complacency.

Adonis and his companions slipped into a narrow hallway, pulling the door shut behind them. Within, a faint light lit the empty corridor. Adonis was surprised to see the white globes in the walls, the same as in the place he had uncovered Maya. Only here they were worn and faded, their magic almost spent.

They moved quickly through the place, finding the

corridors empty, abandoned. Adonis smiled—the distraction had worked. If guards had been placed here, they were involved in the battle now.

The Tangata threaded their way through the myriad corridors, following a staircase up to a higher level, and all the while the fear grew nearer. Adonis kept his senses alert for sign of the Anahera. Even a single creature might ruin everything, for his ten would fall quickly. Unconsciously he picked up the pace, heart racing, struggling to keep the emotions in check.

Then he paused as a faint scent touched his senses. The others came to a stop behind him, and he felt their confusion. It grew as they too detected the scent, one that should have been foreign in this distant place, so far from the lowlands.

*Humans.*

So Maya had been right in that as well. The Anahera they had encountered with the humans had not just been chance—they had already sided with one another. The scent was fresh, crisp amidst the lingering stench of the Anahera. The creatures were still here, hidden somewhere in the twisting corridors. His heart began to race and he glanced at his companions, sensing their anger, their hatred. These were the creatures who had warred against them for years, who had brought destruction to their lands...

*What's that?*

*Who?*

*They're inside!*

Mental voices rose, then shouts that carried down the corridors, pulsing with unconcealed panic. Still distant, but already growing closer.

Adonis cursed, even as his companions' eyes widened, anger giving way to panic. In an instant they were racing down the corridor, making no attempt at caution now. Their footsteps echoed from the cold stone as Adonis focused on their objective. They were close to the source of the fear now. It was the one thing that might save them. They could not outrun the Anahera, could not hide from them here in this city of theirs.

They could only attack.

The fear grew with each footstep, until suddenly he could feel its source, knew it was just ahead, beyond the wall, behind the door ahead of them. With a snarl, Adonis threw himself against it. His heart raced, rage granting him strength, and with a shriek of twisting metal, the door flew from its aged hinges.

Within, voices began to scream.

## ❧ 26 ❧

# THE EMISSARY

The sounds of battle carried from beyond the walls, the distant shrieks of pain, the clash of weapons and thud of blows. Erika shivered, eyes on the sky, expecting one of the Anahera to come tumbling from the clouds at any moment. They were alone now in the yard, the others of the Anahera gone to battle or sent to safety. All but for Farhan.

He stood nearby, forehead creased, his eyes too on the sky. He had ordered his people to arms, to defend their city. Now he listened to their screams through the howling of the storm. Amidst the swirling fog, nothing could be seen but for the occasional flicker as one of the Anahera returned with a report.

Erika shuddered. It sounded as though a thousand enemies had descended upon the City of the Gods. But how was that possible? This place had remained undiscovered for centuries, unknown to human or Tangata. How could the creatures have found their way here? And why now, at the same time as Erika and Maisie? It seemed too great a coincidence to be chance—

"*You!*"

Erika leapt back as she found Farhan advancing on her. Wings spread wide, he stalked through the storm, his face twisted with fresh rage.

"You did this, didn't you?" he snarled, reaching for her. "Treacherous human, why did you lead them here?"

"It was not us!" Erika replied, stumbling over something on the ground.

She tumbled backwards and crashed into the hard stones. Farhan loomed overhead, but whatever had tripped her drew his attention. Lips drawn back in a snarl, he reached down and plucked Hugo from the ground. The young Anahera blinked, looking disorientated, as though he were just recovering from the blow Farhan had given him earlier.

"Father?" he mumbled, his lips twisted in a frown. "What—"

His eyes widened suddenly, as if he'd just been struck, though this time Farhan had not touched him. He struggled free of his father's grip and swung to stare into the storm.

"Tangata!" he gasped. "Where—"

"Your treacherous humans brought them," Farhan declared, still looming over Erika.

"No—"

Erika's protest was cut short as Farhan surged forward. Still on her hands and knees, there was no escaping him this time. His fist closed around her throat, silencing her cries, and she was hauled helplessly into the air.

"This is what these creatures do, my son," he growled. Erika gaped at him, beating at his wrist with her fists, but it made no difference. "They lie, they steal, they *destroy*."

He was too strong. Erika's vision swum as she struggled to breathe, to inhale, but she could do nothing against the Anahera's power. Already her own strength was waning, drained away by the gauntlet...her eyes widened as she recalled its power, forgotten in her panic. Letting her hand drop, she clenched her fist, gathering its magic.

"It is not your fault they so deceived you," Farhan was saying. "It is their nature, to corrupt that which is pure—"

Now it was the Anahera's turn to cry out. Light flashed from the gauntlet as she directed her palm at Farhan's midsection, releasing its magic. She gasped as Farhan released her, and her legs almost collapsed as she struck the ground. Gulping in great lungfuls of air, Erika managed to catch herself before she fell. Then she straightened, arm still outstretched, and unleashed the full power of the gauntlet on Farhan.

The Anahera staggered back from her, mouth stretched wide in a silent scream, the veins on his neck bulging as he strained against her power. But the gauntlet flashed again, and without a sound he crumpled to the ground, wings and arms and legs thrashing. She advanced on him, lips twisted in a sneer.

"At least I never tried to *mutilate* my own daughter," she snarled.

Erika would have said more, but something solid struck her hard in the chest before she could speak. Hurled backwards by the force of the blow, she felt something go *crack*. Then Erika was tumbling across the ground, rocks tearing at her flesh, light flashing across her eyes.

The altar brought her to an abrupt halt, driving the last of the breath from her lungs. Stars danced across her vision and she strained to take a breath, to comprehend what had happened. Cracking open an eye, she searched for what had struck her.

Through the raging storm, she found Hugo standing over Farhan, helping the Anahera to his feet. The youth had re-joined his father's side. Her heart clenched as they turned towards her, and desperately she tried to push herself up. Agony screamed in her chest as the broken rib shifted, but she could not stop, could not give up.

But neither could she fight any longer. Her strength was almost spent, and the gauntlet's power would not be enough to stop the two of them. Turning, she reached for the lip of the altar and strained to haul herself up. The pain in her chest redoubled and other pains made themselves known, but she managed to flip herself onto the awful chunk of stone.

Cara crouched where Erika had left her, one hand and wing still bound. Her back was turned to Erika as she strained against her bonds, but the metal would not give before even her enormous strength. Erika crawled towards her, gauntlet raised. This she could do, this she could manage. Free Cara, and she would save them all. She had to.

As though hearing her silent plea, Cara turned. Her eyes widened as she saw Erika, surprise showing in their amber depths, but then they flickered, shifting to something behind her. Teeth clenched, Erika twisted on the stone, preparing herself to fend off another attack.

But Farhan and Hugo had not moved. It was not the two Anahera that had drawn Cara's attention. Instead, her eyes were fixed on a door across the yard. Through the swirling storm, Erika glimpsed two figures stumble out into the snow.

Dark laughter carried across the yard the two figures advanced, and Erika saw that one had no wings. And the other...the other was Anahera, but smaller than any she had seen before, barely as tall as Erika's waist. A child.

Terror showed in the girl's blue eyes as the wingless

newcomer shepherded her before him. Small wings covered in soft down thrashed against his grasp, but the man refused to release the girl, even as her cries carried through the storm. Erika's heart beast faster as the pair approached, a sense of dread settling in her stomach.

"The fledglings," Cara croaked.

## ❦ 27 ❦

# THE HERO

A fire burned in the king's hearth, crackling gently against the gloom of the fading light. It was wasteful, Lukys couldn't help but think, with the thermal waters warming the tiles beneath their feet. Firewood was a rare commodity in a kingdom that did not cut down its trees, only being collected from what had fallen in the forests. But King Nguyen seemed to appreciate the flames.

Standing in the doorway with Sophia, Lukys stared at the man, waiting for him to announce why they'd been sent for. Instead, the king rose from his chair with a groan and crossed to a table placed near the window. Picking up a decanter, he opened a glass cabinet on the wall and glanced in their direction.

"Whiskey?"

Lukys raised his eyebrows, glancing behind him at Tasha. But the guard only offered a short shake of her head before closing the door behind them, leaving them alone with the king. Letting out a sigh, Lukys watched as the king poured a glass of the amber liquid, trying to decipher his game. If Nguyen was to be believed, this was a man who had lost his kingdom, who had fled to Perfugia with his tail between his legs, his armies broken and defeated.

But the performance he'd given in the court of the Sovereigns had not been that of a defeated man. Had it all been a façade?

Lost in his thoughts, Lukys didn't notice Sophia until she crossed the room and plucked the glass from Nguyen's table. The king's eyebrows lifted into his greying fringe as she raised it to her nose and sniffed, before a smile replaced his surprise. He took several glasses from the cabinet, and poured two extra measures.

*You drink whiskey?* Lukys asked Sophia as the king offered him a glass.

*I'm not sure,* she replied with a shrug. She took a tentative sip, and immediately started to cough.

Snorting to cover his laughter, Lukys raised his drink in salute to the king before taking a sip of his own. The whiskey was dry with a sharp smoky taste and burned as he swallowed, though Sophia's cough seemed an overreaction.

*Poison?* she asked him when she finally recovered, her eyes still watering.

He almost laughed again. *Just alcohol.*

She raised an eyebrow and inspected the glass again, as though expecting it to bite her.

"Fascinating," the king interrupted their silent conversation.

"What?" Lukys asked when the man did not elaborate.

Nguyen gestured at the two of them with his glass. "You're communicating," he said. "Just like Cara said."

"Cara?" Lukys asked. "You said you'd sent her home, to the Mountains of the Gods? What does she have to do with any of this?"

"It was she who told me that the Tangata are not the

monsters we thought them to be," he replied. "That they had some way of communicating."

Lukys glanced at Sophia in question, and she inclined her head. *The Anahera also possess the ability to Speak.*

"Apparently, the Gods can Speak in the same way as the Tangata," Lukys translated.

"I see," Nguyen replied. He sank back into his chair and eyed Lukys. "And what of you, young man? What is your part in all this? How can *you* hear the lady speak?"

Sophia started and Lukys flicked her a glance. She stood trembling in place, grey eyes wide and staring at the king, as though he had suddenly transformed into some foreign beast.

*What is it?* he asked her softly.

She shook her head. *I...no one has ever called me a lady.*

Lukys swallowed, touched by shame, that until just a few days ago he had still thought of her as another species, a creature rather than human. But he knew the truth now, that whatever their differences, the Tangata shared far more in common with humanity than they did differences. He took her hand gently in his.

*You are my lady, Sophia,* he said, filling his Voice with warmth.

She smiled, her eyes fluttering closed at his touch, and for a moment, images of their morning spent in bed flickered into his mind—

"Fascinating," Nguyen said again, and this time Lukys jumped.

He turned an irritated glare on the king. "We're not some specimens for you to examine."

The man let out a booming laugh. "Your friend Cara said something much the same," he replied. Leaning back in his chair, he entwined his fingers. "So...what makes a man turn traitor to his own species?"

Lukys froze at the man's words, drink half-raised to his lips. The glass shook as anger touched him, but slowly, painstakingly, he raised it the rest of the way and downed the burning liquid. Carefully he placed it back on the table and stared down at the man.

"If I am a traitor, I stand in good company."

The king regarded him in silence. "Again with the accusations?" He waved a hand. "Please, enough with the baseless rumours and past grievances."

"Tell that to my friend Romaine, to his people—the Calafe—and his broken kingdom, to—"

"Your girlfriend?" the king interrupted, one eyebrow raised. He glanced at Sophia. "I'm surprised she hasn't torn out my throat and drank the blood yet."

A growl came from Sophia and she took a threatening step towards him.

Laughter came from Nguyen as he raised his hands. "Peace," he murmured. "I only wished to test a theory." He glanced at Lukys. "Though it shows the consequence of baseless rumours, does it not?"

Lukys stood fixed on the spot, his stomach twisted into a knot by the king's words. Not too long ago, he had stood alongside the fearsome Romaine and fought the Tangata on the shores of the Illmoor. Those days he had believed in the righteousness of the war, that he was fighting to protect Flumeer and Perfugia, to avenge the fallen Calafe.

What would Romaine say to him now, should they meet again? The man's family had been murdered by the Tangata in the early days of the conflict, his wife and children some of the first victims that had triggered the disastrous invasion of Tangata territory.

But then…Sophia's partner, the Tangata that had fought alongside her for years, who had been her former… lover, he had died at Lukys's own hands, back on the River

Illmoor. He swallowed, realising for the first time just how great the void spanned between their two peoples.

"Tell me, my lady," the king said, leaning back in his chair. "What do the Tangata say of our southern campaign, of the invasion we led into your lands ten years past?"

Beside him, Sophia stiffened at his words, and Lukys cast her a quick look, wondering at the reaction. She exhaled sharply, the breath whistling between her teeth, and then abruptly images began to flicker into Lukys's mind, faster than he could process, and yet...

*...Lukys was old, his body weary with time, his reflexes slowed, a poor substitute for his youth. Still he thrust the child behind him as the horse raced towards them, steel-tipped lance bearing down, slamming into him, tearing a scream from his lips...*

*...now he raced across the rolling hills, heart pounding in his young chest as he chased after his parents. His Tangatan father carried his human mother, but even so, he struggled to keep pace. Cries came from behind, and risking a glance back, he saw the village, their home, burning...*

*...wind swept through his hair as he stood alone on a hill, looking down upon the approaching column. There were a hundred riders, perhaps more—too many. Yet he had to hold, to halt the enemy march long enough for the children to reach the shelter of Nihelm. The Birthing Ground would shield them, wouldn't it? He closed his eyes and sent a prayer for the Old Ones to grant him their strength. The pounding of hooves carried up the hills as the humans spotted them, and he opened his eyes once more, bracing himself for death...*

Lukys gasped as he tore himself from the lives and deaths Sophia had shown him, a hundred if they had been a handful. A shudder ran through him as he fought to find himself amidst the images, to shake the feeling of unity, of being one among many. Sucking in great mouthfuls of air, he glanced at Sophia, wondering at her again, how she could cope with so many lives entangled with her own.

"Well?"

Looking at the king again, Lukys was unable to tell how much time had passed. A moment only, surely? Shaking himself, he straightened.

"I..." He swallowed, his blood still cold at the visions Sophia had shown him. "She says that her people never attacked Calafe, at least not until after the southern campaign. The invasion, it...came as a shock, a breaking of the unspoken truce they had with humanity."

Beside him, a tear streaked Sophia's cheek, and Lukys felt the power of the images she'd shown him again, the pain of a community, of lives attacked, stolen.

"I see," Nguyen replied, his tone uncharacteristically soft. "I am sorry for the intrusion to your grief, my lady, but I must ask, for these are questions I have carried for nigh a decade now. Do your people know why we attacked?"

Sophia gave a sharp shake of her head, and Lukys sensed the anger burning behind those grey eyes.

A sigh slipped from Nguyen's lips. "Calafe settlements were attacked, men and women and children slaughtered. The survivors spoke of Tangata in the night, slaughtering all they came across."

*My people would never harm children!*

The words reverberated through Lukys's mind as Sophia took a step towards the king, teeth bared. Though he obviously could not hear her words, Nguyen's eyes widened and Lukys caught a glimpse of fear as he raised his hands, as though to fend off her attack.

*Tell him,* Sophia growled, her voice trembling. *Tell him we would never...*

"The Tangata would not have harmed children," Lukys said softly, as he reached out and drew an arm around Sophia's shoulders. He swallowed, choosing his next words carefully. "I have seen it in New Nihelm…the reverence they hold for youth."

A shiver ran down his spine as he considered the implications. The Tangata had *not* been the first to attack. It had been humanity that had started this war, who had attacked the Tangata unprovoked.

But…who, then, had slain Romaine's family?

"If not the Tangata, then who?" Nguyen mused, echoing Lukys's own questions. Rising to refill his glass, he glanced at the pair of them. "I knew King Micah, before the war. I argued against the southern campaign, but he was insistent, believed we needed to strike decisively to protect Calafe. He convinced me to follow his lead, regretfully. But…perhaps the idea was not his own. Micah was always reckless, boisterous with the drink. Larger than life, like most of his people."

Lukys swallowed as he remembered Romaine and the massive axe the man had carried, the way he had fought. Battle was like breathing for the man. He wondered where Romaine was now, whose side he fought on.

"There were those with influence over Micah, ones whose motives I always questioned…" Nguyen continued, then abruptly shook his head. "Regardless, the past must be put behind us. It was a mistake to attack the Tangata. Witnessing her people charge, the decimation they wrought upon our armies…it convinced me a war could never be won against them. At least, not on open ground." He shuddered, as though recalling those days ten years past.

Lukys frowned at the man, unsure how to continue, and Sophia's words whispered into his mind.

*That battle cost my people dearly. Many of the third generation were lost, those who could still partner without humans. Our strength has dwindled ever since.*

Knowing her words were only for him, Lukys remained

staring at the king. He wondered how the man would react if he learned the true weakness of the Tangata, that they could not replace those of them who fell in battle. At least, not without humanity.

"And what about this?" Nguyen asked, gesturing at the two of them with his glass of whiskey. "I've made a few enquiries since my arrival. Seems there are more than a dozen of you who survived the south. Each bonded with a Tangata. Seems there must be a story there." A smile spread across Nguyen's lips and Lukys could see the calculations turning behind his eyes. This was no ordinary man—he already suspected something of Sophia's secret.

Lukys swallowed, suddenly unable to meet the king's eyes. "As I said before, Sophia and her people are just as human as you or I."

"No doubt, no doubt," the king replied, still smiling. "Yet you cannot deny, it is...peculiar that so many would be bonded."

Lukys shared a look with Sophia, but this time they kept their silence, and the king let out a long sigh. "A shame. Perhaps when I learn the secrets of your abilities, you and I can enjoy a true conversation, my lady."

Sophia's face brightened at his words and the king laughed. "In the meantime, perhaps you could tell me more of why you are here. Your Sovereigns spoke of Old Ones?"

Lukys shivered as he recalled his encounters with the creatures—not just in New Nihelm, but the two they had inadvertently woken on the Archivist's quest to the tunnels of the Gods. That time seemed another life now, but the image of the Old Ones stalking him in the darkness was still etched in his mind.

"You have met Cara," he said softly. Taking control of his doubts, he crossed to the king's table and poured himself and Sophia another glass of the amber spirit. "So you know the Gods are real?"

The king raised an eyebrow at his nerve, but held out his glass to be topped up. "I know there are beings in this world who possess extraordinary abilities," he said, then lifted his glass to Sophia in salute.

Sophia snorted and took a cautious sip of her own drink. *I like this one*, she said into the privacy of his mind.

Lukys looked from one to the other. "Well, Cara and the Tangata are not the only ones with these 'extraordinary abilities.' The ancestors of the Tangata still live. They are far more powerful, but possess none of their...manners. We first discovered them in the ancient site we uncovered in Calafe."

"Yes," the king replied. "My spy briefed me on the situation. Your 'Goddess' slew them."

"Those two, yes," Lukys replied. "The Tangata found another."

Nguyen sat up at that. "You have told the Sovereigns?"

Lukys hesitated. "We were...interrupted by your arrival."

A curse slipped from the king's lips as he rose. "If this is true, I can only pray my envoys to Cara's people were successful. If we cannot match the Tangata in battle, what chance do we have against the monsters that bore them," he paused, glancing at Sophia. "...no offence, my lady."

Sophia inclined her head in acceptance. *You are right, Nguyen*, she said, and Lukys repeated her words. *Not even my people could stand against her...she now rules the Tangata as our new Matriarch.*

Nguyen's face grew grim. "I take it then that you and your friends are less emissaries, more political refugees?"

They nodded and the king's face grew grimmer. "This changes everything. Humanity cannot afford to continue with these petty squabbles. We must unite against this threat. Come."

He moved to the door and pushed it open. Lukys and Sophia made to follow him as he stepped into the corridor, but there he paused, looking around in confusion. It was a moment before Lukys realised what had made him hesitate.

*Where are the guards?* Sophia whispered into his mind.

Her question was soon answered, as the sound of pounding boots carried down the corridor towards them. A second later, a dozen men charged around the corner at the end of the hall. Most wore the plain uniforms of regular soldiers, but the man in the lead was all too familiar.

"There they are!" Cleo bellowed, pointing with his silver spear. *"Get them!"*

## ❧ 28 ❧

## THE FOLLOWER

A donis stumbled as he pushed through the door out into the snow, dragging the child with him. She screamed, her wings beating against his face, and almost managed to dislodge his grip. She was strong, almost stronger than Adonis, but he managed to hold on, digging his fingers deeper into her flesh.

Voices cried out through the storm, and he saw half a dozen faces turned towards him. Surprise changed to open fear as they saw who had come for them, what he had done. His stomach twisted but he would not back down now. Keeping the child firm in hand, he staggered through the snow, lips drawn back in a snarl.

The others had already fallen, knocked down by the few Anahera that had remained with the children. Those same guards followed him even now, emerging from the building, keeping their distance, but eyes alert, waiting for their chance to free the girl.

Adonis would not give them that chance. Only he had been fast enough, quick enough to act. While his comrades had launched themselves bravely against the adult Anahera,

Adonis had kept to the plan. The children had scattered at the appearance of the Tangata, separating from their guardians in their panic. In the chaos of beating wings and flailing arms, Adonis had struggled to pick a target.

But he had only needed one.

"Tangata!" a voice called through the snow.

Adonis swung around as an Anahera approached. He was larger than the others, his white wings mingling with the snow, amber eyes fixed on his foe. Baring his teeth, Adonis faced the creature.

*Back!* he snapped, knowing the creatures could Hear. *Or the child will never join her forebearers in the sky.*

His words had the desired effect and the Anahera paused, uncertainty appearing behind those amber eyes. Adonis allowed himself a smile, though his heart was still racing.

*Tell me, Anahera, do you rule here?* he whispered to the white-winged creature.

The Anahera bared its teeth. *I am Farhan. I speak for the Elders of the Anahera.*

*I will take that for a yes,* Adonis replied with a smile.

A scream came from the child and she fought again to break free, begging for Farhan to save her. Cursing, Adonis dragged her back, his hand clamping tight around her wing. She stilled as Adonis squeezed, her cries turned to a whimper as feather's cracked beneath his grip.

*"Stop!"*

Farhan's command struck Adonis like a hammer and he almost released the child. But there was another Voice thrumming in his mind, distant, yet already growing nearer —Maya. The touch of his mate granted him strength, bolstered him against the command of the creature before him.

*I said stay back,* he snarled. Another whimper came from

the young Anahera as he dug his fingers into flesh. *I will not ask again.*

Farhan did not move, but Adonis could see his fear. The Anahera might outnumber him, but standing in that yard with the child in hand, it was Adonis who had the advantage. These creatures would not risk harm to one of their youths.

Unbidden, an image flickered into Adonis's mind, of a child's face with snow upon her lips, freezing in the snow. A shudder shook Adonis and his grip on the Anahera's wing loosened. What was he doing, threatening a child? It went against his every instinct, and yet...

...words whispered into his mind, Maya's promises of a future, for children of his own. None of that would come to be unless the Tangata emerged victorious this day, and silently he restored his grip on the young Anahera. The fate of his species hung in the balance—he could not turn back now.

"Let her go, Tangata," Farhan growled, his voice low, dangerous. "Let her go, and I will allow your kind to leave this place in peace."

*No!* Adonis reached for the Anahera's mind. It had a foreignness about it, not so different as the human, but its flavour markedly different from his own brethren. *No, Anahera, not until we have spoken. Not until you have been made to see the truth.*

"What truth?" his foe snapped, broad wings stretching higher, drawing Adonis's gaze.

For a moment, Adonis wondered at those strange limbs, at the glory of these creatures, at their freedom to soar through the open skies. These creatures had the power of the Old Ones, the minds of humanity, wings. They could produce children, renew themselves without growing weaker each generation. They could have conquered the world.

Instead, they sequestered themselves in these mountains, hid themselves away. Such strange creatures.

"You *can* understand it."

Adonis's sensitive hearing caught a whisper from beyond Farhan. He frowned as a figure approached through the snow, arms wrapped tightly about herself. His stomach roiled as he realised that like him, this creature lacked wings. Here was the human he had sensed in the corridors of the city. Snarling, he tightened his grip on the child, alert for a trap.

*So you have allied yourselves with the humans,* he said softly. *A pity. My Matriarch had hopes for a different outcome.*

A frown crossed the Anahera's face. "You did not come on behalf of Erika's people?" he rumbled, then shook his head, as though to dismiss the question. "Release the fledgling, Tangata. Then we will talk about this truth of yours."

*First, call off your warriors,* Adonis hissed.

"What is happening?" the human called Erika shouted over the wind.

He noticed she kept her distance from Farhan. Then he noticed the spark of light from her fist. Immediately he pushed the child in front of him, recalling the magic he'd witnessed a human wield in the lowlands. Cries came from the Anahera and Farhan swung on the human.

"Stay back, treacherous human," he snarled. "Have you not done enough already?"

The human flinched away from Farhan, raising her magic fist towards him. Adonis frowned at the exchange. Had he been wrong about the connection between human and Anahera? There seemed to be no affection lost between these two.

*Anahera, return to the City,* Farhan's mental voice rung suddenly through the storm.

Adonis lifted his eyebrows, surprised with the ease at

which the Anaheran leader had capitulated. It might have yet been a trick, but moments later he sensed confusion from his own brethren as the enemy Anahera fell back, disappearing into the swirling clouds. A smile touched his lips as he looked again at Farhan, though he still did not release the child.

One by one, Anahera appeared from the sky to land around them. Confusion showed in the eyes of the human as she retreated towards a strange structure in the centre of the yard, but Farhan said nothing, only stared at Adonis, waiting.

Adonis stared back. Slowly the sounds of battle faded away, until there was only the silence of the storm.

And the soft pulsing of Maya, coming closer.

"It is done, Tangata," Farhan said when the last of the winged creatures had landed. "Release the fledgling."

Adonis stood in silence for a while, watching the Anahera around him, their leader. What were their intentions, these strange, secluded creatures? Why had they suddenly returned to the world. He needed to know, to understand.

*All in good time,* Adonis whispered finally. *First, tell me, Farhan. Months ago in the lowlands, one of your kind fought against me on the side of humanity. Why?*

"A traitor," Farhan replied, and for a second, Adonis thought he glimpsed something in the creature's eyes. "My daughter," the Anahera added finally, his voice cold. "She will concern you no longer."

Again there was the flicker, the half-glance back towards where the human had retreated. Adonis frowned, following Farhan's gaze to the strange structure rising from the yard. His eyes caught movement there, the human climbing up upon a block of stone. The snow was slowing and he saw something else now, another figure, lying upon an altar.

Ignoring Farhan now, Adonis started towards the monolith, the child still in hand. He narrowed his eyes as he drew close, realising that one of the Anahera had been chained to the stone. One auburn wing flapped free, but the other was still bound tight. The human was crawling across the altar towards her, but the amber eyes of the Anahera were locked on Adonis.

Belatedly, he realised he knew this creature. Farhan had not been wrong—this was the Anahera he had fought at the river, all those months ago

*I know you,* he murmured, drawing to a stop beside the altar.

"Erika," the creature hissed, and beside her the human spun. Her hand still glowed with magic, but Adonis held the child before him and she did not strike. "Erika," the Anahera bound to the stone said again. "You have to get out of here, you have to leave me."

"*Never,*" the human called Erika hissed. She stood and faced Adonis, though she still dared not unleash her power. "I won't leave you with these monsters."

Adonis raised an eyebrow. Ignoring the human, he looked to the imprisoned Anahera.

*We fought once, you and I,* Adonis continued conversationally. *Tell me, Anahera, does your father speak the truth? Did you act alone, that day by the river?*

*Do not hurt the human,* the bound Anahera's words came to him in his mind, raw and untrained.

*You do not beg for the child's life like the others?* Adonis asked. He gave the girl a little shake to emphasis his point, drawing a scream from her. Nearby, the other Anahera cried out, but a snarl from Adonis kept them from advancing.

"Cara, what is she saying?" the human hissed, her fist growing brighter.

*Please, I spared you that day by the river,* the Anahera called Cara pled again. *Just leave the humans alone.*

Looking at the human, Adonis shook his head. *Such unpleasantly loud creatures,* he said, then turned to the creature bound in chains. *Would that I could, Cara, but their kind leaves us little choice.*

Abruptly he turned his back on the two and crossed to where Farhan still stood, fists clenched, eyes burning.

*I am called Adonis,* he said quietly. *I was sent by my Matriarch to treat with the Anahera.*

*What is it you want, Tangata?* Farhan snapped.

Adonis stared up at Farhan, seeing his rage, a thin veil to his fear. The child—or fledgling as Farhan had called it— was barely moving in his arms now, as though he had already struck her dead. Adonis found himself looking upon her with contempt now, his earlier compassion vanished. No child of the Tangata would have been so submissive. What sheltered upbringings did the fledglings of the Anahera live, to be so weak?

*To survive, Farhan,* he said at least, turning his eyes upon the Anaheran leader. *To see my people survive the storm that is to come.*

"We are no threat to you," Farhan replied.

*No, but the humans are.* Adonis turned his gaze on the creature on the altar. The light had gone out in her fist now. He could sense her exhaustion in the slump of her shoulders, but even defeated, the creatures could prove dangerous. That lesson had been taught to him in New Nihelm.

*They are a threat to us all,* he continued, swinging on Farhan. *You think they will allow your kind to live in these mountains in peace?*

"They cannot reach us here," Farhan grated.

Adonis laughed. *They are a plague upon this world, Farhan. I have seen it. Their greed knows no bounds. They will despoil your most sacred of places, dig up your dead, will bring fire and violence against your people, until you have naught left but ash.*

Silence answered Adonis's words as the amber eyes drilled into him. But finally the Farhan shook its head.

"The Anahera play no part in the wars of human and Tangata," he rumbled, drawing about himself a shroud of resolve, "and only one creature has brought war upon us today. Surrender, Adonis of the Tangata, or you will know the wrath of the Anahera."

Movement came from around the yard as the other Anahera edged closer. Even the child in Adonis's hands seemed to regain some of her fight, as she began to thrash against his hold. Adonis cursed, swinging one way, then another, trying to keep the enemy in sight, to keep them from approaching unnoticed.

"*I thought the Anahera to be lions,*" a voice broke across the clearing, hard, unyielding. The words reverberated in Adonis's mind, reinforced by the powers of the Old Ones.

"*Imagine my disappointment when I woke,*" Maya continued as she approached on soft footsteps. "*To discover they had become sheep, to bow before the human plague.*"

## ❦ 29 ❦

## THE EMISSARY

E rika watched as the new creature stalked across the yard. The Anahera parted before her, as though this newcomer radiated something venomous, some deadly odour they feared would strike them down. She couldn't sense any outward difference to this new Tangata herself, but Erika couldn't help but shiver as she watched it come. Its eyes might be grey, but they were deeper, darker than the other Tangata.

And she had spoken aloud.

Erika's blood ran cold as she processed the implications, recalling the creatures she had encountered all those months before, the monsters they had awoken in the darkness beneath the earth.

No, this was not a Tangata that stood before her.

It was one of the Old Ones.

Struggling just to breath through her fear, Erika watched as the Old One joined the Tangata who held the Anaheran fledgling. Cara had killed the two they'd woken in the tunnels, so where had this creature come from? And how had she come to stand with the Tangata?

Atop the altar with the wind and sleet hissing down around them, Erika swung on Cara. "What the *hell* is happening?"

Crouched with one hand still shackled, Cara frowned, before understanding dawned in her eyes. "Right, you can't hear them." The Goddess gave a visible shudder. "Lucky you—she's practically radiating death."

"Radiating death..." Erika shook her head. Extended use of the gauntlet had drained her of energy and she had more work to do yet. Shaking off the dozen questions that came to her mind, she forced her mind to focus. "What do they want?"

A sigh came from the young Anahera. "Your guess is as good as mine," she murmured, then flicked Erika a glance. "Err, don't suppose you've gotten some energy back?" She rattled her chains for emphasis.

Erika's eyes slid closed, but after a moment she nodded. Farhan and the other Anahera were absorbed by the Tangata and their endangered fledgling—punishing Cara seemed the least of their priorities now. Just a little more effort, one last push, surely she could manage that?

Pain from her injuries swept through Erika and she cursed into the howling wind. Then clenched her teeth, she crawled to the second chain and gripped it with the gauntlet.

"Why...didn't they stop it?" she asked as the magic began to gather. It was taking an age, and she wondered what would happen if she pushed too far.

"Adonis?" Cara hesitated. "Father couldn't, not with the fledgling at risk."

Pursing her lips, Erika said nothing. She had seen the pain in the child's eyes, the fear. Her heart went out to the young girl, but...the Tangata were deadly killers. They might not be the monsters humanity had made them out to be, but even so…Farhan had risked everything by calling off his warriors, allowing the Tangata into the city.

"The Old One changes everything though, surely…" Cara was saying.

Before Erika could reply, Farhan's voice rose through the storm, carrying across the yard to where they crouched.

"It's not possible." The Anaheran leader seemed as shocked as his daughter to be confronted by an Old One. "Your kind are extinct…"

The newcomer's face hardened at that, and she advanced until she stood face to face with Farhan.

"And how did that come to pass, Anahera?" she hissed. "When I began the long sleep, it was humanity who wavered, defeated by the last sacrifice of my people, of my own mother." She paused, eyeing the leader of the Anahera. "Yet now I wake to find humanity ascendant, my own children corrupted. Yet here your kind stand, as sickeningly pure as ever."

"The Anahera play no part—"

Farhan broke off as the Old One turned abruptly, marching to where the first Tangata still stood with the fledgling. Movement came from beyond the gathering, and Erika's heart fell into her stomach as more of the creatures filed into the yard—those Tangata who had been warring outside. They looked to number in the hundreds.

Then a high-pitched cry carried across the yard, and Erika watched in horror as the Old One caught the imprisoned fledgling by the wing and dragged her across the ground to where the Anaheran leader waited. The young fought to break free, but the Old One was far stronger than her Tangatan descendants. Faster as well—Erika had learned that in the depths of the earth.

"So this is a child of the Anahera," the Old One muttered, lifting the child by the wing. Beside Erika, Cara winced at the girl's screams. "Even in my day, your kind kept them secret. I can see why, such pitiful creatures."

"Release her, foul beast," Farhan spat, though he still made no move to intervene.

A smile spread across the Old One's lips, a dark, terrifying thing that sent chills running down Erika's spine. "Why don't you make me, Anahera?"

Farhan's jaw clenched so tight Erika could see the tendons standing up on his neck. Even his feathers bristled, so that his wings seemed to almost double in size. For a moment, she thought he would accept the challenge, but…

…that moment stretched out, seconds ticking past, until finally his shoulders slumped.

Laughter answered his defeat. "I came here to bargain, Anahera," the Old One rasped. "To seek an ally in an old rival. I did not expect to find you so craven. Perhaps I should simply take what I desire."

"My people have nothing to give—"

The laughter came again, echoing from the stone walls, a dark cackling that sent tremors to Erika's very core.

"My Tangata, they still value their children, as they did in times past. They are our future, our hope."

"I will destroy you—" Farhan started.

The Old One gave the fledgling a violent shake and she cried out, fingers scrabbling at the snowy gravel. Farhan took a step closer, arm raised, but the Old One was faster. A scream tore from the fledgling as a boot fell upon her wing. The sharp *crack* of breaking bones brought silence to the yard. The eyes of the Old One swept the Anahera. She was outnumbered, outmatched, but Erika could see the ecstasy in her eyes.

"What was I saying?" she murmured. "Oh, yes." Her

grey eyes fell to the child once more. She placed a boot upon the fledgling's throat. "My Tangata, they cherish their children, but so too have they learnt the price of weakness. Isn't that right, my mate?"

Beside her, the Tangata stared back at the Old One, then bowed its head in silence.

"Yes, that's right," the Old One continued, looking to Farhan again. "They know that sacrifice is necessary, that sometimes the weak must perish to protect the strong." She crooked her neck. "Have the Anahera learned that lesson, Farhan?"

"*Erika!*" A hiss from Cara drew her attention back to the altar.

Her fist was vibrating with power now, and quickly she gripped the last of the chains in her gauntleted hand. The sharp *shriek* of shattering steel followed, and then Cara was throwing her arms about her. Soft sobs whispered in Erika's ear as she hugged the Goddess back, but there was no more time than that for celebration. Breaking apart, they turned to the confrontation in the yard.

"Please…" Farhan's voice had grown weak. Even Erika could hear his despair. Before the fledgling's pain, he stood helpless. *All* the Anahera stood helpless.

"*Enough!*" the Old One snapped, sneering. "Enough of your pitiful whining. Here is your chance, Farhan, leader of the Anahera. Attack me, prove your courage—but do so in the knowledge that the child will die."

Farhan did not move, and the Old One shook her head. "Ah, my poor cousins, how cruel the passage of time has been for you. But fear not, your saviour has come. I will free you of the burden of your freedom." Her sneer grew wider. "But first, I would have you kneel to your new master."

A growl came from Farhan and alongside Erika, Cara tensed. Before anyone could move, the fledgling began to thrash, her face growing pale as the Old One's boot pressed down. Erika's heart twisted as she saw the panic in the girl's face, streaked now by mud and ice, her mouth open, gasping, struggling to breathe. Clenching her fist, Erika began to rise.

The Anahera gathered in the yard acted first. One by one, they fell to their knees before the Old One. Erika stared, aghast, as the creatures that had been her Gods, the most powerful beings in the world, submitted to the monster in their midst. This couldn't be so, couldn't be happening...

Farhan was the last to kneel. He crumpled suddenly, as though his strength had just given out. Mud and ice cracked as his knees sank into the slush and he said not a word, but Erika could see the despair in his eyes as he looked up at the Old One.

"Release the fledgling," he rasped.

The Old One smiled and removed her boot. The girl gasped, her whole body shuddering, but the creature allowed her no time to catch her breath. Grasping her by the wing, she dragged the fledgling through the slush to where her Tangatan mate waited. She handed the sobbing child to the creature, then returned to Farhan. Smiling, she reached down to stroke his face.

"All in good time, my slave," she murmured. "First you must prove your loyalty." Abruptly the Old One turned, and Erika went cold as those terrible eyes fell on her. "First, we must deal with the human."

Fear swelled in Erika's chest, but she did not flee from the creature. With Cara at her side, they stood atop the altar and watched her approach. The storm was breaking now, the first hint of light appearing overhead. None of the Anahera moved as the creature approached, and Erika had lost track of Maisie in the chaos. With her broken leg, the spy could not have gone far. But even uninjured, what could the Gemaho spy have done against a monster such as this?

"Can you fly?" Erika hissed to Cara as the creature stalked towards them.

Erika glanced at her friend when she did not reply, but Cara's eyes were focused elsewhere—on the face of her father, on Hugo knelt in the mud, on the other Anahera, their heads bowed before the Old One's threats.

"I can't leave them like this," the Goddess whispered.

Erika's stomach twisted and she made to argue, then thought better of it. Reaching out, she took her friend's hands in hers.

"Then we'll face her together," she whispered.

Surprise showed in Cara's eyes, but already Erika was turning away, stepping forward to face the ancient creature that had come to wreak havoc upon all of them. The Old One moved through the mud and snow without haste, a smile on her lips, and death in those terrible eyes. Yet it was not her that Erika focused her attention on, but the Anahera. She searched their faces for some spark, some hope that they might yet rise.

"Is this how the Anahera fall?" she asked, voice soft, rising above the dying of the storm. "Is this what becomes of the Gods of men? For centuries we have prayed to you, longed for your return, that we might together beat back the scourge of the Tangata." Her eyes passed over the collection of faces, but none dared meet her gaze. Not even Farhan. Despair welled in her chest and her eyes burned.

"I believed in you," she whispered.

Laughter was her answer.

Clenching her fist, Erika faced the Old One. She could not hope to defeat a host of Tangata, but perhaps her magic might make a difference against this one. But even as she tried to summon the magic, the strength went from her legs and she cried out, almost falling.

Wings beat the air and then Cara was at her side, lending her strength. Together they faced the enemy, but not even Cara could fight all of the Tangata. As Erika watched, the creatures slid through the ranks of the Anahera, moving to support the Old One, their Matriarch. Swallowing, Erika pressed Cara behind her. It was her the Old One wanted, not Cara.

The creature's cackling grew louder as she approached, but as she reached the foot of the altar, she fell silent and leaned her head to one side. "Gods?" she asked, before looking back at Farhan. "You convinced them that you were their Gods?"

The laughter came again, higher in pitch now, as the Old One threw back her head and howled with true mirth. Erika staggered, shocked by the creature's reaction. Finally the sound faded, and Erika found those terrible eyes upon her again.

"You do not understand why I laugh, do you, human?" the Old One asked, still standing at the foot of the altar.

Erika bared her teeth and raised the gauntlet by way of response. A spark of light lit the metal, only a fraction of its usual fire, but enough to give the Old One pause—or so she hoped.

"I understand well enough," she snarled. "The Anahera are not the Gods of our past."

The Old One chuckled. Then suddenly she leapt, alighting on the side of the altar. Erika flinched back, raising her fist by instinct, but it managed only a flicker before the light died. A wave of dizziness struck her, and suddenly she was looking up at the Old One from her knees.

"Do you know why I came here, human?" the creature

asked. "Why I sought out this place, rather than attack humanity?"

Erika could only shake her head, too weak to move, to resist. The Old One's smile grew as she leaned in close.

"Because in my time the Anahera and Tangata were not enemies, human," she rasped. "We were *allies*."

## ✣ 30 ✣

## THE HERO

R oaring, Cleo and his soldiers rushed towards where Lukys stood with the others. A curse came from the king—then he was spinning on his heel and pushing them back into the room, slamming the door closed and throwing the lock.

Heart pounding, Lukys stumbled towards the window, looking from the door to the king.

"What's happening?" he gasped.

The king swung this way and that, searching the room for weapons or an exit, but he paused at Lukys's words.

"It would appear someone has taken it upon themselves to rid Perfugia of our little inconvenience," he said, returning to his search. He winced as something hard struck the door, then added: "That, or your friend out there really doesn't like you."

Lukys swallowed as a sharp *crack* came from the door, one of the wooden panels shattering as an axe appeared through the wood.

*I wouldn't discount the second possibility,* Sophia said wryly as she came alongside him.

"Cleo's a brute," Lukys said shortly, eyes fixed on the door as it shook beneath another blow. "But I wouldn't have thought him capable of this. And Tasha..." he trailed off, recalling the way she had pulled him aside in the room—and her change in manner when she saw the tangled sheets on the bed.

*Bang!*

His thoughts were interrupted as the door finally gave way, shattering inwards to emit the first of those outside. Two soldiers forced their way through the broken wood, spears held at the ready.

"What is the meaning of this?" Nguyen bellowed, abandoning his search and swinging towards them.

Cleo shouldered his way past the soldiers, silver spear held in one hand, shield in the other. In the blue steel of the royal guard, he could have been a noble warrior from legend, but the hatred that twisted his face was pure malevolence.

"The beast, her lover, and the traitor king," he snarled. "A match made in hell. The Sovereigns will thank us when you're gone."

At that, he hefted his spear and thrust the razor-sharp tip at Sophia's throat.

Lukys cried out, but moving with Tangatan speed she twisted away and the blade cut only empty air. A snarl rattled from her throat and for a second it seemed as though she would tear Cleo in two. But his comrades pushed forward, their own spears turning on the Tangata in their midst, and Sophia was forced to retreat.

Standing just outside the reach of their blades, Nguyen finally reacted. As one of the guards stepped out of line, the king darted forward and caught his spear with both hands. The man cried out as Nguyen twisted the weapon, then yanked back with all his strength. Taken off-guard, the spear was torn from the man's hands. Reversing the weapon with a speed that belied his greying hair, Nguyen drove it through the throat of its former owner.

Shock showed in the eyes of their assailants as the king leapt back, flourishing the bloody blade. A dozen pairs of eyes turned to their fallen comrade, even now still grasping at his throat, desperate to stem the blood pulsing between his fingers. Then the eyes returned to the king, and Lukys glimpsed their rage.

"You'll pay for that, bastard," Cleo growled.

He advanced a step, freeing space for the last of their comrades to enter. Lukys clenched his fists, eyeing their weapons. Unarmed, he would be of little use, but perhaps he could disarm another of the guards as the king had—

A soft growl, barely audible, was the only warning Cleo and his companions had before Sophia fell upon them. The breath lodged in Lukys's chest as a man staggered back from her blur of movement, the side of his helmet caved in by an unseen blow. The steel had done little to protect him from the Tangata's strength, and with a gurgling cry, he crumpled to the ground alongside his dead companion.

The other men cried out and thrust their weapons at Sophia in panic, but these soldiers did not possess the same skill as royal guards, and Sophia easily evaded their attacks. Before Lukys knew what was happening, she tore a weapon from one of their grasps and sent it hurtling towards him. At the last second, he snatched it from the air, then moved to aid Sophia.

Not that she needed it.

The freshly unarmed man turned and fled, while Cleo and the rest tried to rush her all at once. It looked like Sophia would be overwhelmed, but she only bounded forward, dodging inside the range of the spear tips, and kicked out at the nearest of the men. An awful *crack* followed as her boot connected with his chest and hurled him backwards.

Snarling, Cleo tried to bring his spear to bear, but Sophia was faster, grasping another of the men by his chain-mail vest. Unable to use his weapon, he dropped it and swung a punch. The blow connected with Sophia's forehead, but she barely seemed to feel it. A growl rumbled from her throat as she spun, flinging the man over her hip and into the path of Cleo. The two crashed together with an audible *thump* and went down in a heap.

As the two struggled to recover, the others came at her, spears held in trembling hands. A hiss escaped from Sophia as she swung on them, and Lukys glimpsed madness in her grey eyes, a reflection of the insanity he'd seen in the eyes of the Old Ones. The remaining men saw it too, and with a final glance at their fallen leader, they turned and fled.

For a moment, Lukys thought Sophia would chase after them. A growl rumbled from her chest as she watched them vanish into the corridor, but then she let out a long breath. The madness seemed to leave her with the exhaled air, and blinking, the tension fled her body. She glanced at him, and now he saw concern in her eyes, sensed it in the yellow fear of her aura.

Lukys said nothing, only crossed the room and drew her into a one-handed hug, the spear she'd thrown him clutched unused at his side.

"Impressive," Nguyen said softly.

A groan from across the room drew their attention to Cleo and the man he'd tripped over. Sophia must have thrown him harder than Lukys had thought, for neither had yet regained their feet. Releasing the Tangata, he levelled the spear at the royal guard.

"How did you get in here?" he snapped.

Cleo drew his lips back in a sneer. "I'll never tell you anything, Tangata fu—"

His words were cut off as Nguyen stepped up and drove a spear through his back. The guard's eyes widened and his mouth fell open, as though to say more, but blood burst from his lips instead, and he pitched face-first to the ground.

"I believe you," the king said softly. He turned to the second man. "And what about you?"

The plain-clothed man tried to retreat from the king, but his collision with Cleo must have left him with injuries, for he struggled even on his hands and knees.

"Please," he gasped. "I don't know anything!"

"I see." The king's voice was cold as the spear flashed out. A moment later, the man lay still in a pool of his own blood.

Lukys stared at the dead men in shock. Beside him, horror radiated from Sophia, and absently he recalled her dismay when he'd told her of the wars that had raged between humanity, how obscene the concept had seemed to her. The Tangata did not murder one another—or at least they hadn't, until the reappearance of the Old Ones.

Silence fell over the chamber as the last of their assailants breathed their last breaths. The king stood regarding them, his green eyes unreadable.

"Why did you kill them?" Lukys finally managed.

"Were you planning to take them prisoner?" the king asked. "I'd rather not have them come against us again while we're trying to escape."

"Escape?" Lukys frowned.

"You weren't planning on sticking around waiting for others, were you?"

Lukys shook his head, still staring at Cleo. The hatred had left the guard's face with death. Shivering, he looked to the door again, the empty corridor. Where had Tasha and her escort gone?

"None of this makes sense," Lukys whispered. Cleo he could imagine giving in to his hatred and going against the wishes of the Sovereigns, but Tasha? She might hate the Tangata, but the woman was a professional.

"When politics is involved, I rarely find things do," the king commented.

"The Sovereigns..." Lukys started.

"Forget the Sovereigns," Nguyen said shortly. "The guards will never let us near them after this, even if they don't have some hand in it. Come, we'd best move quickly if we're to escape with our lives."

Lukys's mind was still reeling from the sudden betrayal and he struggled to keep pace with the king's thinking. "Where are we going?"

"My ships," Nguyen replied.

Lukys and Sophia followed the man into the corridor. Outside, the hallway was empty, all sign of the men that had attacked them vanished. But if the royal guards were plotting against them as Nguyen believed, it wouldn't be long before more came to finish the job. As though to confirm the thought, horns began to sound in the distance.

"We'll never make it that far," Lukys said, turning to the king.

Nguyen grunted. Reaching into his shirt, he drew out a glass orb. Lukys frowned. The object had a strange sheen to it, as though there were some inner light within the crystal...

He jumped as light burst from the globe, raising his spear. But when the brilliance faded, he found the space where the king had been standing vacant. Blood pounded in Lukys's ears as he took a step back, touched by fear. What new magic was this?

"Step closer, and it will hide you as well," Nguyen's voice emerged from empty air, causing Lukys to jump for a second time in as many minutes. "Amina is not the only one with a few tricks up her sleeve."

Lukys swallowed and stole a glance at Sophia. Jaw clenched, her grey eyes were fixed on a point near where the king had disappeared. Without waiting for him to speak, she took a step forward—and vanished as well.

A shiver ran down Lukys's spine, but a moment later her voice whispered in his mind

*It's okay,* she murmured. *This king has an old magic.*

Lukys let out a sharp breath, his skin crawling at the strangeness of this new power. But circumstances left him no choice, and clenching his fists, he strode towards what seemed to be the source of the king's voice. There was another burst of light across his vision, then his companions reappeared before him. The hackles on the back of his neck stood on end as he looked around, finding the rest of the world stained a pallid grey.

"What is this?" he whispered.

"How do you think I was able to sneak into the court of the Sovereigns?" the king replied. "My Archivists and engineers managed to create this prototype from an artefact we discovered. A shame they were lost in the ruins of my fortress—they would have been excited to see how effective it has proven. Now come, we'd best reach my fleet before our new friends decide to up the stakes."

Lukys watched as the man turned in the direction of the harbour, but something held him back. There was a wrongness to all this, to the sudden betrayal of the royal guards, a question he needed answering. More than that, there was the threat of the Old Ones, the need for humanity to unite against them.

"Stop," he said abruptly. The king swung back,

eyebrows lifted with irritation, clearly unimpressed by the delay. Lukys spoke over his objection. "We can't run," he hissed.

"Lukys, if we stay here, we die," the king said, his eyes hard.

Lukys shook his head, surprising himself with the defiance. But Nguyen was not his king. Not even the Sovereigns were now. He was his own man, the Tangata and Dale and Travis and all the others his people.

"If we flee, we die anyway," he replied. "When the Old One and her Tangata come, there'll be nowhere left to run, no safe place to hide. Millions will perish."

His words seemed to give Nguyen pause, and his gaze flickered to Sophia before returning to Lukys.

"The Sovereigns won't listen," Nguyen replied. "Not with the blood of their guards on our hands, not without my soldiers to protect us. It was a mistake coming here, I can see that now."

"No," Lukys said softly. "You were right to ask Perfugia to stand with you. You were right to seek unity. But we cannot turn from the path now, whatever the risk."

"Those who escaped will have already told their tales to the Sovereigns. They will call you monsters, name me a traitor."

"Then we will name them liars. We will make the Sovereigns see through their hatred," Lukys said, though recalling the look they'd given them in the amphitheatre, he struggled to believe the words himself.

The king regarded him for a long while, until Lukys thought the man must think him a fool. Yet he knew in his heart they could not run now. A fleet might wait for them in the harbour, but what use was that with no safe port to dock? If they fled now, all the world would stand against them.

*I am with you, Lukys,* Sophia whispered.

He smiled at her, seeing the support in her eyes. Whatever he chose, he knew Sophia would join him on the road, however long and arduous the journey might prove. Even should Nguyen turn back, he would not be alone in his confrontation with the Sovereigns.

"Very well," Nguyen said abruptly. He waved a hand. "You are right, of course. Though you'd best pray to those Gods of yours that the Sovereigns don't have us slaughtered on the spot. Alone, I fear there's little we could do to defend ourselves."

"They won't," Lukys said firmly, "and we won't be alone."

*The others?* Sophia said.

Lukys nodded, and silently he reached out with his mind as he had before in their chambers. This time, though, he persisted, sending out feelers for Sophia's brethren, for his family. The citadel was filled with minds, with the presence of other Melders, some barely a glimmer in his inner eyes, others a brilliant vortex of colours. But only a handful were familiar.

The Tangata.

*Brothers, sisters,* he called out, touching each of their consciousnesses. *They're coming for you.*

He sensed fear and concern as a dozen voices called back to him, but he thrust their words aside. There was more to say, and he could not afford to delay.

*Escape your quarters and evade the guards. Meet us in the amphitheatre of the Sovereigns. We will make our stand there.*

As he finished, the fear radiating from the others subsided, giving way to quiet resolve. In his mind's eyes he glimpsed images of the Tangata and their human partners climbing from windows, bursting through doors, exchanging blows with blue-garbed soldiers. For a moment he was with each of them, felt the rush of their adrenaline, their desperate plights…

*Lukys!*

Sophia's call drew him back to his own reality. Shaking himself, he glanced at the others. They still stood in the bubble of strangeness, cast by the orb in Nguyen's hand. He swallowed, touched by sudden guilt. The others did not have the advantage of the king's magic. Would any of them survive to reach the Sovereigns?

"Our friends will join us in the amphitheatre." Too late to second guess himself now. He looked at the king. "Do you remember the way?"

## ❦ 31 ❦

## THE EMISSARY

"Stay back!"

Fear gave Erika fresh strength and she scrambled back from the Old One. She found Cara, still standing unmoved, and managed to come to her feet. Grasping at the Goddess, she looked at the Old One, saw the shine in her grey eyes, the amusement.

"Should I tell you the truth, human?" the Old One said, stepping closer. Erika shrank against Cara, feeling the tremors in her friend, but there was no escaping the creature's words. "About what really happened all that time ago, when the world Fell?"

Erika shook her head, trying to deny the creature's lies, her darkness, but no words left her mouth.

"It was so long ago, centuries of darkness. No wonder humanity has forgotten," the creature continued, its voice soft, almost seductive. "Perhaps it has even passed from the memories of the Tangata." She swung back towards where Farhan knelt. "But *they* have not forgotten. Not with their long lives, their isolation. Their Founders made sure of it."

"No," the Old One continued, shaking her head. "My

children may have forgotten the sacrifice of their forefathers, but I have not. For it was my own mother and father who helped light the match of humanity's destruction."

"They were the first of you," Erika murmured, more to herself than the creature. "The ones who stole the magic from the Gods?"

Then she frowned, glancing at the kneeling Anahera. That had been the legend, the tale passed down by human legends for generations. The Tangata had stolen their power from the Gods, the Anahera. But...that no longer rang true, not with everything she'd learned. Then how...

"My parents were no thieves," the Old One snapped. "Their power, the strength that runs in my veins still, even that which remains to the Tangata, it was a gift." Her smile grew. "From humanity."

Erika started. "What?"

The Old One stared back, unrelenting. "Yes, just as the Anahera later received their gifts, we were blessed by the magic of humanity." Her face hardened, the smile turning to a snarl. "Only your gifts came with a cost, one we became increasingly unwilling to pay: our servitude." She glanced back at Farhan, still knelt in the mud, unmoving. "Isn't that right, Anahera?"

Erika's heart throbbed painfully in her chest and she staggered, the pieces of the puzzle finally falling into place. The reason the Anahera had fled into the mountains, why their city was so pitiful compared to the pictures of the past, why the sight of her magic had triggered such a reaction from them. Even the notes from the journal, the regrets, the doubts of the long dead Founder.

Because *none* of it had been created by the Anahera.

The magic, the majestic city, the very existence of these beings, all of it had been created by humanity.

"Do you understand now, human?" The crunch of the

Old One's footsteps whispered in Erika's ears as she came closer. "Yes, I can see it in your eyes, the truth."

Shaking her head, Erika broke away from Cara, retreated from the Old One's advance. Her mind was still racing, the whole of the puzzle taking shape. The legends claimed that the Gods—the Anahera—had thrown down the world to destroy the Tangata, that they had brought about the Fall to stop the stolen magic from spreading.

Lies.

Erika squeezed her fist, summoning the power of the gauntlet. Magic that could cause a Tangata to scream in agony, that could bring an Anahera to his knees. Just a fraction of the magics had once existed. All of it, created by humanity.

Until the Fall.

"My father told me the story," the Old One rasped, her grey eyes boring into Erika's, "about my mother's sacrifice —and the great alliance between our peoples, the union of Anahera and Tangata against a common enemy." Her lips drew back, revealing shining teeth. "Against humanity."

"No," Erika whispered, her whole being trembling.

*No, no, no!*

She stumbled back from the creature, struggling to deny, to reject the tale. Desperate, she looked at Cara. Two of the Tangata had approached on either side of the Goddess, ready for signs of treachery, but the Goddess did not seem to notice them. Her amber eyes were wide, fixed doggedly to the ground, avoiding Erika's gaze. Pain swelled in her chest, a gathering pressure, building, growing, screaming for release.

She saw again that glorious, wondrous city from the painting, rising from the waters of the harbour. The City of the Gods , created by her own people, sculpted by her ancestors hundreds of years passed, by humanity.

All of it destroyed, torn down in the violence of the Fall, by the cataclysm that had reduced humanity to beasts, clawing and warring in the dirt.

Not to destroy the Tangata, as human legends had told for generations.

But to destroy humanity itself.

Erika's entire being shook as she stared at the Old One. Every evil her people had borne, all the death, the destruction, the suffering, it had all been because of the creatures before her, a vile way to keep humanity in check.

And all these while the Anahera had hidden away in these mountains, holding themselves aloof, proclaiming their Divinity because they did not kill, did not lie.

They had committed the greatest genocide in all of history.

A soft crackling lit the yard as she ignited her magic.

"I will destroy you all," Erika whispered.

"Such anger," the Old One murmured, "and yet you call my children mad, have treated them as monsters. No wonder my mother took retribution upon your kind." A smile touched her lips and she glanced at Farhan. "With your own Founders' help, of course."

Erika screamed.

It was a scream unlike any she had ever given, carrying with it all the torment of her life, the betrayal of her people, of a limitless rage. Without thinking, she leapt at the Old One, arm thrust for her face, the magic thrumming in her ears. Light flashed and the Old One stumbled in the snow, hands going to her ears…

…then she was surging forward, teeth bared, fist flashing out to strike Erika's chest. The agony of her broken rib flared back to life and suddenly she was on the ground, mouth stretched wide, straining to breathe.

The Old One gave her no time to recover. Growling, she

caught Erika by the shirt and lifted her into the air. Erika tried to raise her fist, to bring the gauntlet to bear, but the creature caught her by the wrist and grinned.

"A curious thing," the Old One said matter-of-factly as she inspected the metal links covering Erika's arm. "Of all the power your ancestors once possessed, this was but a trinket, created at the end. Yet it is still enough to bring us to our knees."

"I will see your children burn for what you did to us," Erika spat.

Laughter rasped from the throat of the Old One. "Oh, I don't doubt you would try." Her face hardened, and a fresh darkness came into her eyes. "I do not intend to grant you the chance."

Suddenly the Old One's grip tightened on Erika's wrist. She cried out, twisting, trying to break free, but there was no escaping this beast. Iron fingers dug into the gauntlet, squeezing, crushing metal against flesh, until Erika could feel the bones grinding, cracking, *shattering*.

A scream tore from her throat as red-hot agony swallowed her arm. Through the pain, she saw the Old One smiling, the triumph in her eyes...

...then felt a *thud* as a blur of auburn struck the Old One, flinging her back, sending Erika tumbling to the snow.

Light flashed as she struck and stars danced across her vision. She lay in the snow, gasping for breath, screams still ringing in her ears as she fought the pain, sought to stave off unconsciousness. Agony rose in her throat to swallow her, threatening to drown her.

Somehow, Erika clung on.

Across the yard, the thud of fists on flesh sounded from the walls. Teeth clenched, Erika struggled to rise once more, to see what had become of Cara. Two bodies lay on the snow nearby—those of the Tangata that had tried to restrain her. Blood seeped from their shattered skulls, staining the snow.

Auburn and gold flashed amidst the falling snow as Goddess and Old One battled fist and boot and wing. She could barely follow the two as they warred against one another—not even the other Tangata seemed able to keep pace, and Erika's heart soared. Cara had already defeated two of the Old Ones in the caverns beneath the earth; surely she would emerge victorious now.

Snarls rose from the two, each punctuated by the heavy *thud* of flesh on flesh. In moments, the dirt and snow had been trampled to mud by the fury of their assault. Around the square, the Anahera watched on. Not one moved to aid their fellow Anahera—not even Farhan.

The Tangata had no such hesitation. Lying in the dirt, Erika watched as the creatures edged closer to their embattled leader, though they did not yet attempt to interfere. Gritting her teeth, she struggled to push herself up. Pain lanced through her chest but she made it to her knees. Erika could go no further though, could not help her friend this time, not in this battle. Just the slightest shift of her fingers ignited fresh agony in her gauntleted hand.

Horror stole Erika's breath as a sudden cry came from Cara. She watched as the Goddess stumbled, mud slipping beneath her bare feet. Her wings flared out as she sought to regain her balance, but the Old One would not grant her the opportunity. She pounced, boot crashing against Cara's stomach.

The blow drove the breath from the Goddess's lungs and she doubled up, only to meet the Old One's knee as she drove it upwards. A terrible *crunch* sounded across the yard as the blow connected, lifting Cara from her feet, hurling her back. Mud splashed as she tumbled across the ground, staining her wings, drenching her thin clothing.

Still Cara would not surrender. Groaning, the Goddess struggled to her knees as the Old One approached. The familiar laughter sounded in Erika's ears, but she could do nothing but watch as the creature caught a handful of Cara's hair and hauled the Goddess to her feet.

"At least one of the Anahera still has the heart to fight," she said, and it seemed to Erika there was regret in her voice. "A shame; you might have served me well."

Tears filled Erika's eyes as she watched the Old One send her friend crashing back to the ground. This time Cara struggled to rise, her wings flailing, hands slipping in the mud. Heart pounding, Erika searched for someone, anyone that could help. Maisie still lay unconscious, her leg twisted at a terrible angle, and not one of the Anahera even looked at Cara now. Their eyes were fixed to the mud, as though by turning their backs, they might ignore what was about to happen.

Then Erika saw Farhan. He still knelt like the others, but he alone of the Anahera did not look away. His amber gaze was fixed on his daughter, reflecting her pain, her grief...

"Farhan," Erika rasped, struggling to lift her voice above the wind in the mountain peaks. "Farhan, you have to help her!"

The Anahera's eyes flickered ever so briefly towards her, but he made no move to act, to intervene. Watching him sit there, Erika felt her rage stirring, the terrible anger that burned within her, the desire to rend and tear, to punish those that had so devastated her people, humanity.

"*Bastard!*" she screamed, her vision blurring. Agony engulfed her as she pushed herself to her feet, but the rage would not be denied. "You said you only wanted to protect her, to shield your daughter from the dangers without. Now you sit and watch her die, and do nothing? *Coward!* You deserve your slavery."

At that she turned away from the fallen God, from the Anahera and the Tangata. Her entire being in agony, Erika faced the Old One.

"You thought they would aid you?" The creature reached down to where Cara knelt at her feet and patted the Goddess's cheek. "This one has more courage than all the Anahera combined."

Cara still struggled against the creature's grip, but her strength could no longer match her foe. Diminished by captivity, by grief and exhaustion, Cara was all but defeated, the Old One resurgent.

Erika stumbled towards them, lurching from one foot to the other. Each step sent jolts of agony through her chest, her arm, but she did not stop. She knew she couldn't win, couldn't stop this creature. All she could do was stand with her friend. If they were to die, at least then it would be together.

The Old One watched her come, amusement showing in her eyes, in the cruel twist to her lips. She knew the end was near, that soon the city, maybe even the whole world, would belong to her. But it didn't matter to Erika, not now.

Suddenly she was standing before the creature, eye to eye, with Cara at her feet. The Old One made no move to intervene as she reached down with her good hand, said nothing as she helped the Goddess to her feet. She only stood and watched, smiling, always smiling.

Erika swallowed as she glanced at her friend, saw the pain in her amber eyes, but also the love, the warmth of the knowledge she did not face this monster alone. Just as Erika had said, they faced the Old One together.

"Are you ready then?" the creature growled.

A lump lodged in Erika's throat and she tensed, preparing for one last stand, one final attempt at resistance...

"*Old One.*" Erika's head whipped around as a shout came from across the yard. Farhan rose slowly to his feet. "*You will leave my daughter be!*"

Eyes burning, white wings spread, he advanced on them. For just a moment, the Old One seemed surprised. She watched him come, then abruptly turned from them. Her movements quickened as she stepped to meet her challenger.

"So another has the courage to fight," she laughed. "Come then, Farhan of the Anahera, come and meet your death."

Erika winced as the two came together, but she knew there could be only one outcome from this battle. The Anahera remained on their knees, unmoved by Farhan's defiance, just as they had been for Cara. The Tangata still held the child, the fledgling slumped in its hands. They would not act so long as she was in danger.

Erika looked around for Maisie, hoping against hope she might have recovered, but her hopes were crushed as she saw the Tangata had found the injured woman. Half a dozen of the creatures stood guard over her unconscious figure, grey eyes alert. There would be no saving the Gemaho spy.

Despair welled in Erika's heart as she looked to her friend. "Cara," she whispered, reaching out to take the Goddess's hand. "Cara, we have to go. We can't stay here, we can't help them."

The Goddess's eyes were still fixed on her father, on the ferocious battle between the two titans. Erika felt a tremor shake her friend.

"He cares," she whispered. She blinked, and a tear spilt down her cheek. "He...he..."

Her heart twisting, Erika stepped between the Goddess and the battle, cutting off her view of Farhan. "He saved you," she whispered, cupping Cara's cheek. "He saved us both. We can't let it be for nothing. Cara, we have to go."

Cara's face spasmed and she shook her head, a sob tearing from her throat. "No, no, I can't..."

"*You can,*" Erika insisted. "*You must!*"

"No!" Cara whipped her head from side to side, her eyes scrunched closed. "Please, don't make me."

Standing with her back to the two fighters, Erika couldn't see the blows, but she could hear each strike, the thud of pounding flesh and breaking bones. It grew more urgent, more violent with each second. But even if Farhan gained the upper hand, there was still the Tangata. There were enough in the yard to tear the leader of the Anahera to pieces.

"It's time," Erika whispered, hugging her friend tight. "Come on, before it's too late—"

Erika broke off as with a final scream, Cara hugged her back. Agony engulfed her chest, but before she could cry out, the great wings of auburn beat down, striking the air, pounding so hard that stones and sleet and mud were sent whirling away from them. Roars of anger came from all around as the Tangata realised what was happening, but it was already too late.

They were airborne.

## ❧ 32 ❧

# THE HERO

Lukys raced through the twisting corridors of the citadel, surprised at the speed with which Nguyen moved. Sophia had no problem keeping pace, but still weakened by his time at sea, Lukys struggled each time they came to a fresh set of stairs. His heart pounded hard in his chest as they made their slow way up through the endless complex.

For a time, it seemed the king's magic would allow them to pass easily into the amphitheatre of the Sovereigns—until they finally turned a corner and found themselves facing a hallway filled with soldiers. They stumbled to a stop as one, their path blocked. The soldiers stood some thirty yards away, spears and shields held in preparation for battle, their formation tight.

And at their front stood Tasha.

Lukys swallowed, holding his breath as he felt the eyes of Tasha and her soldiers upon them, though he knew they could not be seen. It was eerie, the sun shining down upon those dozens of faces, their brows creased, eyes wide, as though in reaction to their sudden appearance.

"Oh by the Fall," Nguyen swore.

Jumping at the outburst, Lukys swung on the king. He started to raise a finger to his lips, then paused, his heart growing suddenly still. His gaze was drawn to the orb in the king's fingers. Its light was dull—had vanished completely, as a matter of fact...

Suddenly Lukys's heart was racing and he swung back to see the soldiers lowering their spears. Shock showed in the eyes of Tasha, though it was quickly replaced with rage.

"So it's true," she snarled, pointing at them with her weapon. Gone was all semblance of reason. Hatred seethed instead in her eyes. "See, comrades, how the traitors show their true colours? Quickly, we must stop them before they reach the Sovereigns!"

Ice spread through Lukys's veins as Tasha started towards them, the soldiers at her back. A cold wind swept through the corridor as overhead a cloud passed before the sun. Holding his spear close, Lukys swore at the king.

"What the Fall happened?"

"Ran out of steam," the king panted as he tucked the sphere back into his tunic and gripped his spear in two hands. "Don't suppose you had a plan B."

Lukys cursed, but before he could respond, Sophia spoke into his mind.

*I do.*

For a second, he thought his partner meant she would face the soldiers alone. But her eyes were not on Tasha and their foes at all, but rather on the sky, on the walls of the corridor stretching above.

"What are you thinking..." he started.

He broke off as Sophia caught him by the front of his tunic. Before he could so much as cry out, Lukys found himself airborne, hurled upwards by the astonishing strength of the Tangata, up towards where the ceiling should have been.

Only there were no ceilings here, no stone roofs to trap them, and Lukys's cry cut off abruptly as he landed with a thump atop the corridor wall. Gasping, he rolled onto his side, struggling to regain his breath. Shouts and the clash of weapons came from below, then another body followed him.

The king of Gemaho landed with a little more poise than Lukys had managed, though to be fair Sophia had probably given him more warning. He lost his grip on his spear though, and the pair of them watched as the weapon rolled over the stone ledge on which they crouched and disappeared over the side.

Lukys's heart clenched as a scream drew his attention back to the corridor. Below, Tasha and her soldiers were swarming Sophia, pressing her back against the wall. Fear rose in Lukys's throat, and gathering up his own spear, he rose to go to Sophia's aid.

Again though, it proved unnecessary. In a blur of rage, she caught a soldier that stepped too close and hurled him backwards into his companions. Several went down, and in the ensuing chaos, she turned and leapt.

Watching her hurtle upwards, Lukys couldn't help but marvel at her ability. Sophia could have been one of the Gods themselves, the way she moved, the grace with which she landed atop the narrow strip of stone on which they perched. Her eyes flickered from Lukys to Nguyen, a wry smile twitching on her lips.

Shouts came from below and a moment later a spear flashed up from the corridor. But the narrow space and sheer angle of the walls made the throw difficult and the weapon came nowhere near any of them. Even so, Lukys moved away from the edge and turned to survey the landscape.

He swallowed as he found himself looking upon the citadel from an entirely new perspective. The open corridors looped away from the complex of the Sovereigns like the rings of a labyrinth. The covered roofs of sleeping chambers dotted the citadel, creating a unique design when looked at from above—a pattern that only the Sovereigns would ever see, seated on the thrones atop their high balcony.

Voices came from below, drawing Lukys's attention back to Tasha and her soldiers. They were already organising themselves, some attempting to lift others onto their shoulders to reach the top of the high walls, but the majority were retreating down the corridor with Tasha, no doubt to reinforce the guards at the amphitheatre.

Lukys's gaze swept across the loops of the labyrinth to where the palace of the Sovereigns rose above them. They were close, might even be able to reach the amphitheatre before Tasha's soldiers. The way ahead was clear, and after a quick glance at the others, he set off at a jog along the tops of the marble walls.

With the soldiers trapped by the labyrinthine passageways, they soon left their shouts behind. The palace of the Sovereigns rose above them as they neared the amphitheatre. Even from a distance, Lukys could see that the great balcony was empty. The Sovereigns must wait within the dark alcove of their palace. He prayed they would listen, that he could convince them, but...

He pushed his doubts aside and came to a stop atop the stands overlooking the amphitheatre. The ground below was silent, unnervingly so, and he flicked another glance at the balcony of the Sovereigns. Nothing moved there, not even a breath of wind to shift the curtains of their chambers.

A shiver ran down his spine as he looked at the others.

"What is this?" There should have been dozens of guards here already, hundreds even...

Whispers rose from below and he swung around, spear clenched tight in case of an ambush. A moment later, Dale and Isabella appeared, followed by Travis and Keria and half a dozen of the others. He was pleased to see they had armed themselves and his heart soared. Throwing caution to the wind, he started down the stands into the amphitheatre. It might still be a trap, but at least they would be together.

Concern showed in the faces of the others as Lukys and Sophia joined them, followed belatedly by the king.

"Lukys," Dale said, his voice low. "What's going on? The corridors are empty."

Lukys shook his head. A few minutes later, the last of the Perfugian recruits joined them with their Tangatan partners. Lukys's heart pounded in his chest as he turned on the spot, scanning the rim of the amphitheatre, the empty corridors leading into the bowels of the citadel. Something wasn't right. The royal guard could not have simply disappeared. And where were the Sovereigns?

His thoughts trailed off as a distant pounding carried to his ears. For a moment it seemed to match his heartbeat, the racing of his anxious pulse. But it soon grew louder, more insistent, until Lukys knew it for what it was.

The beating of boots on stone.

Standing with his Perfugian comrades and the Tangata and the Gemaho king, Lukys watched as the soldiers raced into the amphitheatre. Tasha led them still, and at a gesture from her, the soldiers spread out, surrounding the Tangata and their human companions in a ring of steel.

Lukys clenched his fists about his spear as he looked from Tasha to the empty balcony. Something was happening here, something he did not understand.

The soft tread of footsteps came from above. Lukys swung on the balcony and watched as the Sovereigns emerged one after another from the darkness of their complex. Others of the royal guard filed out behind them, moving quickly to place themselves on the steps leading up to the balcony. Garbed in their purple gowns with silver crowns upon their young heads, the Sovereigns looked down into the amphitheatre.

"*What is the meaning of this?*" The voices of the Sovereigns rang with anger.

"Your Majesties!" Lukys cried, taking a step towards the balcony. "*We came to beg—*"

"My lieges, blood has been spilt in our halls," Tasha called as she joined her fellow guards on the steps to the balcony. She paused, and then went on: "I left Cleo to guard your…guests, but moments ago word reached me that they had attacked his escort, killing many before they escaped. I led reinforcements to your defence as fast as I could."

"*So the Tangata reveal themselves.*" The words of the Sovereigns carried down to those gathered below. "*Do you think to take us unawares, traitors, to slay us while our backs were turned?*"

"It was your own people who attacked us, Sovereigns," Nguyen called back calmly, stepping up beside Lukys.

"*More lies, traitor king?*" the Sovereigns shook their heads in unison. "*It should not surprise us to find your involvement in this betrayal.*"

"Please, Your Majesties," Lukys tried again. "The Tangata are not responsible for this bloodshed."

"*No?*" the pair growled. "*Do not seek to deceive us, Melder. Against the knowledge of our forebearers, we granted you our trust, invited the creatures into our citadel. But the Tangata have proven their true nature. They are hateful creatures, just as we have always known.*"

"Sophia and her people want only peace," Lukys

responded, shouting to be heard by the two above. "It was humanity who attacked them, who stormed their villages and killed their children." He gritted his teeth. "Now they come to warn us of a new threat, to seek asylum, and what do they find?" He shook his head. "Deceit, treachery, an oligarchy as obsessed with purity as..." He trailed off as a thought came to him, unable to finish the sentence.

Mouth still open, he stared up at the Sovereigns. Something had just occurred to him, an answer to the question that had plagued him since their arrival in New Nihelm. In his mind, he recalled Sophia's words, the story she had told him all those weeks ago in the dungeons of New Nihelm. And later, her claims that he must have Tangatan blood in his veins, to possess their ability to Speak.

"Your people will be enslaved by Flumeer unless you heed to my warning," Nguyen spoke into the silence. "Queen Amina will not stop until all the kingdoms of humanity fall under her control."

Blood pounded in Lukys's ears as he shook his head, trying to blot out the words, to focus on what the Sovereigns had said. Surely it could not be true. There must be some other explanation. And yet...the hairs stood up on the back of his neck as he recalled their words.

*So the Old Ones have returned...*

How had the Sovereigns known that name? Nguyen had not known it, not even Cara had ever mentioned that name to him. Only the Tangata knew, only Sophia and her people.

"Lies," he murmured, then louder: "*It's all lies!*"

## ❧ 33 ❧

# THE HERO

"*How dare you—*"

"*Liars!*" Lukys bellowed over the Sovereigns' objections. He stood staring up at them, hardly able to believe the scale of the deception that had been played upon his people. "You've lied to us all from the start, down through the centuries, you and all your predecessors." He drew in a breath, hardly able to believe what he was about to say. "We're not human at all," he whispered. "We never were."

His words were met with silence, as all eyes in the amphitheatre stared at him in disbelief. Even his comrades cast him sharp looks, as though afraid he had lost his mind.

"What nonsense are you talking, lad?" Nguyen hissed.

"*Madness,*" the Sovereigns snarled.

"Truth," Lukys said.

He turned to Sophia. Standing beside him, her eyes were wide, their grey depths a mystery, though…he could sense a familiar fear from her, that the world was spiralling beyond her control, that if things went wrong, she could not protect him. Smiling, he kissed her gently, just in case…then turned again to the thrones above.

"The Tangata sent us away," he said softly, matching the stares of the Sovereigns now, refusing to back down, "our ancestors. It was never the human wars the first Perfugian settlers fled from. It was the Tangata, in the early days after the Fall. Sophia told me, there was a time they sent away those who were born without the grey eyes, some they sent on ship into the endless ocean, never to be seen again."

"*More madness,*" the Sovereigns hissed. "Why would Tangata be born without grey eyes?"

Lukys hesitated, glancing at Sophia. *Can I tell them?*

She paused only half a moment before meeting his eyes. *I trust you, Lukys.*

He nodded, swinging to address Tasha and her circle of soldiers. "The Tangata are a dying race," he said, his voice touched with sadness. "Their strength dwindles with each passing generation, as fewer and fewer are able to breed amongst themselves."

Frowns creased the faces of his fellow Perfugians as he spoke, though he could not decipher whether their reaction was one of anger or confusion. Their auras, the emotion swirling from each man and woman, had become a bubbling kaleidoscope of colours.

"To survive, the Tangata have been mixing their lines with humans. That is how my friends and I came to know our Tangatan partners, to know their humanity." He drew a breath as he prepared to reveal the truth of their own ancestry. "But it was not always so. Once, those who became too human, who lost the grey eyes of the Tangata, they were sent away. Our ancestors, the first of the Perfugians, were amongst those banished, sent away in a ship to keep the bloodlines of the Tangata pure."

This time, silence answered his proclamation. Atop their balcony, the Sovereigns stood unmoving.

"Sent away, but not forgotten," Lukys murmured. "Sophia and her people, they never knew what became of us, but they never forgot their lost cousins."

Still the Sovereigns said nothing. A stillness had fallen over the amphitheatre, as every soul present stared at Lukys.

"But not all of those the Tangata sent into exile were without power, were they?" he continued. "Some of our ancestors who arrived on these shores, they retained the abilities of the Tangata, their ability to Speak, to communicate mind to mind. Powers that would become valuable through the years, cherished, protected, preserved. The abilities of your Melders."

He could feel the anger behind the Sovereigns' eyes now, the rage, and he wondered why they had not ordered him killed. Clenching his fists, he spoke on.

"Sophia, Isabella, Keria and their brethren, they *are* our people. You *know* they have not come to harm us, that they would be our allies. Why do you hate them so?"

Footsteps came from above as the Sovereigns slowly descended from their balcony. Lukys held his breath, watching as they came. The expression on their faces was unreadable, their aura carefully kept blank. Tasha and the royal guards formed up to either side of them as they reached the floor of the amphitheatre, spears held at the ready.

*"Because they rejected us,"* the Sovereigns finally replied, their voices low, tinged by sadness. *"Because they sent us away for being weak, impure."* Their eyes met Lukys's across the floor of the amphitheatre. *"Because they deserve our hatred."*

Inhaled breaths whispered through the yard as those gathered swung to stare now at the Sovereigns. Lukys felt a rush of exhilaration, that he'd guessed right, that he'd discovered the truth the Sovereigns had kept from his people down through the centuries—that the Perfugians had descended from Tangatan exiles. Though, one question still remained unanswered…

*You were not forgotten,* Sophia's voice carried through Lukys's mind. He glanced around as she joined him, entwining her fingers with his, sharing a secret look before she turned again to the Sovereigns. *The lost ones,* she continued, bowing her head. *We always wondered, always regretted… what became of you.*

"We were the Banished," the Sovereigns rasped. "*The hated ones, judged inferior and forced from our homes, our families.*"

"Yet now you do the same to our own people," Lukys said, gesturing to his friends. "While the Tangata have grown, come to embrace all, no matter their differences."

"*Lies!*"

*Truth!* Sophia responded.

Lukys shivered as images flashed into his mind, of New Nihelm as he had known it—humans living alongside Tangata, children of both races playing in the streets, eyes of grey and blue and brown shining in shared joy. He found his own eyes burning and a tear streaked his cheek as he recalled his days there, what he had lost.

"*No…*" the Sovereigns tried to refute the images, but they spoke in a whisper now, more a plea that what Sophia showed them was false.

*An Old One has returned,* Sophia continued inexorably.

The images changed, and Lukys saw the Matriarch falling to the hands of Maya, witnessed Tangata racing through the streets of New Nihelm, becoming more animal than human as they hunted down the humans living alongside them. He saw again Adonis in their courtyard, using his powers against them, speaking of his desire to rule them…

The images cut off and Lukys swallowed, finding himself looking again at the Sovereigns.

*Your people need you,* Sophia said again. *We will fall to the darkness without your aid.*

The Sovereigns said nothing, only stared at Sophia, brows wrinkled. Then their eyes flickered to Lukys.

"*Is what she says true, soldier?*" they asked softly. "*Have the Tangata truly changed?*"

Lukys glanced at Sophia, hesitating, then straightened his shoulders and faced his Sovereigns. "All my life, I have struggled to find my place, as a student, as a recruit, to find a way to serve my people." He swallowed, giving Sophia's hand a squeeze. "In New Nihelm, I finally found it. With this woman."

There was a long pause as the Sovereigns regarded them, until Lukys thought for sure that he'd failed, that whatever ancient hatred the pair carried would triumph and he and his friends would be slain. But finally the Sovereigns bowed their heads, and when they spoke, there was acceptance in their words.

"*We have clung to this anger for long enough,*" they said softly, "*but that is for past generations. Today, let the peoples of Perfugia and Tangata be reunited.*"

Silence hung over the square at their proclamation. Slowly the soldiers began to lower their weapons, to look from the Sovereigns to one another, confusion in their eyes.

"About time," Nguyen grunted, "And let the Gemaho stand alongside you. We will face our common enemies together."

The Sovereigns frowned at the king's interjection, but before they could respond, movement came from beside them as Tasha stepped forward.

"*No,*" she said softly, and Lukys staggered as her words rebounded inside his skull, amplified by her own power.

The Sovereigns too flinched from her, swinging to face the guard. "*Soldier, it is not your place*—"

"This is *wrong!*" Tasha roared the word this time. She took a step towards the Sovereigns. "How can you call them allies, these monsters that have plagued our peoples for generations?"

The Sovereigns stood staring at her, their strange eyes unwavering. "*We are sorry for your confusion, Tasha,*" they said gently, "*but*—"

"*No!*"

Suddenly Tasha was leaping forward, silver spear raised. The Sovereigns staggered back in shock, but the woman was too slow to escape the blow. A sickening *thud* whispered through the amphitheatre as Tasha drove her spear through the Sovereign's stomach.

Lukys gaped, unable to believe what he was witnessing, that one of the royal guard should so betray their vows. Face twisted with rage, Tasha tore her blade free and the woman Sovereign slumped to the ground, hand clutched at the terrible wound. Blood bubbled between her fingers, as alongside her, the male of Sovereigns screamed and fell to his knees, as though her agony were his own.

"I thought you would realise your mistake," Tasha hissed as she advanced on him. "That you would see the truth when they slew Cleo. I thought it would be worth the sacrifice, driving him to attack, to force the beasts to reveal their nature. But now all here have seen the treachery of the Sovereigns."

"It was you," Lukys gasped, staring at the woman.

Tasha had been the unseen influence he'd sensed, the one that had driven Cleo to attack them. By doing so, she'd thought to turn the Sovereigns against them, to convince the rulers that they'd broken the peace.

Ignoring him, Tasha looked to the others of the royal

guard. "Ever we have guarded the power of the Sovereigns, protected their secrets—but not to treason! Not to the destruction of everything we hold dear. They would sell our freedom to the beasts, would see us become slaves to the creatures of our nightmares." She shook her head. "I will not allow it."

Abruptly she reversed her spear, and drove it down through the back of the male Sovereign. Still crouched beside his partner, he tried to straighten, to fight her off, but the youth was no match for a warrior's strength. Dragging back her blade, she looked again to the royal guard.

"Join me, brothers, sisters, and we will drive these beasts forever from our land."

Lukys's heart thundered in his ears as one by one, the royal guard raised their spears. Hatred shone from their eyes, swirled from their minds, a seething, festering green, so overwhelming that Lukys sensed it could not be natural, that Tasha was using her own powers as a Melder to augment their emotions. And it was spreading, passing from the guards to the soldiers. Metal rattled as the ring of steel surrounding Lukys and his companions began to advance.

Cursing, Lukys gathered his own emotions within, drawing them close, allowing them to build, to swell within him. Then praying their enemies remained open to more than hatred, he released them, broadcasting to Tasha and the soldiers and all those gathered in the amphitheatre, just as he had that day on the beach in Calafe.

But this time, he filled his mind with joy, with the shining hope he had found with Sophia, the love they had forged, with the warmth of companionship, with the sheer elation of existence.

It swept from him to strike the minds of the soldiers, to crash upon the hatred Tasha had fed them. For a moment, the two forces warred, love and hate burning against one another, a swirling vortex of colour.

The roar of voices died as the soldiers broke off their charge. Staggering to a stop, they looked at one another, bewilderment and confusion showing in their eyes. These were common men and women, not Melders. They could not understand the forces warring for their souls, but for the moment at least, Lukys's action had broken Tasha's hold upon them.

Not so the royal guards, and Lukys realised with a chill that all those garbed in blue-armour possessed the abilities of a Melder. With Tasha in their lead, they came on, their hatred more powerful than his hope, nourished by the lies the Sovereigns had fed them for generations. The Sovereigns might have risen above their resentment in the end, but their legacy could not be so easily severed.

Realising a battle could not be avoided, Lukys looked to his friends. "Recruits," he said, meeting the eyes of Travis and Dale. "On me."

His friends snapped to obey, raising spears and moving into place alongside him. Sophia and the Tangata made to follow, but Lukys waved them back.

*No*, he said softly. *This is our kingdom, our fight.*

Sophia hesitated, but after a moment she nodded and he saw understanding in her eyes. In that moment, he wanted to hug her close, to breathe in deep her scent and forget everything around them. Instead, he turned to face the advancing guards.

"It is not the Tangata who committed treachery!" he called, adding his Voice to the words, so that all would hear him. "Sophia and her people kept the peace—it was *you* who sent armed men to attack us, *you* have raised your hand against our own Sovereigns. You dare to call the Tangata traitors?"

Around the great room, the soldiers he had stopped looked to one another, and he could see the depth of their confusion, as they were torn between loyalty to their Sovereigns—and hatred for the cursed Tangata. The royal guards had slowed at his words, hesitating, though he knew Tasha would not turn back. The hatred she had kept so carefully hidden would not allow it.

"I fight for Perfugia," he said softly. "For the lives of all our people."

"Ha!" Tasha spat, a sneer on her face. Spear in hand, she marched towards him, the royal guards formed up behind her. "Don't believe a word from this traitor's lips," she snared. "See the Tangata with him, it is his mate. He has formed a Gods-cursed bond with the enemy."

A sad smile touched Lukys's lips as Tasha came to a stop a few feet from him. "I have only one enemy—and she stands before me. There is no need for any more to die this day—let this end between us two."

Tasha seemed to consider the proposition. Then she shook her head and laughed, gesturing to the other Perfugian recruits. "You think these sorry excuses for soldiers can stand against us? The rejects of our society, sent to die so they did not taint us with their weakness?"

"Obviously some mistakes were made," Lukys shot back with a smile.

Tasha's smirk turned into a scowl and she hefted her spear. "Enough talking," she snapped.

"I couldn't agree more," Lukys hissed.

Their blades met with a flash of sparks and snarls.

## 34
# THE FOLLOWER

The child hung limp in Adonis's arms. She no longer struggled, no longer even cried. She was so still she might have been dead already, if not for the occasional sniff of her nose, the quiet hiccup of her sorrow.

Guilt hung heavy on his soul as he watched the child's despair. They had used her, this innocent of the Anahera, had taken advantage of her helplessness to crush their enemy. Now the spirits of the Anahera hung as low as the child in his arms. All around the yard, his brethren were in celebration. Their inner voices thrummed in his mind, rich with the ecstasy of their great victory.

But standing amidst it all, Adonis remained untouched. He could not lift himself above the shame of what he'd done, the stain upon his soul. Was it worth it, this victory? The Anahera had remained neutral for generations, had removed themselves from the conflict between man and Tangata. Everything they had learned here only served to confirm that truth.

So what purpose then for this conflict, to enslave such

glorious creatures beneath the rule of the Tangata? Beneath the Old One?

His heart twisted, and he found his gaze drawn to where Maya stood above the corpse of Farhan. The Anaheran leader had fought valiantly, had bloodied Adonis's mate with his strength. With wing and fist he had driven her back, until even Adonis had begun to fear for her.

But there was nothing valiant about the way Maya had defeated her foe. Falling to one knee, she had claimed defeat, had begged the Anahera to spare her. But when Farhan had approached...

Adonis shuddered as he looked at the blood mingling with the ice and mud. There was no river here to carry it away, no swirling current to hide the atrocity that had taken place this day. There was only the Anahera lying dead before his fellows, white wings twisted and broken, eyes staring unseeing at the stormy sky.

Movement came from nearby and Adonis frowned. Two Tangata stood guarding a figure on the ground. They withdrew as he crossed to them, revealing a human crouched in the mud. Adonis's frown deepened, but this was not Erika, the human that had escaped. Idly he handed the child to one of his brothers—let *his* hands be stained now—and stepped forward to stand over the human.

She stared up at him, eyes hard, jaw clenched, but she did not flinch away. Unusual amongst her kind—usually even the bravest of human warriors tried to flee when they found themselves face to face with a Tangata. Something was clutched in her hands, but as Adonis knelt, he saw it was only a shattered globe of glass.

Footsteps approached and Adonis rose as Maya drew alongside him, dipping his head in deference.

*Shall I kill her?* he asked softly.

Maya's laughter whispered in his mind. *So eager, my mate,* she replied, then paused, contemplating the creature at her feet. For her part, the human glared back at them, eyes revealing nothing of her fear. *No, our war against humanity will depend on more than simple violence. They are unpredictable creatures, cunning, dangerous. They will not succumb like the Anahera. Their conquest will require…subtlety.*

Adonis frowned. *You wish to interrogate her?*

*Perhaps.*

Maya stared at the creature for a while longer, then flicked a hand. One of her guards moved forward and took charge of the human. She stirred at his touch, but her struggles were rendered useless by the leg lying twisted beneath her. Adonis watched as she was carried away, the Tangata he had handed the child prisoner following. They would join the other Anaheran fledglings—taking the rest captive had been the first priority of the Tangata, after Farhan's surrender.

*This one you may kill, my mate.*

Maya's words drew Adonis's attention to the youth that knelt beside the body of the Anaheran leader. His son, Adonis presumed. His wings lay in the mud as he sobbed into his father's chest. The sight sent another jolt of guilt through Adonis and he looked again at Maya, wondering at her cruelty.

*His sister was the one who fled with the human,* he said absently.

*Is that so?*

Stones crunched as Maya approached the youth and crouched alongside him. He did not look up at her presence, but as Adonis stepped closer, he realised there were words to the boy's sobs.

"I'm sorry…Father…should have been…better."

Shaking his head, Adonis looked again at Maya. Surely the youth had suffered enough. Let him be returned to the other Anahera, to grieve alongside them for their fallen leader. Greater suffering would come soon enough, he did not doubt. The creatures were weak, lessened by their years of peace. They belonged to the Tangata now, and his brethren would take what they wished.

*"Dear, dear, cry not for the departed."*

Adonis shuddered as Maya spoke the coarse language of the humans, though he sensed her Voice beneath, prodding at the youth's consciousness, seeking weakness. They were untrained, these Anahera, vulnerable to her power. Little wonder they had surrendered so easily, with an Old One playing upon their minds, influencing their emotions.

The youth could not resist her manipulations. His head lifted at Maya's words. Anger glinted in his eyes as he saw who it was, but Maya spoke before it could catch light.

*"There was no need for blood to be shed this day,"* Maya continued, her Voice whispering, winding its way into the young Anahera's mind. *"Your father surrendered in peace, with nobility. It was not he who broke our accord."*

Some of the anger went from the youth at Maya's words and he frowned. "What...are you saying?"

Maya leaned close, her fingers reaching out to stroke the young Anahera's cheek, to brush the hair from his face.

*"It was the humans who brought this upon your people,"* she whispered. *"Upon your father. It was they who tainted your sweet sister, who lured her to the darkness."*

"I..." the Anahera swallowed. "Cara..." He looked around, eyes lost, trapped. "She's...gone."

"Yes...*gone beyond my reach,*" Maya said, *"but not from yours. Humanity has claimed her soul, but you can free her, my child."*

He looked up at that, and for just a moment, Adonis

thought he would refuse, that the youth would find the true cause for his hatred. Then the last of the fury faded from his eyes, leaving only a dull blankness, a final acceptance of his new master.

"*Please,*" he whispered. "*Tell me how to free my sister.*"

# 35

# THE HERO

Lukys ducked as a blade flashed for his face, then thrust out with his spear, forcing Tasha to leap back. Immediately he retreated and sensed movement from behind. He grinned as Dale and Travis stepped up alongside him. Tasha had refused his challenge and sought to kill them all. No point in it being a one on one competition.

A frown appeared on Tasha's face as she found herself confronted by a line of spears. Though they wore no armour and only a few had scavenged shields, Lukys had to admit the Perfugian recruits appeared a ferocious sight standing together. Just as Romaine had trained them. His heart swelled and he thought the old Calafe warrior would have been proud to see them now.

Smiling, he faced Tasha once more. She had expected the royal guard to sweep them away with ease. They might have the advantage of armour, but he could see the hesitation in her eyes now, the sudden doubt. Time to press the advantage.

"Perfugians, forward!" Lukys cried, and gripping his

spear with two hands, he stepped forward, trusting his comrades to join him.

Spear tips shone as the line advanced and Tasha leapt back, re-joining her fellow guards. Around the courtyard, the common soldiers stood fixed in place, eyes wide as they struggled to overcome the warring emotions the Melders had cast upon them.

That suited Lukys. The Perfugian recruits were already outnumbered without the soldiers aligning against them. It would take all their skill and determination just to turn the guards back, though…

…perhaps if he could strike Tasha down, the rest might be reasoned with.

He jerked as a sudden roar crashed over the amphitheatre. Then the guards were charging.

Lukys had faced a Tangatan charge before, had felt their voices thrumming in his mind as they sung their chants of death in the face of battle. But this was something different. These men and women, they had no reservations about using their power, and now Lukys felt his legs tremble as fear swept like a gale through his soul. Around him, the recruits wavered, threatening to succumb to the emotion cast by their enemies.

Gritting his teeth, Lukys did his best to lift them, to nurture their courage, but he could feel the cracks spreading through his own strength. He was but a drop in a lake before the collective strength of the guards. Twenty Melders stood with Tasha—too many. In that moment he knew they would break, that the guards would sweep them away, crush them all beneath their boots…

Warmth struck him like a wave, sweeping through his body, his soul. It carried on through those around him, filling them with hope and love, casting off the fear. Suddenly the men and women of his regiment were straightening, their courage restored. Blinking, Lukys glanced back through the ranks of his companions and found the Tangata guarding their rear.

*In this, at least, we can help,* Sophia said, though he could not see her through the press of his fellows.

A smile came to him as he realised that she and her people were protecting them from the guards' mental assault.

*Thank you,* he whispered, and faced the enemy once more.

Tasha and her guards faltered as their powers failed, but that hesitation lasted only a moment. Then the battle was upon them, and Lukys found himself fighting again for his life. Despite their heavy armour, the guards moved with deceptive speed. As a spear almost took him in the throat, Lukys found himself wondering if the guards had retained more than just the powers of a Melder, for it seemed they moved almost as fast at the Tangata themselves.

"Friends, on me!" he called, fighting to keep his recruits in a line.

Dale and Travis formed up to either side of him, and together they pressed forward into the teeth of the assault. The other recruits would not give an inch so long as they three stood. The guards seemed to realise it too, for those nearest turned towards them.

Lukys thrust out a spear as a man came at him, then cursed as the guard evaded the blow. Travis intercepted a riposte that would have caught Lukys in the groin, then attacked himself. This time, his spear found flesh and the guard fell. Two more came at them. Teeth bared, Lukys joined with Travis and lurched to the attack. He felt a satisfying *crunch* as his spear slipped past his foe's shield and found a weak point in his armour.

They weren't so fortunate with the second. Rushing

forward, he evaded their spears and slammed his shield against them. The weight of his blow sent Lukys onto the back foot, and for a moment Travis was left exposed.

Dale was there though, and together they drove the guard back, until finally he fell, dropping without a sound. Lukys glimpsed a flash of white surprise in the aura of the guard standing beyond. The man hadn't even lowered the visor of his helmet. Obviously these guards had not expected such resistance from the rejects of the Perfugian academy.

Lukys offered a grim smile as he re-joined the line and leapt to the attack. He was happy to be underestimated. The royal guard would pay dearly for their complacency. More of his recruits had recovered shields now and one tossed his to Lukys. As the next guard advanced, he found himself presented with three united shields and hesitated.

All along the line, the royal guards faced a similar struggle against Lukys's recruits. The enemy might have been better armed and trained, but they fought as individuals. They weren't used to facing soldiers trained for battle, working together as a unit, protecting one another's backs. Just as the Tangata had once struggled to break the formations Romaine had drilled into the recruits, now the royal guard found themselves under pressure.

They were losing.

Another guard went down before Lukys, and suddenly he found himself facing Tasha across the line of their spears. Anger touched him. This bloodshed, all the death, it was all because of her.

Gritting his teeth, Lukys gathered himself as she came for him. Tasha moved faster than the others, her silver spear flashing at his face so fast he barely had time to raise his shield. The *thud* as it struck wood left his arm numb and instinctively he thrust out with his own blade, seeking to slow a second attack.

A *shriek* followed as the point caught steel, forcing Tasha to retreat. Lowering his shield, he studied her, seeking an opening. Her feet moved like water beneath her, reminding him of the Tangata, of their poise and balance. His fists tightened around the shaft of his spear as he cursed the hatred that had so blinded her. He knew it well, recognised its glow—it was the same hatred that had driven him to attack the Tangata on the shore, that had made him so distrustful of Sophia, despite everything she had done for him.

He wished he could make Tasha see the truth, the similarities she and her guards shared with the Tangata, rather than the differences.

Instead, there would be only death.

Tasha came for him again and he met her with shield and spear. All else fell away as they moved through the dance of death. Lukys sensed his companions retreating to grant them space. The sounds of battle receded, until it seemed they fought alone in the amphitheatre, as though the fate of the kingdom fell upon their shoulders.

She was a better fighter than anyone Lukys had faced before. Lacking the speed and power of the Tangata, she still moved with a subtly that hinted at the blood the Perfugians carried in their veins. Adding to it were the skills of years spent training, of an entire life dedicated to but one task—protecting the Sovereigns.

Against her skill, Lukys brought raw ferocity, a blunt talent learnt in desperation, skills drilled into him by the last warrior of the Calafe. Romaine might not have prepared him to fight someone so skilled, but he had trained Lukys to face the Tangata, to stand against enemies he had no right to resist.

And so he stood against Tasha and defied her with every inch of his soul.

He could sense the hatred radiating from her, the madness that had driven her to such extremes, to break her vows. Lukys reeled from it, shrunk from its fury, struggling to fortify himself against it. Yet still it pressed against him, her power as a Melder crashing against his thoughts, drawing his own anger to the fore, his own hatred.

Teeth clenched, he struggled to fight back with his mind, reaching out for the thrumming of her power. The emerald of her hatred washed over him, its awful power, seeking a home in his own heart, to drive him to corruption, to deal death. Something inside him responded to that power, the piece of him that had loathed the Tangata since childhood, that had been nurtured by the teachings of the Sovereigns.

But he could feel Sophia's presence on the edges of his mind. With her love, Tasha's hatred could find no purchase within him, no soil in which to take root.

Instead, he gathered it up, the twisting threads of her hatred, working by instinct and desperation, rolling it into a ball of darkest emerald, into a focal of hatred.

Then he cast it back at Tasha, hurled it back at its owner.

A scream tore from Tasha's lips as it struck and she lurched back from him, eyes bulging. An awful snarl hissed from her throat, a cry of such loathing that it sent tremors down to the souls of all who heard it.

Still shrieking, the woman hurled herself forward, driven mad by her own hatred, all caution cast aside.

Lukys's spear crunched through steel as it struck her throat.

Then Tasha was staggering back, eyes wide, blood gushing from her wound, staining the blue of her armour.

Lukys froze, his eyes drawn to Tasha's face. Shock

showed in her eyes as the spear tumbled from her fingers, as her hands clutched weakly at the wound, as the strength went from her legs and she slumped to the ground, armour clattering against the stone.

Standing over her, Lukys shivered as she met his eyes, as the glow of her hatred gave way to fear, to the terror of failure. Whatever her deeds, Tasha had thought she stood on the side of right. Indoctrinated by a society that had preached of the Tangata's evil for generations, she had seen no other choice but to stand against the monsters, though it meant betraying the very leaders she had sworn to protect.

Then the light was gone and Tasha was tumbling backwards, lying still upon the stones, blood spreading out beneath her.

Lukys's vision blurred as he shook his head, tears burning in his eyes. He wanted to scream at her, to tell her she was a fool for choosing hatred, for going against her own Sovereigns, her own people. But it was too late now. If only...

The thought trailed away as he realised that silence had fallen over the amphitheatre. He blinked, looking from Tasha's body to the royal guards. At her death, they had staggered back from the Perfugian recruits, weapons slipping from their hands. Shock and horror showed on their faces as they looked to him, and he saw the regret there, the pain.

They too had been caught up in Tasha's hatred, in their own loathing for the creatures of their nightmares. Now that their leader had fallen, her influence had vanished, leaving them to stare in horror at what she'd done.

At the bodies of the Sovereigns, lying still on the amphitheatre floor.

## ❧ 36 ❧

## THE EMISSARY

Erika was flying. Soaring. The mountains flashed by below, little more than a blur to her narrowing vision, the darkness pressing in. But still…she flew.

No…Cara flew. Somehow, the young Anahera held her, clutched Erika tight as her wings struck the air, beating frantically, straining to keep them aloft. Erika frowned as she looked at the Goddess's face. She was crying…no, screaming, the sounds ripped away by the mountain winds. Veins bulged in her neck and Erika realised her friend was at the limits of her strength, barely keeping them aloft.

Then her vision spun, another wave of pain radiating from her chest, from her shattered wrist. For a while she knew only a tide of red, drifting, floating on an ocean, in warm waters, swept away, carrying her to someplace else, to peace…

*Thud.*

A scream tore from Erika's lips as she found herself suddenly back in the mountains. Before she could recall how she had come to be there, she was falling, tumbling towards distant rocks. Arms clutched tight around her waist, straining against the buffeting winds. Something struck her arm and agony laced her mind—

*Thump.*

They slammed into the mountainside in an eruption of gravel, so hard Erika's teeth rattled in her jaw. A cry tore from her lips as stones ripped at her clothing, her flesh, as she tumbled down the jagged slope. Torn from Cara's arms, she rolled over and over, the world a flashing of white and red and black and blue...

...the warm ocean swallowed her again, and for a second Erika felt blessed peace, sinking into the depths of unconsciousness, away from the pain...

...a scream dragged her back. She fought against the call, but there was something in that scream, a need, a desperation, and suddenly the agony returned, forcing her eyes to open again upon the world.

Erika found herself lying on an outcropping of rock in the bottom of a valley. How far they had flown from the City of the Gods, she couldn't say, only that she no longer recognised the peaks rising high above. A stream raced past below, crashing over jumbled boulders lining the valley floor.

A flicker of movement drew Erika's gaze back to the gravel slope down which she had tumbled. A few yards above, Cara crouched, one wing twisted behind her at a horrible angle, face lifted to the sky as she screamed her agony. And above...

...above stood Hugo, shoulders heaving, wings stretched wide as he stared at his sister. His lips parted as he raised a fist. Below, Cara remained on her hands and knees, her screams echoing from the cliffs, only to turn to soft sobbing. Erika shuddered at the pain in her friend's voice. She tried not to look at the broken wing, at the terrible bend to the bone beneath her auburn feathers, at the blood staining the gravel.

Then suddenly the Goddess fell silent. Lifting her head, she looked at Hugo.

"Brother," she rasped, her voice breaking, "why?"

A spasm passed across Hugo's face as he looked down at her, but Erika could see his eyes now, glinting in the flickering light, the grey sheen. There was a madness to him as he stood over Cara, a rage.

"I must avenge my father," he growled. "I must free you from their evil."

"Wha—"

Cara broke off as Hugo surged forward, his boot rising to catch her in the chest. A cry tore from Erika as her friend tumbled down the slope to crash into the rocks alongside her. Desperately she tried to rise, to go to Cara's aid, but another wave of pain broke upon her and suddenly her vision was spinning and the cold rocks were pressing against her face.

"Brother…please, stop."

Sobs came from Cara as she tried to push herself back up, but the fall had only done more damage to her injured wing. The pain seemed to rob her of strength and she slumped, gasping, against the rocky outcrop, watching as Hugo moved towards her.

"I will give you peace, sweet sister," he was whispering as he reached for Cara. He lifted her easily, drawing her up by the shirt, softly, almost tenderly. "I will free you."

The sharp *crack* as he slammed her back to the ground was anything but tender. Erika screamed as Cara struck the rocks, her broken wing flailing useless, the arm she raised to break her fall crumpling beneath her weight. This time there was no scream, only a low groaning as she lay upon the stone, the soft sobbing of her pleas.

"Brother." Erika could barely hear the words from where she lay. Somehow, impossibly, Cara pushed herself to her knees. Agony twisted her face and her body was a mess of torn flesh and broken limbs, but still she faced her brother, amber eyes aglow. "Please, you don't have to do this," she whispered.

A flicker passed through Hugo's face, but he only shook his head. "I do."

Before him, Cara bowed her head, and Erika heard the soft cry of inhaled breath, the depth of her friend's sorrow.

Then abruptly the Goddess surged forward, her bent legs propelling her from the rock. She slammed into her larger brother, and on the uneven slope, Hugo lost his balance and fell. Cara was on him in a second, hammering her fist into his face, her incredible strength slamming him backwards into the mountain.

But Hugo did not have a broken wing. He recovered quickly from the shock of her attack and surged back, his greater bulk threatening to hurl her from him. Instead, Cara clung on, teeth bared, eyes burning, and the two tumbled across the rocky ledge—then disappeared over the side.

Erika cried out and crawled across to where the two had vanished. The drop was only a dozen feet. Below they had landed beside the stream, their battle carrying them into the waters themselves.

Still, neither would surrender, and Cara screamed again, her broken wing trapped beneath the currents. Her face went so pale Erika feared she would collapse, but somehow the Goddess dug beyond her limits and attacked her brother again. The slick stones shifted beneath them and suddenly Cara was straddling the younger Anahera, grasping him by the throat, driving him beneath the waters.

A fist slammed into Cara's face with desperate force, almost dislodging her. Blood ran from her mouth but she clung on, a shriek sounding from the depths of her soul as she drove her brother back beneath the surface. Her eyes were wild, swirling from orange to grey, tears streaming down her face.

"*Erika!*"

It was a moment before Erika recognised her name amidst Cara's cries. Shaking off her shock and pain, she stumbled to her feet. The movement sent her vision swirling again, but gritting her teeth, she swung from the outcrop and staggered down the shore towards her friend.

"*Help. Me!*"

Cara's screams took on a fresh desperation as Hugo surged back, mouth wide as he sucked in fresh air. His wings churned the waters, but weighed down by the currents, he could not bring them to bear, could not quite free himself before his sister drove him back into the icy cold.

Help her? What could Erika possibly do to help against one of the Anahera? Her gaze was drawn to the gauntlet, but she could not even make a fist, did not have the energy to fuel it, even if she could. Her legs felt weak and her vision was blurring.

Another cry came from Cara. Tears streamed down the Goddess's face and blood ran freely from her nose, her mouth. Still she held on, screaming, sobbing, though Hugo might be stronger, though she was injured, though she fought against her own brother. She did what she had to, not because of duty or family or for the greater good.

But to survive.

The blood was pounding Erika's ears as she fell to her knees beside the stream. Rocks lined the shoreline and she clutched at one she could lift. It was only the size of a small melon, jagged and broken, as though it had only recently cracked off the cliff face above.

Fighting back her own agony, Erika stumbled into the

water, the rock held awkwardly in both hands. It hardly seemed enough, but she clutched it all the same. It was all she had.

Cara's face was a bloodied, purpled mess now, her wing twisted so badly Erika feared it might never heal, that after all they had been through, her friend might still lose her ability to fly. It hardly mattered now, not with Hugo here, trying to kill them.

Erika stumbled into the swirling waters, her boots slipping on unseen rocks. Then she was there, standing above her friend, above Hugo. Images flashed in her mind, of the young Anahera showing her to Cara's room, of him standing up to his father, speaking on Cara's behalf. Suddenly she found herself hesitating. Surely this could not be happening, surely they could convince him...

A roar sounded as Hugo's head broke above the surface again, his eyes shining the dark grey of madness, teeth bared. Cara slipped, almost lost her grip as his wings thrashed. She cried out, her eyes meeting Erika's. In that moment, she saw her friend's desperation, her grief, her pain. And she knew there was no other way. They were the only ones who knew what came, the darkness that now lurked in the Mountains of the Gods, the death that marched on mankind.

Hands trembling, Erika lifted the rock and brought it down on Hugo's skull with all her strength. There was a soft *crunch*, a gasp and a groan, before his head slipped back beneath the waters. His fingers clutched at Cara still, but the strength had suddenly gone from his struggles.

The end wasn't long in coming, after that. Sobs rasped from Cara's lips as she held him down, as she watched her brother die, until finally she released him. Swaying in the icy waters, she slumped against Cara. Together, the two stumbled from the stream and collapsed against the jagged stones of the shore. Neither looked back, could not bear to watch as the water claimed its prize.

Instead, Erika found herself staring up at the open sky, at the endless blue above. She'd done it. The Anahera was dead.

They were free.

This time when the darkness rose to claim her, Erika embraced it with open arms.

## 🪷 37 🪷

# THE HERO

Silence had descended on the courtyard. Lukys could sense the eyes upon him, of his friends, of the Tangata, of the gathered soldiers and those Royal Guard who still lived. Even King Nguyen was watching him. They seemed to all be waiting for something.

He swallowed, still looking down at Tasha, hardly able to believe what he'd done. This was beyond anything he'd thought himself capable of, an act that seemed almost blasphemous. He'd used Tasha's own hatred against her, used his mind to practically drive her onto the spearpoint. He could see now why the Matriarch of the Tangata had forbidden her people from such abuse of their power.

A shiver ran down his spine and shaking his head, Lukys looked to the soldiers that still ringed the amphitheatre.

"Throw down your weapons," he said.

It was softly spoken, without hint of threat, but the rattle of steel blades striking stone was deafening. When silence returned, he met the gaze of every man and woman present, and nodded. Exhaustion hung heavy on his shoulders and he wanted nothing more than to lie down and rest, but there was still work to be done.

*Lukys.* He turned and found Sophia standing nearby.

He reached for her, then hesitated, aware that what he'd just done was forbidden by her people, considered a great crime. But she came to him anyway, and he let out a sigh of relief, that at least the two of them were okay, that he had not thrown everything away in a moment of rage. He closed his eyes as they embraced, savouring her warmth, her support.

*She's still alive,* Sophia said into his mind when they broke apart, so that only Lukys could hear.

He nodded. He had sensed the flicker of the Sovereign's aura, though she had tried to hide it from Tasha. Drawing in a breath, he took Sophia's hand in his and moved to where the Sovereigns had fallen.

They found the female Sovereign lying beside her brother, one arm outstretched to rest on his shoulder, as though she could not bear to be separated from him, even in death. For a second, Lukys sensed nothing from her, and he wondered if they were too late. But she shifted at the sound of their footsteps, her eyes flickering open.

*And so ends our reign,* her voice whispered into their minds. It sounded wrong, without the echo of her brother's.

Lukys glanced at her wound and saw it was true. There was nothing to be done for such an injury. Only the fact Tasha had driven her spear through the Sovereign's stomach, rather than her heart, had saved her from an immediate death. Though perhaps that would have been kinder…

*How?* Sophia whispered, crouching beside the Sovereign. *How…can you remember our people, our crime against you?*

The hint of a smile tugged at the Sovereign's cheek. *Without the…strength of the Tangata, we learnt to cherish the abilities of our Melders, in those early days on this wondrous island.* Even in Lukys's mind, he could hear her pain. *Eventually, two of us were chosen to lead...for eternity.*

Sophia shook her head, not understanding.

*It is good...that we could better...those who rejected us...in at least one talent.*

*You would have been welcomed by my Matriarch with open arms,* Sophia whispered, and Lukys saw that tears beaded her grey eyes.

*I think...we would have liked to meet her,* the Sovereign breathed. *Alas...our hatred was the end of us. We should have... forgiven long ago. Should have...led our people forward...rather than looking back.*

Silence fell and the Sovereign grew still. For a moment, Lukys thought she had passed, but then her eyes flickered and her Voice came again.

*This Old One...* she whispered. *You will need...aid.*

Lukys nodded. *The Gods—*

*No,* the Sovereign cut him off. *We allowed their legends, but...the Anahera have already failed humanity once. They cannot defeat the Old Ones alone.*

*Then how?* Sophia pressed. *I have felt her, Sovereign. She is too powerful. I would have slain my...love, had she commanded me to.* Lukys could hear her voice breaking at the admission.

He swallowed, wanting to say something, but the Sovereign was speaking again. *I do not know, children.* It was strange, being addressed as such by someone in the body of a child, but then those ancient eyes...

*But...perhaps we have been wrong. Perhaps we have followed the wrong path, these past centuries. I do not know. Maybe you can do more with the Sovereign gift than we ever could.*

Sophia had been watching her with curious eyes, silent, but now she spoke again. *Who are you?*

The smile returned to the dying Sovereign's lips. *Someone who witnessed rule of the Old One's...first-hand.*

*What—*

Lukys didn't get to finish the question. Even as he touched the mind of the Sovereign, something surged from her, a burst of Voice, as though she'd screamed into his very consciousness. He gasped, trying to withdraw, while beside him Sophia stiffened. But it was too late.

In a flash of white, images burst through Lukys's mind. Voices cried out within him as he saw an inferno fill the horizon, as he saw darkness and light and cities turned to dust. Gods fell from the skies and creatures that looked like the Tangata howled, as hours and days and decades swept past, as the world changed, castles rising where cities had once stood, as the Tangata crept from their holes and civilisations were reborn.

The Sovereign cried out as the images finally faded, blinking against the brilliance of the light above. His vision swirled, then crystallised, and he found himself staring down at a pair of bodies on the marble floor. The Sovereign frowned. One was *his* body, was it not? Images, memories, collided in his mind, and something else stirred. He sensed something...had gone wrong.

Another consciousness slivered through his mind and another memory imposed itself on him, of the Sovereign looking up at...himself? Agony tore at his head like a dagger and Lukys cried out. A hundred other voices cried with him in the silence of his own mind, the voices of the Sovereigns, every one of them from today stretching back to the first settlers of Perfugia—and further even than that. Their minds passed down from one pair of Sovereigns to another, until today, until Lukys.

"Lukys?" a voice came from nearby.

He looked around, finding an unfamiliar...no, a *familiar* face standing over him.

"Travis?" he croaked, looking up at the man. A barrage of images assaulted his senses, flashes of the man who stood before him.

"You okay, Lukys?" Travis asked, reaching out to grip his shoulder.

Lukys shook his head, trying to sift through the memories. So many memories. A hundred lifetimes of knowledge. He felt himself getting lost in them again, felt those other consciousnesses pushing...struggling for supremacy.

*No...*

He pushed back, and reluctantly they sank. Lukys sucked in a relieved breath, struggling to retain his sanity—and his breakfast. Stars were still dancing across his eyes but he nodded to his friend.

"I'm...okay, I think," he croaked. "What about Sophia?"

Travis glanced to his side, and Lukys followed his gaze, finding Sophia hunched in two. But as he watched, she straightened, turning to meet his gaze. For a second, he saw the ancient gaze of the Sovereigns and felt a pang of fear, that somehow they had taken her. Then the gleam faded and when she blinked again, it was Sophia who looked back at him.

"Are you okay?" he asked, too exhausted to use his mind.

Sophia managed a smile. "I'm okay, Lukys."

# EPILOGUE
## THE EMISSARY

With Cara's broken wing and Erika's injuries, it took them almost two weeks to reach the River Illmoor, to finally gain the safety of the Gemaho plains. In all that time, Erika expected wings to darken the sky at any moment, for one of the Anahera to come diving down upon them, for the Tangata to emerge from the shadows.

But none had followed after Hugo.

A tremor shook Erika every time she thought of the dead Anahera, of his battered corpse in the river, Cara's soft sobs as she mourned him. His blood still stained their clothing—no matter how many times they tried to wash in the freezing mountain streams, the red refused to fade.

Cara herself said little during the long journey, though there was no missing the pain, the agony in her eyes. They had used strips of their clothing to bind her broken wing flat to her back, but even after two weeks, the Goddess had not attempted to use them. Erika hadn't asked how long it would take to heal, or whether it would heal at all.

And so they had travelled in silence, haunted by the darkness they had escaped, by the failure of their desperate mission. Banished by her people, her father and brother lost, Cara had no one left, was as alone as Erika now.

Erika could hardly bear the thought of standing before King Nguyen and revealing her failure, that the Anahera now stood allied with the Tangata, that Maisie had been left behind, had surely been slaughtered by the Old One in vengeance for their escape.

The thoughts made her cold. No longer could she imagine hope for the future. Once, Erika had thought she would return to civilisation and find her lost people, gather the refugees of Calafe and lead an uprising against the queen that had betrayed them. But what hope could she offer them now? Their Gods were a deception, cowardly creatures that would rather submit to terror than fight for their freedom.

No, only Nguyen could help them now. He was a true king, would know what to do, how to deliver humanity the victory it so desperately needed. The man was their only hope, their only chance for sanctuary now.

But when they finally stood on the shore of the Illmoor, they found the plains of the Gemaho aflame. As far as the eye could see, the fields were burning. Crops and pasture and livestock, all of it had been consumed by flames. Where before the horizon had seemed to stretch to infinity, now a sickly smoke stained the sky grey, and ash turned the land black.

"What happened here?" Erika whispered as they came to a stop before swirling currents.

She glanced at her friend, but the young Anahera said nothing, only stood with her shoulders hung low, eyes staring into the distance, as though they did not see the destruction. Erika suppressed a sigh. She needed her friend, needed her strength, her determination, but she could not find the words to lift the Goddess from despair. Maybe when they were safe, when she could finally rest, they could finally process all that had befallen them in the mountains.

But for now, rest would have to wait.

Together, they turned and started downriver. It would be a long march north to Solaris, the capital of Gemaho, but there were no other options. Whatever the source of the fires, they would find answers in Solaris. To the south was only fresh wilderness, only Badlands and the Dead Sea. But in Solaris was the king's court, the last bastion of freedom in a terrible world. There they could plan how they would defend their world, how they might stand against the Anahera and Tangata and the Old One that now led them.

Cara must have taken them north in their flight from the City of the Gods, for it was only another three days before they finally came into sight of Solaris. Built on a fork in the great river, it was said to be one of the great cities of the age, more wondrous even than Mildeth.

Looking across waters turned dark by ash, Erika found destruction in place of wonder. After so long on the road, on the run, she could no longer summon the will to be surprised. There had been signs on their march north, burnt villages and the river empty of ships. In her heart, Erika had known what they must find here, though she had clung to the hope she would be proven wrong, that the great Solaris might still stand.

It had not.

The Kingdom of Gemaho had fallen.

The lands of humanity belonged to Queen Amina.

Slumping to the soot-stained grass, Erika sat beside Cara and watched in silence as the great ship floating on the river swung towards them. Men and women scurried backwards and forwards across the deck, rushing to obey the orders of their captain, and soon oars beat the waters, sending them racing towards where Erika knelt.

There was no point trying to run. Erika was tired of running, of fighting, of *trying.* All that remained to her now was despair.

Swinging alongside the shore, a gangplank rose from the galley and fell to the shore with a *thud.* Soldiers garbed in steel and wearing the red of Flumeer rushed to surround them, swords in hand. Erika made no move to rise as the weapons were pointed at her throat, but as a fresh set of footsteps came from the gangplank, she managed to push herself to her feet. Reaching out, she took Cara's hand.

They watched together as the Queen of Flumeer walked down the gangplank, royal armour shining in the noonday sun. A sword was strapped to her side, but she did not draw it. What need did *she* have for a sword, with the might of her soldiers on hand, with an entire kingdom brought to its knees before her?

With the glow of the gauntlet she wore on her fist.

The soldiers parted as she approached, but her eyes never left Erika. Despite her exhaustion, despite the despair that had robbed her of even the will to flee, Erika shuddered at what she saw in those eyes. There was a hatred there, a raw anger kept carefully in check. She drew to a stop before Erika.

"So, my dear Archivist returns to her maker." Amina smiled.

Then the queen raised her gauntlet.

Light flashed, then a sharp, shrieking noise sounded in Erika's ears, so high pitched as to be almost inaudible. And yet...a scream tore from her lips as pain split her skull, as though someone had taken a nail and driven it through each eardrum. Her mouth fell open and she tried to scream, but no sound came out, even as her legs went from under her. Mind aflame, she arced against the ground. Even as she sucked in the slightest breath, Erika knew she did not suffer alone, that Cara lay alongside her, engulfed in the same agony, the same doom.

Then the pain intensified, the nails turning to her eyes, her brain, her very being. White flashed and the world fell away.

Until all that was left to Erika was pain.

———

HERE ENDS BOOK THREE
OF
DESCENDANTS OF THE FALL
The story continues in:
Dreams of Fury

———

**\*Author Note:** If you enjoyed this story, please don't hesitate to scream it from the rooftops over at Amazon or Goodreads— otherwise no one will know! It matters so much not just to me but to other readers that might be interested in starting the series :-)

# NOTE FROM THE AUTHOR

Phew, well, I'm not entirely sure why, but this must have been one of the most difficult books I've ever had to write. With both Erika and Lukys separated in such different environments, AND the Tangata to bring into the conflict, there were a lot of balls to juggle. But hopefully I pulled it off (Fingers crossed!). It also didn't help that I became unwell in the final week of writing, but I got through it!

Now though, I already can't wait to begin on book 4, Dreams of Fury, which will finally see our heroes reunited —and an end to the conflict...one way or another ;-)

**FOLLOW AARON HODGES...**
And receive TWO FREE novels and a short story!
www.aaronhodges.co.nz/newsletter-signup/

## THE KNIGHTS OF ALANA

If you've enjoyed this book, you might want to check out another of my fantasy series!

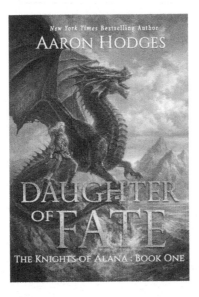

When Knights attack the town of Skystead, seventeen-year-old Pela is the only one to escape. Her mother and the other villagers are taken, accused of worshiping the False Gods. They will pay the ultimate price – unless Pela can rescue them.

# THE EVOLUTION GENE

If you've enjoyed this book, you might want to check out my dystopian sci-fi series!

In 2051, the Western Allies States have risen as the new power in North America. But a terrifying plague is sweeping through the nation. Its victims do not die—they change. People call them the *Chead*, and where they walk, destruction follows.